FROM THE TOP

JAQUELINE SNOWE

Published: 2022

Published by: Jaqueline Snowe

Copyright © 2022, Jaqueline Snowe

Cover Design: Dany Snowe

Editing: Katherine McIntyre

Formatting: Jennifer Laslie

All rights reserved. No part of this publication may be reproduced, stored in a retrieval system, or transmitted in any form, or by any means, electronic, mechanical, recording, or otherwise, without prior written permission from the author. For more information, please contact Jaqueline at www.jaquelinesnowe.com.

This is a work of fiction. The characters, incidents, dialogue, and description are of the author's imagination and are not to be constructed as real. Any resemblance to actual events or persons, living or dead, is completely coincidental.

FROM THE TOP

Cami Simpson is the 'it girl'—at least until a string of terrible decisions leads to no boyfriend, no captainship of the dance team, and no fancy apartment. Due to a mold outbreak at her place, she's forced to relocate to a co-ed dorm as a senior. And to top it off, she finds out she's at risk of not graduating due to an error in her schedule. Talk about the worst senior year ever.

Frederick Brady the IV would never admit the massive crush he once had on the dance darling. Not to anyone. They'd almost had a moment a year ago, but she crushed him, so she's the last person he wants to live next to. It doesn't matter though. He's on his way out to an internship and almost done with school where he can leave his heartbreak and data foes behind.

Neither expected to form a friendship or know what to do about their insane chemistry. With late nights, insides jokes, and the rare comfort they find in each other... lines blur, and the popular girl gets with the nerdy guy. Only, Freddie's done this before and knows how it ends. His insecurities clash with Cami's need to be picked first, so when Freddie has to choose where to attend his internship, he can either pick the job or the girl. And for the guy who's set on protecting his heart, well, he might break hers in the process.

CHAPTER ONE

Cami

When it rains, it pours.
Except this time, the water hit my mascara, so when I faced my dance coach, I rivaled a drowned raccoon. It didn't suit me. Not one bit. The walk to my coach's office in a downpour was a clear sign of a bad omen.

I had a reputation to uphold, and looking like a soaking wet rodent wasn't the way to do it, but I could fix myself up before going back out in public. Right now, I had bigger concerns.

"I'm not going to be the captain," I said, making sure I heard her clearly. I'd busted my ass to lead the dance team for the last three years, and I had plans. I had a vision. My fucking mood board was plastered on my bedroom wall with all the ideas and mission statements to live by. Cami Simpson— captain of the dance team. It had a ring to it, but as Coach Audrey lowered her gaze and slumped her shoulders, I knew. I knew in my gut her decision was final.

"Why?" I asked, my voice taking on the dangerously low tone that was a dead giveaway for the simmering frustration boiling inside me. I crossed my arms over my chest and tilted my head to the side. One thing I'd learned early on was to never let anyone see your insides. Coach Audrey might've crushed my very soul with her choice, but she'd get nothing but indifference from me. Life was way easier when everyone assumed you were untouchable.

"Because Daniella exemplifies what it means to dance, serve, and lead. Your recent *incidents* put our team in the spotlight, Cami. Not in a good way." She wore disappointment on her sleeves, and I couldn't find it in me to feel bad.

Did people think I didn't understand I was on a rocky path? Did they just believe I was stupid and naive? They did. They saw a pretty face, killer dance moves, and the tight uniform and assumed I was a bendy little bimbo. I let them believe that too, so it was partially my fault that it was the go-to judgement for me.

My twin sister had the brains, and I had the boobs.

My eye twitched, and I arched my perfectly drawn brow. Yes, I did some dumb shit, but after a recent scare with a date, I'd backed off. I didn't say any of that though because Coach didn't know about *that* stuff. "I'm not allowed to make a mistake?"

Her lips pressed together, and she shook her head, causing my heart to beat faster and my hands to clench into fists at my sides. "Not like this."

The latest incident wasn't even my fault. Not really. Someone had handed me their drink to hold onto for a photo. Sure, it was outside the bar's patio, so within two seconds an officer saw me, and bam. Public Drinking citation. I gritted my teeth and tried a different approach. "Coach, that was—"

"I'm sorry." She pressed her lips tight together for a second. "You work hard. I know you do, but I'm not changing my mind." Audrey sighed and fidgeted with the ends of her fishtail braid She was adorable in every sense of the word but intelligent as hell and tolerated no bullshit. She'd been the queen bee of her high school and dance squad, and even now, as my shoulders hunched and my stomach rolled with heartbreak, I couldn't fault her logic.

It was a common theme these days. Me not being enough. Not smart enough. Not leadership material. Not the kinda girl you bring home to meet the parents. And until recently, my twin sister thought I was the kind of person who would steal guys from her. My throat tightened, and I pursed my lips, refusing to break down. I was a Simpson. We were ice cold and tough. "So that's it. Three years of busting my ass and it goes to the junior."

It was like my brain stopped working. I knew I should leave, should just walk out her office door and cool down, but I kept poking the fire. Pushing. I'd dreamed of being captain of Central's dance team since I was a preteen. I'd visit campus where my dad coached and watch them practice, buying their calendar and hanging it in my room. All those years wanting this, and it was taken away from me. By fucking Daniella Donavan.

Audrey narrowed her eyes. "You're going to respect my decision *and* Daniella."

"Seems like a threat, Coach," I fired back, unable to stop myself. Even though my heart pounded against my ribs and my eyes prickled, I couldn't shut my mouth. Did she not care how this tore me up inside? "I'm one of the best dancers on the squad. It's the truth."

She groaned, that sound worse than anything she'd said so far. It was filled with the disappointment I'd heard so many times before. I straightened my shoulders back, pushing away the pinpricks over my body that would surely come. I could handle it. I had to.

"Cami, you have all the talent in the world, but the way you attract trouble holds you back. I can't fix that. Only you can."

My temples throbbed from how hard I clenched my jaw. No response was better sometimes. Made people nervous. The silence. The eye contact that went on two seconds too long.

Audrey didn't flinch though. She eyed her phone and jutted her chin toward the door. "I have to meet with the director in a few minutes. Will I see you at boot camp next week?"

Boot camp was the kickoff for the school year and one of my favorite things in the world. 24/7 dance, teammates, and working muscles. Sweat and glitter and collaboration. However, with the new turn of events, the magic dulled. I'd planned on running bootcamp as the captain—all the bonding activities and drills and pep talks. Plotting our goals as a squad and how we could support each other. Having to sit through Daniella leading it? I was close to crying, and I needed to get the fuck out of there. "I guess we'll see, won't we?"

I brushed past Audrey and went straight to the bathroom nearby. I focused on taking deep breaths as I reapplied my red lipstick, wiped under my eyes, and smudged the mascara to give myself a smoky eye look. My chest constricted, but I powered through. Once that was fixed, I made sure my crop top stopped above my belly button. With my short cut-off shorts, always black, and my hair falling into waves on both sides, I had my uniform on. That was what my dad always called it.

It gave the impression I was unflappable, and I preferred it that way. Mean girls never went away after high school, and displaying weakness was unacceptable. Being vulnerable meant someone could use it against you, so I held my nose up high and straightened my shoulders. The midwestern summer air was thick and heavy after the rainstorm, but that was why I owned so much black--never showed you sweating. My conversation with Coach stood at the forefront of my mind, but no real decision took root. Would I actually quit, or did I just need her to want me?

Story of my fucking life. I just wanted to be wanted. By my parents. Friends. Boyfriends. My sister. Damn. Now dance? The squad had been my saving grace, and now it was gone.

I smiled at some of the football players jogging down the sidewalk and winked when one whistled at me. I liked attention. Sue me. Always had. Probably always would. Some might say it had to do with my upbringing where my sister got all the academic accolades and then the divorce... what a fucking mess.

That relationship shit? No thank you. Dating? Flirting? Hooking up? Yeah, I'd do that all day, but *committing* to someone and opening your soul for them? Made me gag. I'd take my flings any day over a *boyfriend* every single time, even though people judged me for it. I was always being stereotyped though—my makeup, my clothes, my looks, and my dancing.

Haters were always gonna hate. Might as well enjoy myself while they dissed me.

"Ms. Simpson?" A middle-aged woman with graying hair stopped me as I entered my kick-ass apartment building. I moved in two weeks ago, and it was the dream—right in the center of campus where there was always a party nearby. The bricked walls were beautiful, and it had a clean, fresh carpet smell. The natural light was top-notch, and I'd even bought a plant.

"Yes, ma'am?" I said, putting on my *smile.* It was my show-smile. The one I used when we danced at games or had a photoshoot. I knew exactly how to tilt my head and pressed my tongue to the roof of my mouth to prevent double chins.

She blinked. "U-um, did you get a call from us?"

I frowned. "No?"

I scanned my phone, and yes, there was a spam call, but I received a million of those a day. I didn't have a car, and I didn't need a fucking warranty. "Why? What happened?"

"There's been an incident with mold, and well, we're relocating everyone for a few months in the dorms. Ledger Hall. Health inspection..." I tuned her out as the words LEDGER HALL went off like a glitter bomb in my head.

The bricked, *non-air-conditioned* co-ed dorm? The one of far too many horror stories? "This can't be right," I said, my voice tight with tension. How much could a girl handle in one day before my hair would fall out from stress?

"It is. I'm sorry."

She looked it too, but that didn't help me. I'd saved every penny teaching dance classes over the last two years to live here. It was my dream apartment for senior year. The place where I would be able to study and be myself, away from the sorority life and drama of my last roommate. "I don't understand."

"It's just for two months. You'll get your rent back, obviously, and we're hoping the remodel can finish before then, but here's the memo you should've received." She handed me a slip of paper, and I stared at it, refusing to cry.

No captain position.

No bad-ass place to live.

What was next? Would I break an arm or start getting acne?

I scanned the memo and read the instructions—talk to the R.A. in Ledger Hall to get my room. My throat clogged, and I met the woman's gaze again. "Everyone in here has to live in the dorms now? Even if we aren't… underclassmen?"

She nodded and chewed her lip. "Yes. Graduate students are relocating there too. You could stay at a hotel, but we won't refund for that." She cracked her knuckles and gave me a pitying look, her eyes downcast like she hated what she had to say. "You have until the end of today to remove your stuff."

"Got it." I pinched the bridge of my nose just as the elevator dinged. The doors slid open, and Frederick Brady IV walked out. Tall didn't accurately describe the gentle giant of a man as he strode into the apartment foyer. If he was a coffee drink, he'd be a trenta, something not even shown on the menu because the guy was massive. At least six and a half feet tall with broad shoulders and a jawline that was dangerous to the human population.

His sharp gray eyes hid behind thick black glasses, and his gaze landed on me for one second before sweeping over me like

I was nothing. He had thick, dark lashes and black hair that fell just right on his face, and while my breathing hitched for a beat, it had nothing to do with my attraction to Freddie. The blip was at the blatant dismissal in his gaze. Like I wasn't worth his attention. Freddie wasn't a fan of me. Despite one night where I thought... maybe... he was such a *nice* guy. But the moment had been a second in time that hadn't worked out, and now he avoided me every chance he got.

Being ignored wasn't great for my ego or my pride, especially not today. Something about his tightened stance made me open my mouth, desperate to ruffle someone else's feathers instead of my own.

"Looking good, Freddie," I said, winking at him as he stopped in his tracks. He gave a slight shake of his head, like I was a pesky little fly before he walked up to the counter and rested his very large palms there. That put him a few feet from me.

He smelled like evergreen and coffee, as if he lived inside a Taylor Swift album and made a home in the woods. I wanted to inhale the scent and listen to Folklore. It also might have something to do with his blue plaid shirt.

"Hey, Erica. You'll keep me in the loop once the unit is available again?" he asked the woman in his deep, husky timbre. The grumpy giant had a voice for blues or the radio.

The woman nodded. "Thanks for being understanding, Mr. Brady."

He sighed and set a key on the counter. Then, not bothering to say a *hello* or acknowledge my existence, he strode back out the front doors.

Jerk. My ego could only take so many hits in a day, and I propped a hand on my hip, jutting it out to the side as I eyed Erica.

"He loves me—he just doesn't know it yet," I said to her, giving what I thought was an easy smile.

The woman frowned and adjusted her weight side to side. I

almost laughed. She was uncomfortable. Another thing I was really good at—making people feel weird.

"Um, right." She cleared her throat. "You'll get your things and move out?"

She sounded too eager for my liking, but what could I do? I nodded. It wasn't like I had a ton of stuff since I moved in two weeks ago and was too busy planning boot camp to unpack. Another sharp pang of betrayal grew in my chest, and I gritted my teeth together, forcing the dance team situation out of my mind. One step at a time.

Focus on packing.

That was what I did for two hours--shoved my clothes in a duffel bag and toiletries in another. It was weirdly therapeutic. Packing only took an hour or so to have all my shit in bags. Keeping busy was good. If I wasn't at practice, I was at the gym. Or putting on makeup or doing my hair. Or out at a party. I never stopped to be alone and feel because *that* wasn't fun for me.

So, I packed. Next stop—Ledger Hall.

The horrible, aged airless dorm had to be a punishment for all the dumb things I'd done in my life. Sweat poured down my temples, chest, arms, and legs. Carrying my stuff across campus worked my muscles, but I did it. The universe decided this dorm was meant for me this year when I was already hitting rock-bottom, and I went through all things I'd done that could've merited this punishment.

Cheating in eight grade math, laughing when a teammate accidentally shaved her eyebrow off, or the fact my sister thought I was a heartless bitch for six years? Maybe it was a combination of the everything that put me in *this* fucking dorm when my senior year was supposed to be the best one yet.

Don't break down. Don't do it. Keep busy. Distraction.

I sucked in a shaky breath just as a familiar voice called out my name. I turned, flashing a grin at my sister's boyfriend,

Michael Reiner. "Hey, what are you—" I slammed my lips shut when Freddie crawled out of the compact car.

A flash of irritation danced along my spine. Freddie had Michael help him with his stuff while knowing I was right there? God, the guy had to hate me. Michael frowned at me, and I covered up the awkward silence with a fake laugh. "I get to relive my wild freshmen days in the dorms. How exciting, right?"

"You can stay with us, Cami," he said, rubbing the back of his neck and showcasing his sleeve of tattoos. "Seriously, we have a couch, and it'd only be for what? A few weeks?"

"Two months," Freddie said, walking by us and not daring to spare me a glance. "I take it the couch-option is only available for siblings?"

"Dude, you wouldn't fit on the thing. Plus, couldn't you stay with your brother?"

Freddie stopped, spinning around and making eye contact with me. It was unnerving to be on the end of his full stare, and I hated how I was covered in sweat. I looked like a sweaty opossum, and he was... perfect. Gray shirt that hugged his pecs and black jeans that led to white chucks. He rocked the nerd-chic thing really, really well.

He cleared his throat, his gaze turning to ice as a light blush covered his cheeks. "I would kill him. We learned early on we weren't meant to share a living space."

"Then Ledger Hall, it is." Michael clapped and grinned at us. "You'll be dorm buddies. How cute." He reached down and picked up two of my bags, his smiling dropping. "Did you walk here with these?"

"Yes."

Freddie tensed his jaw and moved his eyes from me to the bags. "I'm going to talk to the R.A. Thanks for the ride, Reiner."

"You got it." Michael held out a fist to him then faced me. "Seriously, any time you need an escape, come over."

"And ruin y'alls honeymoon period of living together? I

wouldn't do that." He had no idea that his offer and genuine words meant the fucking world to me. I was judged constantly, but Michael never stereotyped me or made me feel inferior. He was a wonderful human. Naomi was lucky. "Thanks though, really."

He nodded and dropped my bags off at the end of the dorm hall before heading back toward his car. I went to find the R.A. Might as well discover what room was mine before hauling all of it somewhere. My footsteps felt like weights as I padded through the stifling hallway to see Freddie walking my way with a key in his hands. Our gazes locked for a beat, but before I could decipher what his look meant, he glanced at the ground, like the boring brown and white tile was better than my face.

"Maybe we'll be neighbors, Freddie. Could you imagine all the fun we'd have?" I said, unable to stop goading him, just to see if he'd ever smile at me again.

I wanted to break through the anti-Cami shell he wore like armor. Silence greeted me like I figured it would, so I went to meet our R.A. to get my card. 5G was my room. Right in the center. I made the joke that I better have good cell service, but Betty the R.A. didn't think I was cute.

I could only imagine how well she and Freddie would get along. I went to my room and opened it just as Freddie walked back into the dorm and headed to the door *right* next to mine. What a fucking day. I wasn't the captain of the dance team, and I wasn't living in my dream apartment. I shared a wall with a guy who hated my damn guts.

Senior year was *not* starting off with a bang. It was my own version of hell, and I didn't know how I was gonna survive.

CHAPTER **TWO**

Freddie

The dull buzz of my phone going off had me plopping onto the twin bed to answer my brother's Facetime call. "Oh, convenient that you're free now after I'm moved in," I said, narrowing my eyes at Camden. One of his talents was always disappearing when anyone needed him. At least when it came to anything physical. Emotionally? He'd be here with ten pints of ice cream and a notepad to make a list of who he was going to hurt.

Cleaning the kitchen as kids? He'd have something *come up* that *couldn't be avoided.* Yardwork when our mom asked for help? Same thing.

He responded to my jab with a sheepish grin. "I wanna see the place. Give me the tour, Freds."

Freds. The terrible nickname he coined a decade ago. It was a combo of that and FB3. Either one made me sound like a tool. He swore it was endearment, but I always saw the glint in his eyes. He enjoyed my suffering. He really had the whole youngest child syndrome down pat.

"You could actually walk here and see it." I sighed, eyeing

my living space for the next two months. It was roughly the same size as my closet in the new apartment I was supposed to be staying in. Not ideal. Not awesome. My back muscles clenched with tension about the damn heat already suffocating me, but it wouldn't help to panic. The size of the bed alone was worrying, but I tried to not think of the negatives. "But let me guess, you have a pressing appointment."

"Sensing a tone, Freds. Don't be pissed at me that you've had some shit luck the last year and two months." Camden grinned, as if it was funny my life had been a string of bad luck. He wasn't wrong, but he didn't have to look like he enjoyed it so much. "Stop being shy. Show me the abode. I promise to only laugh twice."

I panned around the room, making sure he got the full extent of the place. The bed, the built-in two drawer dresser, and the desk that was way too small for me. "This is so weird. I'm twenty-four and living in a dorm."

His eyes bugged out, like I'd personally offended him. "I offered my place, like the amazing younger brother you've always had. It was so kind of me, honestly."

"Which we both know was a pity invite." I flipped the phone to face me again. "Did you legit call to see my new place?"

"Yeppers. Legit the only reason." He shrugged and looked off into the distance. "Oh, I gotta go. Roommate needs an extra set of hands with groceries."

"So, you do help others, just not your family."

"Food first, family second." Camden hung up, but I caught the smirk on his face. *Brothers.* He was the easygoing one and had too much charisma. He'd charm the wallpaper right off the drywall if given the chance while I preferred to hang out solo. It was like all of the extroverted genes skipped me and went to him. Some days, it bothered me how easy it was for him to talk to anybody. Other days, he annoyed me because he never shut up. But most of the time, I was thankful we were close.

Just... not close enough to live together.

He was chaotic where I had a plan. He had endless parties and people over, where I preferred silence. Salt and pepper, positive and negative. We were opposites in every sense of the word. *Speaking of plans...* I opened my backpack and started taking out highlighters, notebooks, and my laptop to get them all set up. Even after that small of a task, my shirt stuck to my back from sweat, so I propped open the door to the hall. The constant movement of people would distract me, but it was a small price to pay to escape the stifling heat.

A deep voice and a sexy laugh caught my attention, and my muscles clenched. *Her.* The guy said something, the tail end of the conversation heading into my room. Cami responded with another giggle.

Awesome. Just, fucking awesome. Here she was, flirting with guys on the floor already, not having been there an hour even. And next door to me, no less. I really did have shitty luck. It was the universe laughing at me for thinking someone like her would be interested in me that one night. For believing I had a shot with her. It was a joke, and the shame from that night made my mouth dry up.

I could count on *one* hand the number of people who had the unique talent of flustering me. Cami Simpson was one of them. Kate Beckinsale was on that list because my god, she was my dream woman, but in real life... it was just Cami. My palms sweated, my stomach somersaulted, and I turned into a blob. A thoughtless blob who couldn't even speak to her. Even when we were outside with Michael, she stood there, and it should've been easy to say something. Anything! But nope. I got awkward, my thoughts crisscrossed, and a whole lot of nothing came out. Images of her touching me that night and her teasing smile that made my heart beat twice as fast clashed with the memory of her leaving with someone else.

A year later, the embarrassment was just as fresh.

My ears heated like I'd sat out in the sun for too long, and I ran a hand over my hair before adjusting my glasses on my nose. Cami defined the word stunning. If someone handed me a catalogue to create my perfect woman, it was her. Her wavy dark hair, her large brown eyes, her full, always red lips, and her toned body. I bit the tip of my knuckle, picturing her in her shorts and cut off shirt.

She was strong and worked on every muscle and moved with such grace that it was hard not to stare at her all the time. Even when I saw her across the quad or at a bar, I avoided her. For two reasons. The first—she flustered me. The second... the ever-present embarrassment.

I couldn't look at her and *not* think about that night a year ago. Fuck. My face flushed, and I wiped my hands on the back of my jeans. Living next to her was going to be a special, Freddie-made version of hell. The party girl. The popular girl. The girl who'd flirted with me and left with another guy, crushing my confidence after I'd spent months trying to get it back. I'd foolishly thought for a moment that we had something between us. We clearly didn't, and I should've known better. I had my heart broken once by someone like her, and I had no plans to repeat myself. My future as an environmental engineer wasn't sexy enough, and I was living proof that *nice guys finished last*.

Ask my ex-girlfriend. She'd tell you. She up and left me because I was too boring, too simple, too...sweet. The stress grew in my chest, and I rubbed a hand over my heart.

Having a knot there wouldn't do well with the new arrangements, and I focused on some deep breathing to try and ease it. The exercise didn't help since it was one million degrees outside, so I stepped into the hallway to see if it was any cooler.

It wasn't. But something struck me.

I didn't hear *anything* next door, which was weird. Cami was loud. Her laugh, her voice, her body. The entire time she'd been here, music carried toward my room, but now it was gone. Why? Where was that guy?

Don't do it. Don't look. The co-ed restrooms were just past her door, and I could try and see if she was in her room. If not, she'd left the door open, and that wasn't smart. There. It was a safety check. Michael would want me to make sure his girlfriend's twin sister wasn't getting robbed. *Sure, yeah, okay. It has nothing to do with your crush.*

Unrequited crush, my brain hollered back at me, putting me right in my place.

Content with my almost genuine rationale, I walked by with the appearance of heading to the restroom when I snuck a glance into her room.

She sat on the floor, her legs crisscrossed, with an empty gaze. The image counteracted any preconceived notions I had of her, and I stopped and stared at her unmoving form. Her eyes were sad, and her red lips were flat in a line as she tapped her fingers in a rhythmic pattern on her arm.

She didn't wear headphones, and I couldn't hear any music playing, but it was mesmerizing to see her so still and quiet. The sunlight streamed from her window, reflecting off her belly button ring and showcasing the glistening sweat on her skin. Perfection. She was gorgeous, and a burst of lust made my stomach clench. *Shit.* I gulped, and she snapped her head in my direction.

Within that millisecond, the sadness evaporated from her face, and she twisted those lips into a smile. "Oh, are you here to tell me how happy you are that we're neighbors?"

"What? No," I stammered, taking a step back. Having her full focus was a lot to handle, and it made my thoughts jumble together. I swore she could see into my mind. "You didn't close your door," I said, sounding like a damn robot.

This is why guys like me don't talk to girls like her.

"Why would I do that? I'm still in here." She pushed herself up and put her hands on her very trim hips. I appreciated muscles on anyone because it took work, but my mouth almost watered at the sight of her stomach. So toned and tan. She was different than me, all extra-large limbs and no coordination.

I forced myself to stare at her brown eyes and *not* her skin. "You were quiet, and that's not you," I said, appalled at how direct I was. It had to be the damn temperature making me this way. I didn't have the body to enjoy the heat.

"Oh," she said, her tone getting low and dangerous. "So, *you* think you know me?" She cocked one hip out and rested one foot on the other, reminding me very clearly that she was a dancer. I couldn't stand like that if I wanted to.

Shut your mouth. Don't answer. My brain shouted, but my mouth didn't care. Thoughts of *that night* came back, the same hurt and embarrassment causing me to lash out. The way she smiled at me before she left with another guy. The promise to meet up with me later just a joke, a tease. The hurt made my stomach twist like a pretzel, uncomfortable and painful.

"I know enough. I *hear* enough." My face burned red, and I regretted stopping by her door. It was pointless. We could never be friends and certainly never more. She was popular, and I was a dork. I was way too boring for her, and *what was I doing?* Rationalizing why I couldn't be with her? Jesus. I didn't even want that. Yes, she was beautiful, but that was it. If I'd learned anything from Madelyn, my ex, it was that I learned, the hard way, the type of partner I wanted.

Stable, reliable, safe. The complete opposite of Cami Simpson.

I shook my head, ignoring the angry look on Cami's face, and returned to my task—which was pretending to use the bathroom.

I went through the swinging door, the familiar smells of soap and cleaner greeting me. It reminded me of freshmen year, and a wave of nostalgia hit me. I'd be moving after this year. Six years at Central State and then adulthood.

What a trip.

I barely got two steps into the bathroom before a girl

screamed at me. Bloody murder type of scream, not a cute one. She clutched a towel over her chest, her face turning bright red. "Get OUT! RIGHT NOW! GET OUT!"

My heart leapt in my throat, and I slammed an arm over my eyes, trying to retreat only to have small hands press into my back.

"What the hell is going on?" Cami's voice penetrated my overstimulated brain.

"I don't... she started yelling." I stood in the hallway now. The narrow hallway with Cami just a foot away from me and my brain absolutely spiraling. The girl had yelled at me... screamed... what the fuck?

She furrowed her brows as she frowned at the door for a beat. Her top lip pursed up, and she wet it with her tongue before she snapped her fingers. "Ah, my guess is she's like us—just got put here and didn't realize the bathrooms aren't gendered."

"I didn't intend to scare anyone. I know I'm a pretty big dude, but still." I blinked a few times, willing my accelerated heart rate to return to normal. The chick had let out a high-pitched wail like I was about to kill her.

"Pretty big? Nah, you're massive, Freddie." She gave me a half-smile, and I *hated* how my name sounded from her lips. Seductive, teasing, like she was flirting with me. Which... she'd called me *massive*.

That wasn't necessarily a compliment, and she definitely wasn't flirting. No way. Not with me of all people. Cami liked athletes, frat presidents--the guys who didn't sweat in her presence.

I slouched my shoulders to seem shorter, swallowed hard, and tensed when Cami took a step toward me. Her petite frame came up to my shoulder.

"I'll go talk to her and settle her down. Possibly assure her you're not a murderer. It'll go great, trust me." She sighed like I annoyed her and walked by me. I didn't move out of the way, causing her side to brush my arm, and I sucked in a breath. She smelled like peaches and vanilla.

Two of my favorite flavors.

The shared bathroom didn't bother me at all, but I wanted to be mindful if others were nervous. I was a large guy, and that could be intimidating as hell. Bathrooms should be a safe space for everyone. But what could I do? Knock? Put up a sign? I scratched my head as the seconds went by and Cami still hadn't come out.

I wasn't sure how to proceed.

Wait here? Go back to my room? Go in there?

What if I actually had to *use* the bathroom?

Luckily, I didn't have to answer my snowballing questions because Cami came out with a smirk. I didn't like the twinkle in her eye or the way she let her gaze linger on my chest and arms. My simple blue shirt wasn't special, but the way she stared at me was sinful. How did this five-foot and change girl have the superpower to make everything she did dirty? And I *knew* better than to assume she meant anything by it. She was a tease —something I very much learned last year.

"Well, she's calmed down. She had no idea it was a shared bathroom."

"That was clear." I glanced at the door, ready to bolt if the girl walked out. "I'll knock or announce my presence next time."

"Lord Brady the Third entering the washroom facilities," she said in a horrible English accent. She laughed at herself before the tips of her ears reddened.

For whatever reason, seeing that blush made me almost smile. Our gazes met for a brief second, her leftover laugh and my smile colliding, and *what the fuck was I doing?* I broke eye contact, took a large step away from her, and walked toward my room. I needed space. To be alone. To settle down from the screaming girl and the aggressive attraction I had for my neighbor. To focus on my final year before choosing an internship and career and a city to settle down in...plus... Maddie's last message weighed on me.

No, don't think about her now.

"Um, bye? You're welcome for helping you? For fuck's sake," Cami said, attitude shooting out with each syllable.

My gut tightened because she was right. But for the life of me, I couldn't turn around and look at her again. She made me think stupid things, and it was better to avoid them. Instead, I waved a hand in the air in thanks and hoped that was enough.

"Whatever, asshole."

I went back into my room, leaving the door open as I fell onto the shitty twin mattress. It squeaked under my weight, and my room felt like a microwave, but it was better than being in the hall or around her.

All this drama because I'd wanted to see why Cami Simpson was quiet. This couldn't happen again. I pushed up from the bed, deciding to head to my brother's place to use their pool. I was almost to the point I'd sell my soul to cool off. It had nothing to do with my attraction to Cami. I was ninety-percent sure of it. That girl had trouble written all over her, and I needed to stay the hell away. She could break my already-battered heart with one blink of her long eyelashes, and she totally knew it too.

CHAPTER
THREE

Cami

"What?" I repeated for the fourth time at my counselor the next day. "I'm at risk of not graduating because *no one* told me I was missing a science and a philosophy class?"

Mrs. Applebaum nodded and eyed her watch. I'd booked a twenty-minute slot with her, and I still had eight minutes left. My eye twitched at her obvious lack of manners, and I recrossed my leg over the other.

"Since you changed your major three times and added a business minor, it's no surprise you're not on track. Plus, with the dance thing." She waved her head in the air like my *dance thing* was an errant fly.

"The dance thing? You mean being on the school's dance team?"

"That." She cleared her throat and eyed me over her big round glasses. Her gaze moved toward my tank top and shorts, the judgement in her eyes quite obvious. It wasn't new to have adults scoff at my outfits or sneer at my small straps. It wasn't their body, and they could kiss my ass. It wasn't like my nipples were out in the open. All the necessary parts were covered. Their reaction wasn't new, but it still hurt anyway.

"If you actually put your mind to it, you could add both classes to this semester. You'd be at twenty-one credits, which..." She sucked her teeth and looked down at me. "We should be realistic about your success--"

"Thanks for your vote of confidence. Such a voice for your students." I stood, annoyed at her attitude, and I jotted down the classes I needed on a sticky note. "I'll be fine without your help. Say, where's a comment card? Not all girls have my moxie, and they should be warned about your judgmental attitude."

She blinked and blustered, but I didn't wait around. I had my course names and knew there was a self-transcript report I could pull to figure out what credits I needed. Plus, my twin sister would help me if I asked. I barged out of the counselor office from the arts building, irritated as hell. People had coveted the fact I was on the dance team my whole life until now. I was majoring in dance and minoring in business, and people thought that was dumb? Whatever.

I wanted to open my own dance studio and run it. That was my dream, and I eyed the list of classes on the note. Twenty-one credits—first semester. During football and the start of basketball season. The most I'd ever taken was fifteen, and it was tough my sophomore year. There was the real possibility that I wouldn't succeed.

The itch to do something irrational danced down my spine. This happened more and more frequently when my life was out of control, and I wanted something risky. I scanned the quad and frowned. There was nothing dangerous on campus unless I counted eating at Hank's. Their food was trash.

I'd promised my sister I wouldn't go on dates with sketchy men after the incident last year where she picked me up from a strip club. But the excitement, the adrenaline, and the thrill of being scared was inviting. *It's just your need for attention.* My dad's voice of reason clashed with my need to take a risk, and I hung my head. *This* was why Coach didn't want me being captain.

I knew better.

I forced myself to walk back to the hot ass dorms to make sure I had all my shit for the semester to start next week. The addition of the two classes meant I needed books, and I had a budget for that.

Another thing people never thought I could do—handle money or do math. Pretty dance girls could use their brains sometimes. Who knew?

My navy blue crop top and white shorts stuck to my skin like they were soaking wet. I liked how the material felt on my skin, and I was proud of my body. It was a doozy outside, so I propped my dorm door open. I had two boxed fans now, but they weren't working. I needed more airflow. Stat.

I set my bag on my desk, kicked off my sandals, and moved the chair toward the windows. The fan *could* maybe fit there. I unplugged it and tried shoving it into the screen, but my muscles burned, and *shit*. I dropped it.

The fan crashed against the tiled floor. If it broke, I'd probably cry.

"You alright?" a deep voice asked, the sexy owner leaning against my door frame. Freddie had no business standing like that with those biceps on display. He was too hot for his own good, and my skin tingled just from being in the same room as him. Such a gentle waste of muscles. According to Naomi, he didn't play sports. He read and studied and liked trivia.

We were *so* different.

But our differences didn't matter. He was a jerk who I was pretty sure hated me. So, I did what I always did when confronted with someone who thought poorly of me. Flirted and teased. With him, his eyes would flash with anger, and that emotion did something to me. Lit me up, enticing me because I wanted more of that.

"You able to use your large muscles and help me get my fan in this window or would you prefer to glare at me?"

A line appeared between his brows, and he pushed off the frame to join me. He wore another dark fitted shirt and black jeans with chucks. Nothing fancy or exciting, but my pulse doubled when he stood *right* next to me. Maybe it was the thick glasses or the way his hair fell onto his forehead. Heat radiated from him as he picked up the fan and hoisted it toward the window, the movement causing the delicious scent of firewood to waft my way.

"I can't see the edge. Could you make sure it's wedged there?" he said, his arm brushing mine as he pushed the fan into position.

That brief touch offered a *zap* of heat, and I made sure to avoid contact as I helped adjust its angle. After a few pivots, it was in.

"Thank you," I said, jumping down to plug it in and turn it on. The temperature decreased by one degree, but it was worth it.

"Yeah, sure."

I closed my eyes as the wind danced over my face and hair. It smelled like fresh-cut grass and summertime--a scent I couldn't pinpoint the exact smell of. It was a combination of sunshine, sunscreen, sweat, and fun. Freddie cleared his throat, reminding me he was still in my tiny room with his arms on display, and I snapped my gaze to him. The dark glasses and dark hair worked so well on him. And the gray eyes... *if* I was back to my old bullshit, I'd see how far I could get with him. But his position on me was clear, and I was trying to stay away from problems, not jump naked into their arms.

He studied me with slightly narrowed eyes and a tight jaw. The muscles around his neck were flexed. Bunched up. Like he was stressed, too. I chewed the side of my lip, and before I could overthink it, I asked, "You doing okay?"

"I'm fine." He stepped back, and bam, the open expression I

saw was gone. We were back to McAsshole again. "Don't leave your fan plugged in when you're gone. It could cause a fire."

"I'm not an idiot, thank you." The comment reminded me of my not-helpful counselor. The rage I kept right under the surface bubbled out at his judgmental gaze. "God, I'm sick of people assuming I don't use my brain. Can a girl dance, be pretty, and be smart? Apparently not. Just get out."

"I didn't… I don't think you're an idiot." He hesitated, those gray eyes blinking fast. "Did someone tell you that you were?"

"I'm a big girl, Freddie. I can handle it." I put on my fake performance smile, the one I wore more and more it seemed. The same one on the campus billboard. "I appreciate you helping me though."

He frowned hard, and firm lines appeared around his mouth. "Careful with the fan."

"Of course. I promise to not stick wires in it or play with matches too." I smiled again, jutting my chin toward the door, and he listened this time. Once he was out of view, I collapsed on the bed, tired of everything.

Of pretending to be okay. Of pretending that not being captain didn't destroy me. Of the assumptions and looks and the fact I didn't have a circle of people to lean on. Even my friendships in the sorority weren't deep. We kept it simple. Fun. That was me: simple and fun and wild.

My eyes stung, and I sniffed before I could will the tears away. My nose got stuffy, and pressure filled my head. Fuck. No. Not now. My anxiety took weird forms, and my stress headaches would spiral into bad decisions.

I grabbed my towel and shower shoes, yanked my shower caddy with me, and made it to the bathroom before the tears started.

I couldn't afford a splotchy face tomorrow—if I wanted to show up with the team, I had to look my best. I stripped down, tossed my clothes on the floor, and blasted the hot water. This was my cure to avoid puffy eyes or bags. Steamy shower through the tears. I allowed myself to sniff and cry here. The hot water grounded me, and I could focus on the sensations. The water dripping down my back. The way my hair stuck to my face. The cold floor and loud splashes.

Once I settled my heart rate, my mind processed everything.

Audrey didn't believe I was captain material. My counselor assumed I was dumb. Guys said I was easy. My dad didn't think I was going anywhere. I might not graduate if I didn't pass all my classes. I had to decide if I wanted to be a part of the dance team anymore. Thought after thought, emotion after emotion. My shoulders shook as tears flowed out of me. I let them out, damn well knowing when I got out of the shower, I'd go back to being the flirty princess the world wanted me to be.

I scrubbed my hair and face then shaved my legs. The stall next to mine opened and shut, but I didn't think twice. I'd stripped down so many times from dance competitions that being naked really didn't get me nervous. Plus, call me vain, but I was proud of my body. I worked hard to be fit.

I finished in the shower but let my face rest under the water for a minute before I turned it off. I wrapped the thin towel around my chest and opened the door just as the person next to me did too. I hesitated for a beat, thinking there was some unwritten bathroom rule to not leave the shower simultaneously. Silence greeted me, so I went first. Maybe they were expecting me to leave first.

Oh shit. They were *not* waiting for me. Freddie Brady exited the shower next to mine at the same time, and my stomach swooped at all of his bronze skin. Heat radiated from his body, and I struggled to breathe. From the steam, obviously. Because I didn't get flustered with guys. Attention and flirting were my safe zones, but seeing him standing there, whoa momma.

He was so handsome it knocked the wind out of me. He cleared his throat and reached for the glasses he set on the stall, and when he put them on, they fogged up. It was equally endearing and hot. God, it had been way too long since I was last with someone because my body went into hyperdrive. Thoughts of biting his collarbone and kissing down his pecs to the light dusting of a happy trail crossed my mind, and I might've licked my lips.

My god. He'd be the perfect distraction from my life. One night with him, that body. He'd be worth it for a few hours. Mm.

His nostrils flared, and his mouth opened then closed. The air stilled around us, the steam from the shower trapping us in the moment. Freddie swallowed hard, his throat bobbing with the movement before he stepped back. "I'm not... I'm not going to sleep with you, so *please* don't eye me like that," he said softly, his cheeks reddening as he marched away from me.

Well, damn. That was a harsh slap of reality. The familiar tingle of embarrassment swept down my face and neck, my skin flushing at the blatant dismissal. I didn't even say anything to him. How could this be the guy who flirted with me for hours a year ago? *That* guy didn't look at me like I was nothing. That guy listened to me, seemed interested in what I said.

I swallowed down the regret. No one wanted to peek beneath the surface when it came to me. I was never worth the effort. Straightening my shoulders, I kept my head held high. Yeah, sleeping with the guy next door to me wasn't the best idea. It wasn't even close to being the worst, but I would follow his lead.

If I couldn't distract myself with him, I'd find something else to fill the gap in my soul. It was a constant itch that couldn't be reached, and the idea that I'd never figure out what would make it better scared the fuck out of me. There was only one thing that provided me relief, and that was dance. And with that in limbo...who would I even be if I wasn't a dancer?

With a resigned sigh, I left the bathroom and went to get ready in my room. The gym we practiced at was next door to the hockey rink, and I figured I could stop by to see my dad before blasting some music and going over the routine I'd planned for years. The one I wouldn't be able to show the team because I wasn't named captain.

Fuck. Even my *escape* was turning into a nightmare.

Wearing spandex shorts and a hot pink sports bra, I adjusted my wet hair into braids and applied mascara and lipstick. The day I didn't apply mascara was the day I stopped breathing. It was my security blanket. I drew eyes the entire walk toward the studio, and I winked, smiled, and waved at all the lookers. Students thought I couldn't hear their whispers about the *wild* twin or *she's down for anything.* Another fun fact about me—I allowed people believe that. I never questioned them or told them anything. The world decided to make me out to be this person, and I let them.

I'd had three one-night stands and a handful of casual flings since coming to college. That was it. My bedpost didn't have a million notches on it, and I didn't give blowjobs to every guy who breathed my way. The rumors were brutal, and it wasn't until Naomi told me she thought I'd actually tried to steal guys from her that I realized my *reputation* hurt people I cared about. I hadn't intentionally wanted to be *that* girl, the one who people hated on the inside.

Like her and my dad.

Having that talk with him almost killed me, but I was glad I did. He might be disappointed in me for other reasons, but he knew to ignore the rumors about one of his daughters.

"Hey, Cami girl," he said, smiling from behind his desk as I walked into his office a short time later. He set his paperwork down and gave me his full attention. Something we'd agreed on because both Naomi and I had leftover anger from how he'd treated our mom before the divorce. "You heading to the studio?"

"In a bit, yeah. Thought I'd say hi." I plopped down at the chair in front of his desk. "You'll never believe I'm living in the dorms now."

"What? How? You saved all year for that new place." He

frowned and leaned onto his forearms. "You can always move back in with me if you need a place."

"We'll see how bad it gets, but it's only for a month or so. Mold issue." I shrugged, even though I was still very much pissed.

"Don't love that."

"You and me both."

We shared a smile, and the real reason I came here bubbled up. I didn't talk about my shortcomings often because a) who did? And b) who wanted to? But my soul didn't know how to function without dance, and Audrey's choice weighed on me. "I'm not captain."

He stilled, and his dark brown eyes stared right through me. "What?"

"Audrey said I didn't exemplify what it meant to be a leader. Daniella did." I exhaled and waited for the disappointment to show on his face. I focused on a chip on the side of the desk, wondering how it got there instead of looking at him.

"Are you okay?"

Wait—that didn't sound like disappointment. I glanced at him and saw anger there. On my behalf. Whoa. "Uh, no. I've dreamed about this my entire life." My knee bounced up and down, and my stomach tightened. "I don't know if I want to do the season."

He exhaled and leaned back into his chair, the squeak due to his size, not the condition of it, and he shook his head. "I'm sorry, Cami. I really am."

"No discussion about how I'm being a shitty team player and how coaches can do what they want and I have to respect it?"

"You've made some mistakes, sure, but anyone who understands you like I do would have no doubt that you're meant to lead. Fuck, look at all the shit you've done with that team. If this was high school, I'd have half a mind to go talk to her."

My chest felt like it had too much air in it, and I blinked a few times to prevent any sort of moisture from pooling in my eyes. "Dad, no."

"I won't now, but Cami, I mean this. You get to decide what you want. Not me, not Audrey," he said, sneering her name, sending a wave of gratitude through me. "She chose wrong. I know that, and you know it. But now it's up to you. If you can live without dance this year, walk away. But if you can't... that's your answer."

I nodded, already feeling the answer in my gut. I couldn't *not* dance. It'd be like asking Naomi to go a week without a spreadsheet or my dad to live without hockey. It couldn't be done. But that meant taking a backseat which would be the hardest thing. "I'm going to think about it."

"Good. Do that." He stood up and walked over to me, placing his hands on my shoulders. "I'm proud of you. No matter what you do, I'm proud of who you're becoming."

"Thanks, Dad," I said, the ball in my throat doubling in size to the point my voice sounded weird. I cleared it and broke contact. "I'll see you later, yeah?"

"Sure thing, kid." He waved me off, and I left, not exactly feeling better about the season, but at least I knew what I had to do.

Stay on the team.

I left his office, content on dancing out the negative feelings. I put my headphones in, and as Taylor Swift rocked my ears, I closed my eyes and bobbed my head a bit. Music had a way of settling me down, and I moved my hips left to right. God, it felt good.

Then, *smack*. I ran into something very large and very hard. I snapped my eyes open to see Freddie staring down at my fingers on his chest. He reached out to settle me, his massive hands wrapping around my arms as he said, "Hey, you okay?"

I looked up, my heart pounding against my ribcage. He wore a black V-neck and ripped jeans, plus a backwards Central

State hat with those damn glasses. He smelled like mint and outside and *damn*.

The concern in his eyes went to irritation real quick as he let go of me so fast I lost my balance.

"Dude, what the hell?"

"Me? Why are you dancing in the hallway?" he asked, his tone sharp. His gray eyes seemed more like charcoal in the dim lighting, and I swore I could still feel where his fingers had touched my bare skin. A heat lingered there.

"Or you could make more noise and stop slinking around everywhere." I rubbed the spot where he touched, curious as to why it felt like he zapped me.

"I don't... I don't slink." He adjusted his glasses on his nose and stared at his feet, the tips of his ears reddening.

"I beg to differ," I fired right back, gesturing to his entire body. "For someone your size, *bro*, you should make more noise."

He frowned but not before his gaze dropped to my stomach for one second, sending a little thrill through me. He took a step back and shook his head, like I disappointed him by just existing. I couldn't deal with another insult, so I spoke first before he could. "What are you even doing here? You don't play hockey."

He swallowed hard and looked over my shoulder. "You don't either."

"Thank you, I'm aware."

"I came to see Michael, just..." he paused, doing the weird head shake again where he almost seemed in pain. "I gotta go talk to him." He walked by, awkwardly pressing himself against the wall like being too close to me was unbearable.

It would've been comical seeing someone his size trying to avoid me, but the tension in my chest grew at how blatant his dislike for me was. I put on my music, changed to a more upbeat song, and focused on dance.

The thing all these people didn't realize was that from

growing up with Legally Blonde as my hero, I would succeed out of spite. Sure, my incredibly hot wall-buddy wanted nothing to do with me, but that was fine. I could focus on me this year. I'd prove them all wrong—Freddie, Aubrey, my counselor. I *was* worth believing in damnit, and I'd make them regret doubting me.

CHAPTER **FOUR**

Freddie

I might've crossed a line.

No, I did. I definitely did. It'd been two days since I'd spoken to Cami, and I shouldn't have let her get under my skin, but goddamn, that girl was so hot it made me stupid.

It was my issue, not hers. I knew that, but fuck. With classes starting soon and Maddie's unanswered text still on my phone, my emotions were all over the place.

I miss you. Come back to Chicago.

She dumped me for being too boring, dated a string of guys who were the complete opposite of me, and *now* she missed me?

I chewed my bottom lip as I stared at the list of companies I could apply to receive an internship for second semester. That was my plan for the day, and I needed to stick to it. The firm in Chicago was run by Uncle Martin, a great guy who'd been texting me each week with a *fun fact* about their firm.

I loved my dad, but he talked about the internship like I'd already chosen to move back to Chicago and work with Uncle Martin when I wasn't sure *that* was what I wanted. But letting them both down? The thought made my stomach clench with worry. My head throbbed as I scanned the list again, my phone lighting up with a reminder of her text.

Unable to focus on my internship, I let my mind wander to my ex.

Why did she miss me? What did it mean?

More importantly, why did I care? She broke my heart when I knew she was a risk in the first place. I scratched my chest a few times, my shirt sticking to my skin from the damn heat as the continuous sounds of sex distracted me from my career search.

Dull thuds of a bed hitting the wall, overdramatic moans, and choruses of *yes, yes, yes* came from the right of me. Cami was to the left, but at first, I'd thought it was her.

My reaction wasn't ideal, picturing her dark hair all over the bed, pleasure written all over her face and that strong, tight body trembling. I had to adjust myself after that image went through my mind because damn, even her collarbones were sexy. After seeing her in a small towel, my lust for her had only grown.

Even when she gave me her signature look. The one she used to get her way all the time. The one she'd sent my way the night a year ago that I'd fallen for. However, I'd learned quickly that she wasn't interested in a guy like me—not when she left with the alpha-jock.

Still, the sex noises carried on from next door right in the middle of Friday afternoon.

People laughed in the hall as the screams got louder, and a dull thud came from Cami's room. Then something scratched. Like metal on tile. If I was a better human, I'd head over and apologize about the incident at the hockey arena or *something,* but I couldn't find the courage. Hearing the sex sounds and thinking about her body didn't put me in the right mindset to go and chat casually with her.

I rarely let my libido get the best of me. I was a relationship kinda guy while she was summer flings and hot weekend nights. So, to entertain the idea of sleeping with her was ridiculous in a number of ways.

I rubbed the back of my neck, seconds away from yelling to get the damn couple to stop when a squeaky wheel rolled right outside my room.

Then, without warning, Smashmouth's All Star started blaring, so loud the walls shook. The scratching sound returned, and there Cami was, walking down the hallway in cut off shorts and a crop top, dragging a huge portable speaker behind her. The lyrics drowned out the sex sounds, and everyone's doors opened up, all of us wearing equally confused expressions. I joined the crowd, watching as Cami set the speaker right outside the sex room, and some people laughed softly. A guy on the other side of the sex room high-fived her, and two girls from across the way did as well.

She leaned against the wall, avoiding my gaze entirely as she crossed her arms and propped one leg up while she waited.

Before I could ask what she was doing, the door flew open, and Chase yelled, "What the fuck?"

She paused the music, taking her time bending over to shut it off. Her crop top showed the curve of her spine, and my fingers twitched at my sides as I wondered what she'd do if I trailed a featherlight touch over her.

"Oh, I'm sorry. Is my music annoying? Is Smashmouth a real mood killer for you and Emelia?"

"Why are you being a bitch right now?"

"It's a part of my DNA, so I'm technically one all the time. Since y'all clearly don't give a shit about the rest of us hearing you fuck, I don't give a shit if you think I'm a bitch. See how that works?"

Chase groaned and slammed the door, making everyone in the hallway applaud.

"Girl, thank you lord. I couldn't take another second," a girl said, going up to Cami and hugging her.

"I feel weird about complaining about free porn, but come on, there's no air, and sometimes I don't want to hear that shit," a guy said, his appreciative gaze moving up and down Cami's body. It was easy to do with her long legs and short shorts. She chuckled and pushed her long wavy hair over her shoulder.

"Well, I don't have to be anywhere for an hour, so I'll be on fuck-patrol."

The doofus laughed way too hard at her joke, but what did I know? I must've snorted or scoffed because the guy glanced my way. He jutted his chin out in greeting before moving his attention to Cami.

She didn't miss a beat. She tilted her head slightly to look at me, her tongue wetting her bottom lip. Then, she dismissed me without saying a word.

"You're on the dance team, right?" the guy said, leaning one arm up onto the doorframe and clearly flexing. Her face lit up, and she spoke faster.

"Yes, I am."

"Sick, yeah, I think I've seen your face around. You're gorgeous. Cami, right?"

"That's me." She rocked onto her heels as something loud came from Chase's room. The door twisted, and both he and Emelia walked out, heads held high. Their hands were joined, and a blush covered the girl's entire face.

Cami arched a brow, making a real show about hitting play again, but the couple left without saying a word. She sighed, adjusted her hair, and gripped the speaker. "Thank god. I love a sex show now and again, but not in this armpit of a room."

The guy laughed and moved closer to her, but she was already en route down the hall. This was my shot. The chance to casually apologize for snapping at her outside her dad's office. I could avoid her, but I didn't want to be rude. I wasn't a mean guy. Never had been, and it didn't sit right with me. Insecure, sure, but I could own my actions.

"I need to talk to you," I said to her, not looking at her

exposed belly ring and focusing on her rich, brown eyes instead.

"Ah, sorry, I'm too busy being a ditz, and I don't have time for you right now." She forced a fake smile that made my blood turn cold because damn, there was no longer the interest or teasing glint to her eyes. It was pure dislike, and I didn't like it. She loved everyone. That was her thing.

I swallowed the horrible taste in my mouth. "It'll only take a second, please."

"Thanks for your quick thinking," the guy said. Her gaze shifted to him and away from me. "I'm Nathan if you need anything."

"Nice to meet you, Nathan." She smiled at him before letting go of the speaker and waltzing toward me because Cami didn't walk. She didn't strut either. She waltzed like the shitty tile was her dance floor and we were all her audience. She was grace and core, while I was meat and strength.

"Talk," she said, standing right outside my door. People still lingered in the hall, and I carefully touched her elbow, guiding her further into my room. I had three fans going which only caused her hair to blow all over, sending her sweet scent right into my face. Made me want dessert.

It'd be so much easier if she didn't smell so good. I ran a hand over my face and focused on the first thing. Cami was bold, but that rubbed people and insecure men the wrong way. "If Chase bothers you, let me know."

"It's fine. I can handle an inflated ego prick. Pretty used to them, actually."

"Look." I scrubbed a hand over my face. "I'm sorry about how I snapped at you outside of your dad's office. I shouldn't have." There, I apologized. The weight lifted off my chest. Things could go back to normal now, with me ignoring my attraction to her.

She met my gaze and tapped her foot on the ground. Her toes were bright orange, like our school colors, and she had a fancy toe ring that was the same color as her belly ring. Fuck, if that wasn't hot. "No, I need more. This isn't good enough."

"I'm sorry I've been a little bit of dick. There's no… you haven't done anything to deserve my anger." My face heated because it was the truth. I let my own hang ups about that night alter my behavior toward her, and it wasn't right. My face burned with the harsh reality that *I* was in the wrong here.

She narrowed her eyes, pursed those red lips, and shrugged. "Fine. I accept."

"Typically, fine doesn't mean *fine*." I might've had limited experience with women since Maddie and I broke up, but we both knew that specific f-word was the opposite of the truth.

"It means just that. Okay? You said sorry for being a dick, I accepted it. We're square," she said, her tone edged with ice that had never been there before. My chest tightened, and I wasn't exactly sure why I didn't want her to go. We weren't friends. We didn't like each other. And yet…the shimmer of *something* that always lingered in her eyes was gone. Like she had an inside joke or a mischievous thought she wanted to share.

She stepped to the right to leave, and I tried to say wait and hold on at the same time, the awkward sound of *wold* leaving my mouth. She arched her brows in response, making my stomach flop with embarrassment.

I cleared my throat. "Wait, please," I said, my voice sounding off and foreign to my own ears. I didn't do this. Confrontation. Things that made me nervous. I steered clear of the limelight and left room for people like my brother, Michael, or even girls like Cami. I wasn't sure what else I wanted to say to her, just that I wanted that shimmer back. Her gaze moved from my left eye to my right, her lips twisting up in amusement as the silence went on. It felt heavy, tense. Loaded, but I wasn't sure why. Nothing came out, and my entire body flushed. I slammed my lips together, the gesture ending her patience with me.

She rolled her eyes as she strutted out of my room, her hips swaying from side to side and drawing my attention to her ass. The shorts were made for someone like her--hugging every curve and showcasing how ample her ass was. Flashes of seeing her in just a towel came to my mind, and I slammed my eyes shut, like it would push it out of my head.

I could *not* be lusting after her. Not now, not ever. I needed a distraction from my neighbor, and thank god it was Friday night. Camden always knew somewhere to go.

Part of my and Camden's relationship was pushing the other outside of their comfort zone. That meant I brought him to trivia nights and he dragged me to house parties. It was weird to be twenty-four at a house party. I felt too old when the music shook the entire foundation and red cups were everywhere.

The smell of beer, perfume, and weed hung in the air while everyone let loose. It was the weekend before classes, and people were raging. Girls danced on a kitchen table to my right, and couples grinded on a makeshift dancefloor to my left.

I sat on a leather couch with Camden and his buddy Preston. They looked right at home with their beach shirts unbuttoned. The theme meant I had to dig through my brother's closet for a blue and white beach shirt that was a little too tight. It felt weird to not button it up, but Camden insisted.

Despite telling him I felt too old to do this, he'd dragged me here. This was mainly junior and seniors and even some grad students getting drunk before the school year started.

There were positives though. Free drinks, air conditioning, and distance from the dorm.

"So, you text Murdery Mads back yet?" Camden asked, not even bothering to fill Preston in. His roommate knew everything.

"No."

"I'm surprised, I figured you'd pine over what to say and end up typing you miss her too."

"I miss what we had, not *her*." That was the truth of it, even though she'd been on my mind with Cami living next door. The similarities between them were alarming—personality wise. When it came to looks, Maddie had been beautiful in her own way, but Cami stole the show. "I don't know what to say."

"Tell her to go bother the guy with the face tattoo or the asshole who cheated on her."

"Cheated on her?" I asked, hating that it interested me.

"Yeah." Camden laughed, but the humor didn't reach his eyes. "What's-his-face played her hard, but that's what she wanted. Those kinds of guys."

"Yeah," I said, already wondering if the cheating was why she texted me. She got burned so she wanted the safe guy to lick her wounds? The reliable one? The one who planned his weeks and would never get on a motorcycle? *Fuck.* I took a large sip of the beer and welcomed the burn. I came here to not think about my wonderfully sad love life, yet here we were talking about it.

I wanted the tables to turn on my brother, to analyze his love life, but he loved talking about himself too much. He was a bisexual egomaniac but had a heart of gold buried deep down. I scanned the room for a familiar face to go chat with to escape my brother, but my gaze stopped on a familiar figure. *Fuck.*

Why the hell was Cami here?

Right. The party. She was always at a party.

My neighbor wore a top that couldn't even be described as a bikini. It was more pieces of fabric placed over her nipples. My entire body tightened with need, and as I trailed my attention from her tits to the tiny bottoms she wore, I took a deep breath to settle down. No matter what type of look she gave me in the shower or in the hallway, she'd leave with someone else.

I gritted my teeth together, my knee bouncing up and down as I pictured how close we were that night. How we'd leaned against the wall and her lips were just an inch from mine. Her laugh, her perfume. The way my body hummed around her and how lucky I'd felt. Me. The dork who had his heart shattered pulled the interest of Cami. The party had been kinda like this one, rowdy with a buzzed charge in the air. I swallowed down the memory and pulled at a fray on my jeans for a second.

After a deep breath, I glanced at her again, but she'd moved on. She didn't look at me for more than a second and put her arm around a tiny little thing with red hair. Cami was a petite woman, but this other chick was smaller and totally sloshed. Her head hung at an angle, and her top twisted to the side, exposing her tits. Cami frowned, adjusted the girl's top, and started walking toward the door. It was a struggle, and each tendon in Cami's body tightened with her movements. Her back muscles were impressive as they bulged. She carried the entire weight of the redhead.

Without thinking about it, I bolted up. "Hey, let me help."

"It's fine, Freddie, I can handle it." Her shoulders bunched, but she let her guard down. She winced.

I didn't want to cross a line or do something disrespectful, so I put my arm around the girl, *only* touching her shoulder. She was blacked out. "I'll support her weight. Where are we going?"

Cami sighed as we got out the front door. Music blared all around us as the party went on, and the summer humidity greeted us the second we stepped outside. Damnit. The heat. Made me do stupid things, like letting my gaze linger on her up close. Her lips were so full and soft, and she had freckles on her shoulder I'd never seen before.

But why would I notice? Jesus.

"Seriously, go back in. I'll get her home."

"I'm not letting you both walk *alone* at midnight while you're wearing this," I said, angry that she would even consider this a good idea. "Don't be dumb."

She showed her teeth in a growl. "Fuck right off."

"I'm trying to help. Why are you being so difficult?" I asked, annoyed I was in this situation but unwilling to walk away. We stood on one of the busiest streets on campus with a girl passed out between us.

"Daniella, hey, where do you live?" Cami asked, ignoring me completely. "Put her down." She shuffled us toward a bench a block away, and once we got the poor girl set on the bench, Cami pushed Daniella's hair out of her face.

God, the streetlight hit her just right, showcasing all her curves, and my throat dried up. The things I wanted to do to her. The heat and beer must've been getting to me because she was not the girl for me. She'd led me on and ditched me. I needed to remember that. Cami was heartache wrapped up in a bow, my special form of kryptonite.

"Daniella, wake up." She flicked the girl's forehead and groaned. "This would happen to me. Of all the people." She pinched the bridge of her nose and crouched. "Daniella," she said again, louder, but the girl didn't move.

In her crouched position with her spine curved, it was the second time I thought about touching her skin there. She had dimples at the base, and my god, I was a back man now. Especially Cami's.

I cleared my throat, desperately needing a cold shower the second I got back. "Is there someone you can call?"

"Her friends left her, and no one else on the team is here. I'm sure they'd all love to see their new captain like this. Passed out on a fucking bench. This is leadership right here. Sure, I party but never like this."

"What are you going on about?"

"Oh, didn't you hear? Coach says I'm not leadership material, so this chick got the captain role." Cami sat on the bench, crossed her arms, and pushed her tits up so high in the process I couldn't focus on her face. They'd fit in my hands but barely. And why were they so perky? It wasn't cold out, and yet her nipples strained against the fabric.

"Wait, you're not the captain of the team?" My words were strained, almost hoarse as her eyes flashed with hurt. *That* snapped me out of my lust.

"Nope." She swallowed, her throat making a clicking sound. Her entire body seemed to slump, the sadness radiating off her almost palpable, and I had the most aggressive urge to hug her.

"*Swanna go home,*" the girl mumbled right before she hurled on the side of the bench, splattering all over the ground. I jumped back, but some clearly got on Cami. I tensed, waiting for her to freak out or squeal or yell, but she did none of those things. She took a hair tie from her wrist and pulled the girl's hair back.

"Get it out now, but can you tell me where you live? Is your roommate here?" Cami's tone wasn't nice or mean.

"No," the girl said, sobs coming out. "No, I don't know. Cami, are you going to tell Coach? Or the girls? I can't... I might die."

If I wasn't watching Cami so closely because I was obsessed with her facial expressions, I would've missed the shadow and *misery* crossing her face. Her ice-cold shield lowered for half a second, and the emotion rooted me to the ground. My insides clenched with how wrong I'd been about judging her. Here she was, taking care of this mess of a girl when she didn't seem to like her. But the misery... I understood that. There was a slight chance I didn't know Cami at all, and that didn't sit well with me because the most intrusive thought kept going on repeat.

I maybe sorta wanted to learn more about her.

Cami blinked and tilted her face up toward the sky. When she opened her eyes again, they were wet, but it was over so fast. She sniffed, sat up straighter, and patted the girl's shoulder. "You'll come back with me. It's hot as fuck, but you can't be alone."

"The team. What will Audrey say?"

The muscles along Cami's jaw clenched as she swallowed hard. "We'll keep it between us, but we're talking in the morning. Come on, get up. We're walking back, and you're not puking in my room."

"Thanks, Cami," the girl said, slurring her words as Cami pushed her up to her feet. The girl swayed, and her top shifted again. Cami met my eyes for a second before I took off my shirt and handed it to her.

"Cover her up. I can get it back tomorrow."

"Good call. Thank you." It took a few tries, but Cami got it around the girl's shoulders, and I didn't feel as weird with my arm around her since she had fabric between us. We looked like we were competing in the world's pathetic three-legged race as we headed down the party street on campus toward the hot as hell dorms.

I wasn't sure what would happen when we got back, but I knew one thing—I wasn't going to let my misconceptions about her linger anymore. Cami Simpson had layers, and I wanted to peel them back.

CHAPTER
FIVE

Cami

"U*nnn*, I'm dying."
"Drink the water, and if you puke, don't miss the trash can," I said, unable to believe my *night out* ended with taking care of fucking Daniella. The girl who stole my dream because she was a better *leader*. God, my blood boiled.

When I saw her passed out with a bunch of bros around her, I knew I had to help her. No question about it. But damn, I was pissed. And she'd puked on my feet. Gross. I grabbed my towel and caddy and went toward the bathroom for a quick rinse. It only took fifteen minutes to walk here with Freddie's help, and I refused to think about his bare chest.

Sure, he was hot, but my self-esteem could only handle so many hits. She was a fragile bitch lately, and while I was proud of my vanity most days, the digs on my intelligence and leadership qualities stung.

I started the hot water, letting it burn my face and chest. Some people liked cool showers, but I craved the heat. The cloud that surrounded me in the stall. The way I could focus on the water hitting my skin instead of my life. I didn't think about the first day of practice where *just call me Captain Dani* led the warmup and stretches.

She had no plan for our performance. No routines lined up. Just, *we'll figure it out, right?*

Fuck. Why did I think I could do this?

I scrubbed every ounce of makeup from my face until the water ran cold. Could I live without dance this year?

My mind drifted to Daniella and Audrey and the fact the captain of the dance team was drunk on the floor of my dorm room. Maybe I could live without it.

I could focus on school or volunteer? I wasn't sure, but no answers were going to be found today. I wrapped the towel tight around my chest and walked out of the stall to see Freddie standing at the sink, brushing his teeth. His back faced me, but our gazes met in the mirror, and those gray eyes dragged from my face all the way down my legs.

I felt his attention between my thighs, but it was past time for me to stop letting guys like him take up space in my life. It'd been fun teasing him and flirting with him when I knew it annoyed him, but it was different now. Teasing wasn't fun.

I was sick of myself, enjoying that flicker of lust only for it to hurt later on. My skin tingled from his intense stare, and I swallowed hard.

My feet weighed a million pounds as I walked toward the exit. He trailed my movements, and my heart raced from his attention, but I managed to walk out of the bathroom with dignity and barely got to my room before he was out in the hallway.

A little bit of toothpaste was on the outside of his mouth, and damn, it was cute. His entire appearance from the strong bare chest to loose gray shorts that hung low on his hips *almost* had me smiling at him. But he didn't deserve my smile.

Just a thank you. "I appreciate you helping us walk back. I could've done it, but you're right. It was better that you were with us."

"Of course, yeah, glad I could help." He grabbed the back of his neck and never broke eye contact. "Do you need--"

"I guess I should--"

He flashed a quick smile and shoved his hands in his pockets. "I was going to say, if you want to uh, talk or hang out or avoid your temporary guest for a bit, you could chill in my room."

"In my towel? What a fun offer," I teased, unable to stop myself. The tips of his ears turned pink, and it was just another thing to add to the *FREDDIE CUTE LIST*.

DELETE THE LIST, CAMI. I shook my head to settle my thoughts.

"You can change," he said, letting his gaze drop to my legs and linger there.

"How thoughtful of you."

He let out an exasperated sigh. "I'm trying to be nice."

"Why start now?" I fired back, my attitude returning. I'd been beaten down lately, and I missed the sassitude I'd carried like an accessory as a child. Seeing him recoil made me stand taller. I had none of my armor on (lipstick, mascara, perfume) and yet, I felt powerful. I arched my still-wet brow and waited.

Freddie worked his jaw like he chewed on food before he let out the softest sigh. "Because you look sad."

Whoa. Honest answer.

Real observation too. But the familiar feeling of *get out now bitch* took over. I didn't want to talk about why I was sad. Not with him. Not even a little bit. "Trying to be a hero, Clark Kent?"

He flushed, took a step back, and shook his head. "No. Not at all, I just--" he paused and ran a hand over his face. "You took care of her even though it was hard for you."

"Because I'm not a cold-hearted bitch." I scoffed and felt that fire dim a bit when the realization hit me. Freddie assumed I was just that--cold-hearted. Like Naomi did…

"Look, thanks for helping tonight, but I'm not friends with

people who think the absolute worst of me. Goodnight, Freddie."

I didn't wait for a reply before going into my room and shutting the door. Daniella reeked of beer and vomit, and the heat of the room was enough to make me gag. It was already two am, and we'd have to be up for practice at seven, so did I tough it out or try to sleep a little in the shoebox room of horrible scents?

This was what I got for trying to be a decent person. It was exhausting. I put on a purple sports bra and loose black shorts and went back out into the hall. There was a couch at the end of it, and it'd be better to catch a few hours here than in the hot room that smelled like armpits. The temperature wasn't any better in the foyer, but I didn't have to hear Daniella breathing like an ox.

My body didn't react well to stress, even though I acted like I did. My 'ice princess' shell was built to protect myself, starting when my parents got divorced, and it only solidified through the years. But it was getting more and more exhausting being that way, seeming totally fine all the time when really, my soul hurt.

My twin had a tight circle of friends who had her back for life. She had a boyfriend who saw her, loved her, and brought out the best in her. A twinge of jealousy worked its way down my spine, making me hate myself. Envy was okay. I was allowed to be envious of my sister without wishing her anything but the best. She deserved the world, but when had our lives become so different?

I pinched my nose and stared at the ceiling fan, watching the blades move in a circle for a full ten minutes. My body ached from the stretches and routines, and tomorrow would be worse. Thank god I could come back and nap.

Unless… I didn't go.

"*What* are you doing?"

Freddie. I didn't move from my position to stare at him, but my muscles tightened. "Trying to rest in silence."

"You're not sleeping out here."

"What world do you live in where you think you can tell me what to do?" I pushed up onto my elbows and hit him with my meanest glare. I used it once a day, but this time, I meant it. He stood, shirtless, with his hands on his hips and his gray eyes narrowed in annoyance behind his frames. Him being angry was beautiful. Made me want to rip those glasses off his face.

"Look at you." He waved his hand up and down in the air, heat mixing with the irritation in his eyes. The gray color reminded me of a summer thunderstorm. "*You* can't sleep out here. You don't know who lives here or what weird shit could happen. Like Nathan or Chase."

"Well, I'm a light sleeper, and my room smells like armpit vomit."

His mouth twitched, just a bit. "Armpit vomit? Creative."

"Not lying about it," I said, moving back toward my position on the couch. "Feel free to leave."

"Use my room. I can sleep here."

"No."

"Cami, please," he said, trailing off. Something shuffled on the floor. I didn't bother seeing what it was. Stay in his room? No way. It had nothing to do with my attraction to him and everything to do with what he thought of me.

I'd probably sleep-talk or do something horrible in there. Whatever. The silence went on, and a thud sounded to my right. I bolted up, aware that I was alone in a lobby with three doors that led to the rooms. Maybe it wasn't the smartest decision to sleep exposed to everyone.

I was being *that* girl. The one in movies that made me roll my eyes. Fuck. I couldn't go back on my word to Freddie. That was a hard no still, but I should tough out the vomit smell. Before I made up my mind, Freddie was back with a pillow.

To say I was relieved was an understatement. Did I share my gratitude with him? No. Hell no. But I rested against the cushion as he positioned himself on the other couch. His frame was too large to fit, and he groaned and grunted quite a few times.

"No one asked you to stay with me, you know," I said, a little softer than before. It was clear he did this to protect me. Whatever his reasons were, this was a nice move. I could acknowledge that without overthinking it.

"I imagined this week being chill as hell at the apartment. Probably going to a few parties. Hanging out on balconies. Never did I think I'd be in this shithole."

I guess we were having a talk. Cool. I rolled onto my side and made the mistake of facing him. His gray eyes were open and staring right back at me. "Bad luck for both of us."

"You didn't have to take care of her. You did."

I shrugged, closing my eyes. "Shh. I'm trying to sleep."

"Okay." He sighed, and I snuck a quick glance at him. He rolled onto his back, and his legs hung over the edge all the way up to his knees. Freddie put his arm over his eyes. Exhaustion won, but my last thought was how weird it felt to be protected by him.

The gentle giant in glasses. Despite all the reasons he pissed me off, the overwhelming sense of peace I had around him was a bit alarming. I couldn't remember the last time someone looked out for me.

I woke with a crick in my neck and my abs clenching. Sleeping on a couch was a terrible idea, but damn, the view of Freddie sleeping might've been worth it. His legs sprawled out at an awkward angle, but his face... It was all soft, and there wasn't a single *annoyed* line anywhere. He was handsome. No other word for it with his strong brows and jawline and slightly off-centered nose. His full lips parted slightly as he breathed deep, and for a moment, I wondered what it would feel like to cuddle against him. He'd be warm and comforting. Like my favorite hoodie.

His eyes opened. He blinked a few times, put on his glasses, then said, "Watching me sleep?"

"Jesus, not really." My face heated, and I pushed up to a sitting position. The sun woke at six am in the summer, and it was no different today. The beams crashed through the window and lit up the small room. They also showcased his chest. There was a line with sweat on it, and damn if that wasn't sexy. "I actually was thinking how nice your face is when you're not being mean."

He scrubbed a hand over his face and mirrored my sitting position. The lines I was so used to appeared all around his eyes, and he frowned. Those full lips curved down at the sides. "I might've misjudged you, Cami, and I'm sorry."

"Not the first person to do that, won't be the last." I got up, stretched my arms over my head in a yawn, and watched as Freddie's eyes traveled the length of me. It was weird to know he was attracted to me yet thought I was the worst. When I was done, I met his gaze head on, and there was no denying the heat there now. It made my throat feel tighter than normal, and my scratchy voice was a dead giveaway to the raging feelings inside me. "You didn't have to stay out here with me, so thank you."

"You're welcome." He ran a hand over his jaw a few times and opened his mouth like he had something to say, but a door flew open with a loud bang. Someone--Daniella--ran into the bathroom.

"Hoping it's a good sign she's in the bathroom. Fingers crossed it's my lucky day and there's no puke in my room." I cracked my neck from side to side and glanced one more time at the sleepy and sexy Freddie.

His eyes were darker in the morning, like he was still waking up and they didn't take on their light gray color until later. Very interesting. Not that I had any business wondering about his eyes. With a little wave, I left the lobby and went into the bathroom. The lovely sounds of retching had to be from Daniella, so I waited against the doorframe. "You gonna make it?"

"I'm dying inside," she said, throwing up again. I cringed, definitely relating to how a hangover felt, but I'd learned to never drink like that when there was dance the next day.

"You'll survive but listen, if you want to be someone in the dance world, you can't do this shit before boot camp. You're going to sweat and smell like alcohol, and the girls will know. It sets a terrible example."

She flushed and walked out of the stall and toward the sink. Her skin was pale and gross, and she met my gaze in the mirror as she washed her face. "Why is this place so damn hot?"

"No air. It's hell."

"You live here?"

"Temporarily." I held up a finger. "Wait here."

I went into my room and got mouthwash and a washcloth for her. I gritted my teeth, but I also grabbed a pair of workout shorts and a sports bra she could wear too. It was difficult to help the person who stole my dream. I rubbed my chest, a pang of envy and bitterness forming behind my ribs. No other way around it though. It was my reality. "Rinse up, change. Then, we're heading to camp."

"I can't... I can't go. I'll throw up."

"Yeah, you probably will, but this is on you. You're captain of the squad," I said, my voice getting a little louder. "You'll own up to it, be embarrassed, and power through it. What if this was halftime while our game was live on TV? Would you just let a teammate not dance because she was hungover? No. You tough it out for your teammates. Today is like that."

She blinked a few times and rinsed her mouth. "I can't believe Coach chose me. I swore I thought it'd be you."

"Yeah, well, I did too." I crossed my arms, already feeling

my temples pounding with all sorts of emotions. Lack of sleep, anger, annoyance. "Put on these clothes. Drink some water. We leave in five minutes."

I wasn't sure *what* I planned to do once I arrived, but I got ready *just* in case I decided to stay on the team. I was always prepared for anything.

We got in the hallway finally, and she leaned onto the wall for support. "Could you lead warm-ups today? I don't... I can't."

My hands formed fists at my sides just as Freddie propped his door open. The look in his eyes had my stomach tightening because I was pretty sure he was upset. Not *at* me this time.

For me.

Time froze for a beat when Daniella waited for my answer, and Freddie stared at me with his mouth slightly open, like he planned to say something. I desperately wanted to know what was going on in his mind, but he blinked and took a step back, the moment splintering like a rock in the windshield.

I knew better than to think that support would last long. It never did. Turning my back on Freddie, I sighed and faced my *captain*. "Sure, Daniella, I'll lead warm-ups."

CHAPTER
SIX

Freddie

Being an engineer brought me a lot of joy. There were black and white rules, non-negotiables where the world made sense. I thrived in a world of binary. Even my own rules that I created for myself. Camden and Michael gave me shit for them, like how I color-coded my highlighters with my Skittles or how I had a specific spot in the library that I preferred to study. Not like a certain table, but a certain position.

Back to the window, the entrance in view, and on the edge because I was left-handed. I had to have my coffee black and a water bottle on hand. Getting set up took a few minutes, then I could dive right into my studies.

I'd work for two hours, take a break, then keep going. Maddie used to make fun of me for being so regimented, and looking back, it was a red flag that she didn't understand me. The ache in my chest returned, a dull throb of confusion. I didn't love her anymore, but the wound was still there. The betrayal. The way I'd given her my heart and she crushed it.

It'd put me off relationships for a while, and that was fine. I could focus on my schoolwork, where everything made sense and was easier. I got set up in my spot and wrote out my routine.

It was the first day of classes, and most students weren't hit with thesis projects or career-breaking assignments. The library was filled with nerds like me. My people. I assumed most of the students here were grad students because everyone seemed a bit older, but as I scanned the room, one wavy brown head stood out.

Cami.

The swoop my gut did made no sense. It wasn't the appropriate response toward her. Polite indifference was best. I ignored her and went to my laptop, forcing myself to narrow down my dream agencies to ten. I'd work on my resume and submit intern requests for next semester...including the one with my uncle.

My jaw clenched thinking about the text from my dad that morning.

Dad: Can't believe you're going to be working with my brother. I'm so damn proud of you!

God, the support and guilt was enough to make me insane.

Sure, his office would be cool, but there were nine other choices that I could see myself picking. I kept a detailed list of the intern requirements, how to submit, the timeline, and anything else that stood out. Like the energy firm on the north side of Chicago had an office dog. That was awesome.

A light laugh had me craning my neck, wondering what had made Cami happy. Was it the dance team? Did she still like it after not being named captain? If I'd learned anything after living with Michael, it was the dedication and passion that lived in sports. I couldn't relate to being an athlete, but I saw the pain in her face when the redhead asked her to lead warmups. Cami had more expressions that I could count, and that flash of hurt lived in my mind, sending an uncomfortable urge to protect her through me.

Protect Cami Simpson? The pretty party girl? *Please.*

I tried to focus again, but I kept wanting to see if she was okay...for reasons unbeknownst to me.

A tall guy who was easily my size leaned against her table, a football logo on his shirt. Of course.

It was a football guy she left with at that party a year ago. The night I finally got the nerve to go out and flirt. I'd thought we hit it off, a lot. She was so easy to talk to. I was smart enough to not bring up past relationship baggage when flirting, but she made it so easy. She talked about her parents' divorce while I shared about a bad breakup. She pushed me out of my shell in an hour—that wasn't something that happened to me. Ever.

An instant connection that had apparently meant nothing to her.

Even at the memory, I swore my forearm burned from where she touched it that night with her delicate fingers. I gripped it, rubbing my fingers over the spot. She'd excused herself to get a drink, and I'd waited in the same spot for fifteen minutes, desperate and excited to keep talking to her.

She never came back, and when I saw her, her arms were around a large football guy. Cami had flashed him the same teasing smile she used on me, only directed at someone else.

The fluttering feeling I first got when seeing her disappeared, and I went back to my tasks. I'd gotten over the dismissal, but when I had to see her all the damn time in the dorm, the reminder of being second-best returned, making me think about Maddie and my shit luck.

I turned my music up louder, drowning out the memories and weird emotions. I told myself I could eat Skittles after I got through half my agenda.

Yes, I made an agenda every time I went to the library.

The hour flew by as I narrowed down my list, six of the agencies in Chicago and four of them in the Central area. That felt like a good balance. A fair list to consider. My uncle's firm kept jumping out at me, causing my stomach to tighten, but I pushed it away. Of course, I'd apply to it and likely get in.

It was what happened *after* that had my palms sweating.

I rolled my shoulders and glanced at Cami again, maybe to distract myself or because I was a glutton for punishment. This time, another guy was talking to her. She had on a pretty smile, but the lines around her eyes were tense. She had her arms crossed, and she kept pointing at her laptop.

Something went off in my mind, and I couldn't explain how I knew, but she was annoyed. Her posture was off, and her face…yeah, she was pissed. I watched her saying *I'm busy*, but the guy wasn't leaving.

My first assumption was that people came to the library for attention or for studying. It'd be easy to guess she wanted attention because she got it everywhere she went with her tight outfits and killer smile, but this time… I wasn't sure.

Her gaze moved from the guy toward me, and recognition and relief flooded her face. The fact she seemed happy to see me did odd things to my mind, and I lifted a hand in a wave.

Then, shocking myself, I beckoned her over.

She closed her eyes for half a second, her shoulders relaxing before she stood fast and gave him what I would call an apologetic smile. She didn't even pack her stuff into her bag. She held it against her chest as she pointed in my direction. "I'm meeting a study buddy here, but it was nice chatting with you."

The guy slid his gaze to me, annoyance flaring in his eyes, but it dimmed once he eyed me. Dudes were strange and used physical attributes to judge too soon. He might assume I could kick his ass due to my size, but I couldn't. Not even a little bit.

Cami rushed away from him and walked toward me, the motion of her hips sending my brain to that weird place again. She wore cut off white shorts and a bright orange top that showed off her arms and collarbones. Her nails were blue and her lips bright red, making me wonder how she tasted.

My stomach growled as she sat at my table, the familiar scent of peaches and vanilla crowding me. The library had a pastry counter, and I really wanted to go order something.

She set her stuff down on the other end, knocking my Skittles out of order, and she tensed. "Shit, sorry, here—" She reached over and lined the candies up in the wrong sequence.

I didn't like Skittles in the rainbow color. I put them in my least favorite to most. My brother thought I was wack, but the reward system was fine for me. The more work I did, the bigger the reward. "It's fine," I said, stilling her hand.

Seeing my extra-large fingers on top of hers spurred a tight feeling deep in my chest, but I blamed it on the change of routine. I tolerated sharing a study table with someone else. It was never a choice, but the gratitude on her face made it worth it.

I pulled my hand back fast and felt my face flush an embarrassing red. I adjusted my glasses and found her watching me with her large, expressive eyes. "You can study here if you want."

"Please, yes." She nodded and took in my notes and candy. "I won't make a sound."

"I doubt that," I said, blinking fast as I worried about her reaction.

She smiled and narrowed her eyes, like we had a little joke. I found I liked that mischievous look on her face. It wasn't one I saw often. "Fair, but I'll try really hard."

"Good."

Our gazes met again, and a slight blush covered her cheeks. God, I wanted to know why. What was she thinking about?

She pushed her hair behind her ears, the silver ring on her finger catching the light, and she sighed. "Thank you."

"For what?" I couldn't stop watching her as she arranged her notebook and laptop. Pretty handwriting was at the top, and for some reason, it was so her. Bright purple pen and loopy letters.

"Letting me come over here. I know I give off a certain… vibe," she said, looking at the ground so her long lashes fanned on her cheek. "But I'm taking twenty-one credit hours this semester, and I really need to focus."

"Twenty-one? Why?" That was a lot. More than a full load.

"Because at some point I missed a science class." She gave a tight smile and pointed to her device. "It's an online biology class which should be fine, but I've never taken more than fifteen credits. I need this to graduate."

"Oof," I said, wincing. "That's a bummer."

"Yeah, well, the saying *bad shit happens in threes* has been true. Between the apartment, this class, and not being captain, it's a been the Bermuda triangle of bad luck." She gave a self-deprecating laugh and reached into her bag for headphones. "That's enough feeling sorry for myself. I'll leave you alone."

"You're not bothering me," I said, wanting to figure out *how* to make her bad luck better. I felt the same but in different ways.

"I told you I wouldn't make noise, Freddie." She snorted before looking at her notebook. Worry lines appeared between her eyebrows, and I had the strangest urge to reach over and smooth them out.

Cami Simpson was utterly breathtaking, but witnessing her like this, focused and organized... it caused my heart to beat a little faster. I was privileged to see parts of her that the rest of campus didn't, and in a weird way, it made me feel special.

With a new lightness to my chest, I went back to work. We sat together, both doing our own thing for a good hour before she slid out her headphones and stretched her arms over her head. "Unnn," she said, the sound something like a moan. "This chair is killer on my posture."

"Breaks are important." *Breaks are important?* My god, could I be more of a loser?

"You know, you're right. Is that what your Skittles are?" She pointed to them with a wicked grin. "Do you share?"

"No."

The lightness in her eyes dimmed, and I immediately

regretted it. I cleared my throat, waving my hand in the air like it would wash the words away. "No, I meant, they aren't my breaks. I do share them sometimes."

"How does one get on your sharing-Skittles list? I have a guess it's a very short list." She did that bewitching smile again, and my own lips quirked up. "Oh, I got a grin from the gentle, grumpy giant."

"Shut up," I said, my ears burning hot.

"It's a nice smile. You should do it more." She reached over but paused before her delicate little fingers touched a candy. She arched a brow, her lips still in a bewitching grin. "Can I?"

"Well," I said, adjusting my weight in the chair. "They're a reward system. What have you done today?"

"Oh, yeah, sure." She squinted at her laptop. "I wrote down everything I need to do by next Monday with guesstimates of when I can work on them. Time management is one of my best skills, even though people don't think that."

"With dance, I'd imagine you have to be good at that."

"Thank you," she said, her eyes going all wide. "That's what I've been saying. So, anyway, I made a chart for the week and briefly glanced at the syllabus for this bullshit biology class. I have weekly quizzes which seem horrible."

"Okay, you can have one."

"One? All that work for *one* lone skittle?"

"That's my rule."

"You're a cruel, cruel man." She took a yellow one and popped it into her mouth, her red lips enclosing around it and sending a million dirty thoughts my way. Like how her lips would feel on mine, how she'd taste, and how she'd move her toned body as I pulled her against me.

Seriously, what the fuck? I wasn't driven by lust. I'd acknowledge people I was attracted to, but feelings this strong? The fact Cami had crossed my mind so much that my fingers twitched to touch her collarbone? I wanted to see another sly look on her face or hear the sounds she'd make.

It made no sense. I cleared my throat as my jaw clenched, regret weighing me down. I shouldn't have invited her over to study. She was a distraction. She stared up at me, questions in her eyes as she gave me a little smirk.

"I love the yellow ones. Everyone always chose the red or purple, but not me. The lemon ones? Mm. I'm the same with Starbursts too. Give me alllll the yellows."

"Do more work, and you get more," I said, sounding absolutely barbaric. What was wrong with me? I should give her the bag, indulge her. Make her smile again.

Her eyes flashed with something like interest, and she licked the corner of her lip. "Yes, sir."

Shit. The way she said it...sounded delicious. I put my headphones back on, refusing to think about all the ways she got my blood pumping harder. I had been completely wrong about Cami which was dangerous with a capital D. She was my physical kryptonite, but throw in this badass side of her? I was screwed.

I could be friends with her without falling for her. I had to or else...well...she'd just pull a Maddie and break my heart.

CHAPTER **SEVEN**

Cami

Three days later, sweat cascaded down my spine, the sun hit my face directly, and I chugged my bottle of water like my life depended on it. Hydration was important for my body, skin, and hair, but there was also something delicious about a cold drink after a dance sequence.

Even if the routine wasn't mine.

"Seriously, like, why does she think this routine works?"

"I know! And of fucking course she's putting herself at the front."

Every muscle in my body tensed at overhearing two freshmen talk shit about Daniella. My blood boiled at the lack of respect. Not only from the way the girls talked about her but also over how Daniella led the team. We hadn't bonded yet. There were no ribbon days or moments of her showing her leadership.

My temple hammered like a little guy lived inside my skull and was renovating it with a jackhammer.

"Come on, girls, one more time running through," Daniella

said, her voice lacking conviction. It was like she was a substitute teacher trying to commandeer another person's class. Horrible and uncomfortable.

Coach Audrey met my gaze for a second, her knowing stare rooting me to the spot. How dare she try to make me feel guilty? Like this was my fault? I blinked and focused on the grass at my feet.

She had to realize the decision to choose Daniella would gut me, so she had no right to want me to fix the situation she caused. If this were *my* team, this shit wouldn't fly. But it wasn't. It was Daniella's to lead.

I was too much a mess, a bad influence, a girl filled with mistakes to have that role. *Okay, down in the pity party parade again?* I shook my head to rid myself of the thoughts, and instead, I focused on what I had to do later. Studying and rewarding myself with Skittles. I'd gone to the library at the same time each night, and Freddie was there, smiling at me with his soulful eyes when I joined him.

We didn't talk, but he did bring an extra bag of Skittles for me to use. Just thinking about it made me smile, and I ran my right foot over the grass a few times, the tightness in my chest loosening just a bit.

Audrey barked out instructions, and I bit back my smile.

"Do you want to embarrass yourself at the game next week? If so, carry on. It's not my face on the field wearing the school colors." Audrey's cheeks had red spots on the sides, and she redid her hair a few times, a sure sign she was stressed.

Not my fault. Not my circus.

Well, it was my team…just not one I was leading.

Did that mean I was being too selfish? Was I letting my beef with Audrey get in the way of our team respecting Daniella? That didn't sit right, and when Daniella called for us to get in formation again, I went right to the front.

Three other girls did, but that was it.

"*Listen* to your captain," I said, the threat clear in my voice. I glared at the clique of girls who thought they were hot shit. Ego had a time and place, but this was *not* it. "Get in line now. It wasn't a choice."

The three girls stood straighter and went to their spots. My heart beat so fast I could feel each pounding breath all the way in my throat. The potential ramifications of this were bad. Audrey could be pissed. Daniella could be mad.

But the second one didn't bother me so much. She needed to get it together.

I focused on the stadium in the background. It smelled like fresh cut grass, and the air had that delicious new school year smell. This time of year always excited me, right before football kicked off and homecoming arrived. Formals and parties all over campus. It was exciting, like new opportunities were just out of reach, and I focused on the good.

"Okay, girls," Daniella said. "We're going to run through the sideline routines four times before our half-time performance. Any questions?"

"Yeah, why are you in front? It should be the most talented girl on the squad," Sloan said, making me snap my attention toward Daniella.

Daniella was… not horrible. If she was a decade, I'd pick the 70s for her. She'd be a total hippie and go with the flow which was great. A team needed all personalities. But to lead this group of feisty females? I watched as her face reddened, and she swallowed, hard.

"And you think that's you, Sloan?" she said, her voice shaking on the end.

"No." Sloan laughed. "It's Cami."

The answering silence was as horrifying as it was validating. I put in the time to make sure I was the best, and to hear it come from someone on the team felt validating. But it was the gross nagging feeling in my chest that had me shaking my head and facing Sloan.

"Thanks for your confidence, but since Daniella is captain, she gets to make the calls."

"Even though we all know you're better?"

My eye twitched, but I kept the rest of my face neutral. *Ice queen.* That was me. Unphased. The party girl. "It's Daniella's call."

Sloan shrugged and returned to her spot. Daniella narrowed her eyes at me for a beat before moving along practice, and I avoided both her and Audrey's looks the entire time. For two hours of repetition and unimaginative routines, I danced through the motions because it was all I knew.

I craved to get back to the gross ass dorm and decompress, to think about Skittles and Freddie's little quirks. But I'd barely wiped sweat off my face when Daniella walked up to me.

"Hm?" I asked, keeping my tone as unbitchy as possible. She was my semi-nemesis, so polite was going too far.

"Can we talk?"

"About what?"

She blinked, her large green eyes seeming sad and unsure. Her shoulders slumped, and she looked weak. Our fearless captain. I fought the eye roll as she frowned so hard she aged five years. "Why you hate me."

"I don't hate you, Daniella." I let a guarded smile break through. "If we're being honest, I don't think you should be leading this team, but I'm going to respect Coach's choice. You lack conviction and planning, and you're too afraid to push the needle."

She let out a puff of air and hung her head before her gaze met mine. This time, her cat-like eyes were filled with anger. I tensed, preparing for whatever verbal attack she had. How I was a slut and would never be a leader and blah, blah, blah. I'd reward myself with one hour of watching Law and Order. Then I could get started on the damn science homework. After, I could try to find time to sign up for teaching classes at the studio, and oh shit. She said something, and I'd completely tuned her out. "Say that again?"

"I'm sick of being told I don't have what it takes! You think I don't know that I lack leadership? Or that I haven't thought about this role every second of every day since Coach told me?"

"Are you letting fear hold you back or what? Because you're not doing anything like a leader." I put my backpack on my shoulder, making it clear this conversation wasn't dragging on. "Stop trying to figure out how you can fit into other people's version of you and figure out what you are. Who are you as a leader? Why you?"

She stared at me as I left her there, but I refused to feel bad for her. She'd gotten what I wanted. She was given my dream and was struggling because it was hard? Fuck. This was some bullshit.

"Cami, a word?" Audrey said, right before I was out of earshot.

Jesus. The world was testing me today. I faced her, keeping the same blank expression on my face as I had with the girls. I arched one brow. "Yes, Coach?"

She grimaced and ran a hand through her hair, pulling the ends of it a few times before sighing. "I'm going to talk to Daniella about making you co-captains. I think it would be best for the team."

"No."

She frowned, tight lines forming around her eyes as she let out a long sigh. "The two of you together would be great."

Hell no. A consolation prize? A runner's up trophy? She made her decision, and it didn't work out so *now* she thought it'd be a good fit for me? I swore I saw red. My legs shook, and I needed an outlet for all this rage. My knee bounced as she studied me with a slight smile on her face. Like she was hopeful that her pity invite would be the solution to the team.

The smile pissed me off to the next level. "It's not *my* fault your choice was incorrect. I'm not leadership material, Coach.

You made that clear. Nothing has changed in the past month for your opinion to shift, so, no thanks."

I didn't wait for a response and shoved my headphones into my ears. Co-captains? Fuck. *Fuck.*

I stomped all the way back to the dorm, making sure every square inch of pavement felt my anger. I ignored the looks and smiles thrown my way. Everyone thought they understood me. They all had me pegged and refused to accept that their impression could be wrong.

What made it so much worse with Audrey was that she knew me more than most. She saw the amount of time I put into the team, into being ready and wanting us to be the best. She absolutely understood how badly I'd wanted this.

I could handle most people judging me, but her? When she saw my blood, sweat, and tears? The betrayal hit deeper.

My eyes stung as I used my keycard to walk into the dorm. The hot ass air just fueled my temper, and I almost ran straight into a large body. A familiar, woodsy scented body.

"Hey, whoa, whoa," Freddie said, gripping each of my arms with his massive hands.

I forgot to mask my emotions as I looked up, and his entire face crumpled. The easy smile fell and was replaced with a frown. "I was going to head to the library to study, but you weren't back. Are you... okay?"

Was I? No.

I couldn't talk about it. It was like a hand gripped my throat, preventing me from speaking because once I did, I'd cry. And that wouldn't do. I brushed past him, hell-bent on getting to my room.

The ball in the back of my throat doubled in size as his heavy footsteps followed, and I barely got my door open before he was behind me. "Cami, what happened?"

"Everything's fine." I *knew* I sounded bitchy and shrewd. I didn't care though. Daniella and Audrey took the final fucks I had to give, and I was running on E. "Just leave me be."

"Sorry, I can't do that." He shook his head and leaned against the doorway. There was something about his huge body and that doorframe, his black glasses sliding down his nose as he stared at me with his mouth pressed in a thin line. He looked good doing that simple gesture, and I threw my bag onto my bed and fell onto it, face up.

He moved to sit next to me, not once asking if it was okay to enter.

"I want you to leave," I said, staring at the one light in the center of the pale yellow ceiling. It was so damn hot it was horrible. My skin beaded with sweat, and my heart raced. He smelled like outside. "Why are you here, Freddie?"

"You're upset, and we're friends now. I shared my Skittles with you. That's... a big deal to me. And friends don't let friends be upset alone."

I shared my Skittles with you.

Those words were like a Freddie-sized version of a blanket. My face flushed at the genuine concern in his voice, and I so badly wanted to hold onto the sentiment. Friends.

Friends don't let friends be upset alone.

I had been alone for so, so long. I could call Naomi, and she'd be there for me, but she was my sister. A friend... I was friends with Frederick Brady the Third.

He shifted his weight so his thigh touched mine, and I tensed, waiting for him to move it. He didn't, and the room felt hotter than the dark pits of hell. My brain got fuzzy with who the enemy was anymore. Daniella? Audrey? My reputation?

Me?

I slammed my eyes shut to try and prevent the tears from spilling, but the movement did the opposite. Too much moisture pooled there, and they fell down my cheeks in two lines.

I didn't cry. *Fuck.*

My nose was stuffy, and it was horrible. I sniffed, the sound causing Freddie to bring his hand to my face. The movement had him at an awkward angle, so his body was half-covering mine, and I couldn't help but imagine how he'd be in bed.

But attraction was fickle, and feeling safe was more important. I was starting to *trust* this large man, and that scared me. He wiped the tear and then stilled, like he too realized our position.

He snatched his hand back, holding it close to his chest as he opened his mouth and closed it a few times. His lips were full and slightly wet from his tongue, and I squeezed my thighs together at the aggressive draw I felt toward him.

It had to be because of the growing comfort I had with him. I wasn't used to giving trust to people, and it was making me feel absurd things. He sighed and ran a hand over his hair, adjusting his glasses. "I don't like this. Tell me what I can do to help," he said, his voice low and coarse and *right* in front of my face.

"Nothing." I pushed myself up, steeling my spine to seem tough. "Really."

"Do you want to go study with me?" he asked, the evident plea in his voice causing my insides to get squishy.

"No, I don't know what I want. A distraction. To not feel," I said, groaning and standing up from my bed. It was easier to think when we weren't so close together. I still wore my practice outfit, which was a sports bra and short-shorts, and I caught Freddie eyeing my stomach.

"What do you like for a distraction?"

"Partying. Being around people so I can hide from my thoughts. Making bad decisions to not feel the pain." I let my gaze travel down his broad shoulders, not bothering to hide my clear intent.

His eyes lost some of the warmth and concern, and without saying a single word, he shut my flirting down. If anything, he looked pissed. "It's not a party or around a ton of people, but I have an idea."

"Is it a bad decision?" I asked, pushing my luck.

"It's illegal, so I would say yes." He smiled, a full-faced, real grin, and I wanted to live in this moment of receiving Freddie's grin. My insides fluttered. I smiled back, and suddenly, all the urges to do something stupid flew away. I wanted to hang with Freddie and his Skittles, and I just *had* to learn what he thought was illegal.

"I'm in."

CHAPTER **EIGHT**

Freddie

I should've hesitated or come up with something else instead of taking Cami to the tunnels off the engineering building. It was a campus legend that we'd explored five years ago to find the barely concealed wall that led to an underground tunnel system. I'd only gone down a handful of times, often with a pack of beer, and it had a hauntingly energizing feel to it.

I'd almost gotten caught each time, which was a real rush, and after seeing Cami so sad... this would be a better distraction.

Bad decisions to not feel pain. There was so much more to her than I'd originally assumed. What happened for her to act this way? Was that why she partied so much, to hide her feelings? What feelings did she hide?

I wanted to piece together the puzzle pieces of her when I knew I shouldn't. She was a tempting mystery, and now we were alone in a dark tunnel, and she still wore her tiny workout outfit.

This was probably a mistake. Not only was it dim lighting, but it was narrow and warm and *just us*. The quiet let me hear each time she swallowed or popped her lips together. She took in the surroundings with a curious wonder on her face, and her eyebrows moved with whatever was going on in her mind. It was insanity that I once thought she was an ice queen full of teases and flirtations. She was so much more, and I craved to pull each thought out of her pretty head. Did she think it was cool I took her here? Or was it disgust on her face? I wasn't sure, and it was *maddening*.

"We have a series of tunnels underneath the campus? This is for real?" she asked, turning in circles and eyeing the entrance. The stairs were covered in graffiti, and the lingering smell of pot clogged my nose. The damp air made my limbs feel heavier and my mind foggier.

"Yeah." I rubbed the back of my neck before pulling out the small bottle of whiskey I'd grabbed at the last second. I wasn't a huge drinker. I didn't like how the alcohol dimmed my thoughts, but I had to be honest with myself—between the heat at the dorms and my growing attraction to Cami, my mind was already spinning.

I wiggled it in the air, and her eyes lit up.

"You rascal. Skittles, secret tunnels, and whiskey," she said with a hint of warmth in her voice. "Who even are you, Freddie?"

My face got hot at her words, and she came up to me and placed her hand around the bottle. Her fingers lingered on mine, the touch almost erotic with how tense I was. Her skin was soft and smooth, and I gulped, hard. She took the bottle, unscrewed the lid, and swallowed, wincing at the end as some dripped down the side of her mouth.

I wanted to *lick* the drop. But I did no such thing.

This was another moment of stupidity. Getting tipsy with Cami was the last thing I should do, but damn, the girl had cried. Tears made me forget all rationale except to STOP them, and so here we were.

"How did you find out about this?" She walked up to a wall

and dragged her finger down it. Someone had written in dark marker TREVOR AND SHAE FOREVER. I mentally rolled my eyes but wondered if they were still together.

"Being a nerd has its advantages. We heard rumors about the haunted tunnels in the engineering building, and we found a map, then the fake wall you saw. We broke in five years ago. Not sure where it actually leads as all of us were too chickenshit to explore," I said, laughing at the fact I was a total wimp. We clearly weren't the only people who'd discovered the underground world here, but I had no plans to find out who else or how many others knew about it as well. I took a swig of the bourbon, the sharp sting burning my throat as she snapped her gaze at me.

Cami was a striking woman, but her brown eyes widened, and she sucked in her bottom lip in a way I hadn't seen before. "Haunted? This is *haunted*? You brought me into a haunted hallway?"

Oh, shit.

I cracked a smile at her growing fear and couldn't stop the laughter from bubbling over. "You're afraid, huh?"

"I don't fuck with ghosts, Freddie. They can keep to their business, and I'll keep to mine." She marched right by me back toward the stairs, and I caught her elbow in my fingers. Gently, of course. Our size difference couldn't be any more apparent, and I never wanted her to feel threatened by my body. She glanced at my fingers on her skin, and I let go.

"It's not haunted. I swear. Mostly. This tunnel leads toward the southern part of the quad. Right around that good coffee shop." I didn't mention that there were branches of other tunnels that we had no idea where they ended because hello, I was also scared.

She reached for the whiskey in my hands, brushing her fingers against mine, and took a large swig. Then another while eyeing me in a way that reminded me of my grandma. Her brows furrowed, and her gaze was skeptical. "If you're lying, I will *never* forgive you, and given the chance to haunt you, I will without question. I'm scrappy and hold grudges. Ask me about Nancy Ancy."

"Nancy Ancy? What is that?"

"My third grade nemesis. She stole my Lisa Frank folder with unicorns and had the audacity to tell the teacher she had no idea how it ended up in her bag. She didn't get in trouble, but I never forgave her for that sneaky shit." A slight blush worked up her cheeks, and while I could stare at her face and admire her features for hours, it was the lack of tears in her eyes that had my chest feeling light.

She wasn't sad anymore.

She frowned at my silence and pointed at my chest, her little finger connecting with my sternum. "Don't end up on my Nancy list."

"I understand," I said, raising my hands in the air in surrender, making sure my grip on the bottle was solid. "This helped get your mind off things though, right?"

"Yeah, but now I'm thinking about ghosts *and* the bullshit with the team." She sighed long and hard, her eyes meeting mine for a beat that sent a ripple of awareness through me. I had a feeling this was the *genuine* Cami Simpson, the version she never showed others. It was an addicting feeling to see her like this, raw and real.

She stretched out her hand, and for one second, I thought she wanted me to hold hers. Which was *not* what she wanted. The whiskey. She wanted the whiskey. I handed over the bottle, and she took another drink, this time not spilling any. Once she swallowed, she ran her hand over the center of her chest, pushing into her skin and rubbing it.

It wasn't sexual. I knew that, but god, my cock swelled a little at the continued motion. Sweat beaded at the base of her cleavage, and it took all my willpower to look the other way. Focus. *She's upset. The team bullshit.* "Do you want to walk or sit?"

"Yes? Both?"

"Let's sit first." I went to the cement wall and plopped down, using the wall as a backstop and stretching my legs across the dirt. She eyed either side of the tunnel, both options fading into darkness, and she shivered.

"This place is creepy as hell, but I don't want to leave. If that doesn't describe how fucked up I am, I don't know what does." She joined me against the wall and sat so close to me our forearms brushed. She went for the whiskey again, but I snatched it out of reach. "Um, excuse me? This is my pity-party, and the rules are that I drink when I want."

"Fine, but this is my place, so I get to make a rule. You get some when you answer a question."

"Two way street then, bro." She leaned closer to me, her breasts hitting my arm as she tried to grab the bottle. "I didn't agree to this torture."

"Torture? Please." I rolled my eyes as she went for the bottle again, this time placing her hand on my thigh. It was like a blast of electricity through my veins, causing my cock to stir again from her proximity. Even with sweat covering her, she smelled delicious. "Question, then drink," I barked, my throat rough and filled with desire.

"Whatever," she said, falling back down next to me. It was odd seeing her bring up her shields. She sat straighter, crossed her arms and legs, and stared off into the distance.

What type of question did she think I was going to ask? I hated how the blank expression changed on her. She was full of life and energy, and this was...not that. I didn't want to go as far as to say I missed flirty Cami, but hell, that was a better version than a sad one. *Lighten the mood.*

I snapped my fingers. I wanted to badly to ask about the team, about why she was so upset to the point of tears, but I didn't. I pulled a Camden trick—avoid the issue at all costs. "Okay, what's the most *useless* talent you have?"

"That's... that's your question?" She eyed me, blinking a few times.

"Is that yours?" I fired back.

She grinned, scrunched her nose, and let out a snort. "No, it's not. Not even a little bit. Okay, well, most useless talent. I can flip a pen around my thumb. Like, what's the point of it besides being super cool?"

"Alright, you earned a drink."

She took it from me and held eye contact, the tunnel suddenly seeming smaller. There was something sexy about her throat moving and the way she held my gaze. "My question."

"You want to know my most useless talent? Okay, well—"

"No. I'm not wasting a question on that shit. Tell me about the best sex of your life."

"Cami," I said, choking on her name as images of her body flashed through my mind. "What are you... that can't be your question."

"It is. I want to know." She shrugged like she didn't intentionally cause my pulse to skyrocket.

"Is this payback?" I dropped my gaze to her mouth, wondering why the fuck it was a bad idea to kiss her. My breathing got heavier as she also eyed my lips. My entire body tensed like the time I'd tried running a half-marathon without training. My muscles were sore from holding myself so tight, like if she leaned any closer to me, I'd explode.

"Payback? For what?"

Think. I was so focused on the curve of her upper lip and the light dusting of freckles on her nose that I had no idea what she was asking. Payback... *oh.* "Uh, forget it."

"Okay." She shrugged and arched a brow. "It's my question, so...are you afraid to answer or have you had lackluster sex your whole life?"

"Not holding back any punches, huh?" I coughed into my fist, buying myself some time to get my head on straight. "Here

I thought I'd talk you through what happened to get you all upset, not bring up sex."

I ran a hand over my face and thought about Maddie. The sex wasn't crazy hot or wild like stories I'd heard, but it was sex. So, I enjoyed it. The emotional connection with her made it better somehow though. It made it...more. But then she dumped me because I was too boring and broke my heart, so was it even good then? I rubbed my eyebrow with my pointer finger. "My girlfriend. Ex, I should say. There, happy?"

"Was she into freaky shit?" She raised her brows and wiggled them. "Good for you."

"No, it was our connection, actually." God, why was this so hard to talk about? It made my skin prickle with vulnerability, like another round of that night a year ago. "I don't sleep around," I said, an edge of defensiveness leaking into my words. She'd probably think I was a loser for saying it, but I couldn't lie to her. We were so different—her wild and sexy and free, and me... a nice dork. "I like being in relationships before having sex with someone."

"Relationships," she repeated, no intonation to the word to give me any clue what she was thinking.

"Yes. I'm not..." I paused, adjusting my glasses and hating the rock in my gut. "Super cool or probably like the guys you hang out with."

She sucked in a breath, and I swore, she looked sad. Why? How did that upset her? I blinked and tried to backtrack. "Because I'm a nerd. I hang out in the library and do trivia nights and don't sleep around. I've only slept with like..." Shit. I blushed hard, hating how stupid I felt. My entire body felt too small for my skin, and I let out a shaky breath. History repeating itself—her ability to make me overshare everything.

I took another drink, damn well earning it. I snuck a glance at her, my breath catching in my throat at the wounded expression on her face. Her eyes lost that shimmer that was there a minute ago, and her shoulders slumped, like my words had hurt her. It was a horrible feeling to know I put that sad look on her face. "Hey," I said, desperate to see the twinkle of mischief in her eyes. "I'm sorry I upset you."

"No, it's... I deserve it."

"Deserve what, exactly?"

"Your opinion of me." She pulled her legs up to her chest, wrapping her arms around them. She rested her chin on top of her arms and exhaled so hard her breath tickled my arms. "I've only slept with a handful of people, all who were temporary flings and always safe. It was so easy to create this persona, this unfazed badass who charms and flirts with everyone. I wasn't always like this."

"Why do you do it?" I asked, hanging on every word as she showed more Cami layers that were *just* for me. Maybe I wasn't the only one opening up tonight. The idea pleased me more than I cared to admit.

She let out a sad laugh and stared at me with pain in her eyes. "It's easy to pretend you're not hurt or sad or upset or anxious. I'd throw all my emotions into creating Cami Simpson, the cool girl, the party girl, the girl who everyone wants to be so I wouldn't acknowledge how I was feeling."

"And how are you feeling?"

"Jesus, this is worse than therapy." She held out her hand, and I gave her the bottle. She took a small sip and handed it back. "My sister assumed I'd intentionally dated guys she liked. My coach says I'm not leadership material. My counselor even laughed at my dance degree with a minor in business. Everyone thinks exactly what I wanted them too, but it hurts. I'm utterly alone with just my carefully crafted reputation I formed."

Something aggressive and terrifying surged through me, a need to protect her at all costs. But she wasn't done talking. She still wore that blank look on her face as she scratched a scab on her knee.

"My coach, Audrey, chose Daniella to be captain after I've dedicated hours to getting that role senior year. It's not going well at all. She has no leadership skills or clout. The girls are annoyed at her, and now... Audrey wants me to *co-captain* with her. She acted like I should be thrilled. I'm never anyone's first choice, and I'm supposed to be happy being second?"

She looked so small pulled up into that ball that my heart clenched tight. She'd opened up to me in this gross underground tunnel. My heart hammered at the notion, but a heavy throb started in my chest too. Cami clearly wasn't her reputation. She was battling everyone else's perception of her, which made me want to be there for her. Really there for her.

"I'm sorry you're feeling this way." I squeezed her hand.

"Yeah, me too." She sighed again, leaning back on the wall just as something thudded in the distance. She tensed and reached over to grab my arm. "Did you hear that?"

I nodded, hardly able to think with her tight grip on me. The sound repeated, and Cami jumped into my lap, her chest heaving.

"Freddie, Freddie, there is *something* that way." She clung to my neck, her tits almost in my face. "Is it a ghost? Are there other people down here? Should we go?"

Sensation overload. The sweet mixture of sweat and peaches flooded my nose, and her body pressed against mine so hard I could literally feel her toned muscles. I wrapped an arm around her waist to what.... keep her from falling off my lap? To protect her? Because I was selfish and wanted to prolong this moment?

"Not a ghost," I said, my voice husky and a dead giveaway to my attraction. She didn't notice though. She clung to me harder as the sound grew louder.

"We should run the fuck out of here."

Yes, before I get a boner.

"Sure, yeah." I tried to move her off me, but she bore down, not loosening her grip at all. Okay then.

I stood up, making sure I held her and the bottle tight. She wrapped her legs around my waist, causing me to touch her ass. *Jesus.* It was tight and perfect. The urge to dig my fingers into her globes was enough to drive me crazy.

"A little hustle, Freddie. Please, it could kill us."

"You could walk yourself, you know," I said, teasing but not wanting to stop touching her. Her petite, strong body felt so good against mine.

"Absolutely not. I'm using your large frame as a shield. I thought that was obvious." She looked over my shoulder and tensed even more. "They have a flashlight! Run!"

CHAPTER
NINE

Cami

I clutched my throat, my breath coming out in heavy pants. I wasn't sure who held the flashlight, but Freddie set me down, and we *ran*. Not like a cute jog. No, we sprinted as if we were about to die.

Freddie wiped his brow with the bottom of his t-shirt, his breathing coming out erratically like mine. A flash of his stomach greeted me, but the building was too dark to get a good glance. My stomach swooped at the thought of touching him there though.

"What a rush. Wow." Once we were back in the engineering building, I put a hand over my heart. I wasn't scared of a lot of things, but ghosts? Hauntings? Fuck that. The few sips of whiskey combined with the adrenaline rush, and a pleasant, tipsy feeling overtook me. This was what I needed.

I smiled, ready to thank Freddie, but he had a dark, angry expression on his face as he put his hands on his hips, staring daggers at the fake door.

"What is it? Do you think it'll follow us?"

He glanced at me for a second. "No."

My stomach sank, and regret flowed through me like a leaky faucet. I'd jumped on top of him. I'd clung to him for dear life. My ears burned like fire as I cleared my throat. He had to feel so awkward. "Freddie," I said, waiting for him to look at me. It took a few seconds, but when his beautiful gray eyes met mine, I swore there was some flash of emotion in his eyes. "I'm sorry."

"Why?"

"For making you uncomfortable," I said, adding a little laugh at the end. "I didn't mean to climb you like a tree. If you couldn't tell, ghosts freak me out."

"I noticed." He shoved the whiskey into his pocket and adjusted his glasses. He was giving some serious Clark Kent vibes with the size of his chest and his dark swoopy hair. I wanted to ruffle the fuck out of his locks just to see it messed up, but I didn't.

Freddie had boundaries, and I needed to respect them. He was a relationship, meaningful sex kind of guy. I wasn't that way. No matter the feelings he stirred in me, I couldn't cross the line. For his benefit.

"Uh," I said, pushing my hair behind my ears. I was suddenly embarrassed I was still in my workout clothes. It was almost the same size as a swimming suit, and I showed so much skin. "Thank you, for this. The distraction. The rush."

"You're welcome." He gave a tight smile and nodded toward the door. "Should we head back?"

Did I want to return to the hot ass dorm to sit in my room alone? No. I didn't at all. I frowned and chewed my lip before I shook my head. "I don't want to go back."

He stilled, and a line appeared between his brows, like my answer bothered him. He opened his mouth a few times, closing it without saying anything. "Okay. Where to then?"

There was ten feet between us in the classroom, and yet it felt like we were touching as his gaze roamed my body. I knew then that the flash of emotion on his face was heat. Seeing he was attracted to me sent a thrill through me, lighting me up inside even though nothing would ever happen. At least I knew it wasn't just one-sided. "Oh, don't feel obligated or anything. If you need to go home, go ahead. I'll figure something out."

"I don't feel pressure." He pulled on the edge of his shirt, almost to fan himself before he studied me with the same intensity I'd witnessed in the library. Like I was a project. An assignment.

"Seriously, you don't have to hang out with me." I waved my hand in the air. "There's always a party going on."

It was important to create some distance between us. To put some walls back up around my soul. I'd shared too much, showed him too much of me. It made me feel bared and naked.

"Is that what you want? To go to a party to not deal with your emotions?" he asked so casually, like we were talking about the weather.

His question was a dagger straight to the gut. I should *never* have told him that. It was the magic of the tunnel. The feel of his large body next to me, the thick air, the whiskey. He caught me at a temporarily vulnerable time.

"I was just blabbing. It's nothing," I said, flashing my fake smile. "This was great. Love that you know about a secret tunnel. Very un-Freddie-like of you."

"Cami, cut the bullshit, please."

Whoa. I'd never heard Freddie raise his voice, and there was a ring of authority to it. The gentle giant had a bit more to him. Layers. Layers I kinda wanted to peel back slowly to see how he'd react. He stepped toward me but not close enough to touch. His mouth twisted in a scowl as he looked down at me.

He had to crane his neck to see me, and I matched his stance, crossing my arms and preparing for whatever he was going to say.

"Don't do this," he said, a softness to his tone that had my resolve weakening. "Don't give me this version of yourself when I've seen the true one."

"I'm not," I said, the lie thick on my tongue. "This is the real me."

"If you want space because you shared too much, I understand. I'll give you space, but please don't go to a party alone right now. You're upset and had some drinks. I'll worry."

"I don't need you to *worry* about me."

"I know, but I will anyway. Friends care about each other."

Fuck. The silent plea in his eyes, the way he made a fist at his side, the undeniable feeling of safety I had around him... It was all too much, and it'd be cruel to intentionally hurt him. Friends.

It was the second time that night he'd referred to us as friends. How pathetically sad that I couldn't recall the last friend I had? Sure, I had teammates, roommates, and sorority sisters who were fake and temporary. But friends who cared about each other? Who *ever* admitted to caring about me that wasn't a family member? My throat tightened.

I had one in high school who fell out of contact after we went to college. My roommate from freshmen year never responded yes when I asked her to grab dinner together. After a while, it got easier to live in my lonely ice castle. Even when Naomi and I grew apart, we had such little in common that *friends* wasn't what I'd use for us.

Now? We were working on getting better, but Freddie was the first person in years to say that about me. *Shit.* My eyes stung a little, and I pursed my lips, refusing to let the tears fall. "Want to come with me?"

Whatever he thought I was going to say, it wasn't that. He blinked in surprise before he repeated, "Go to a party *with* you?"

I wasn't sure why he said it like that, like he was accusing me of something. I nodded. "Yeah, let's get into trouble together."

He scratched his head and gave me a long look that had me squirming because he was so unreadable. The dark hair, the eyes hidden behind the glasses, and the absolute softness from a man his size was a lot to deal with.

"Promise me something."

"Anything," I said, before realizing how desperate that made me seem. He had to know though that his support, his insistence on being my friend...well, that meant everything to me.

"Please, don't leave with someone else." The tips of his ears turned redder than ketchup, and my stomach sank at his insinuation.

"Wow, way to let your real opinion of me show." I straightened my shoulders, hating how his words stung. "I'll have you know I attend parties and keep up appearances, but I haven't fucked anyone in months, Freddie. I might not do relationships because I think love is a poison, but I'm not the girl you think I am, and I find it—"

He silenced me by putting one long finger on my lips. I had no idea how he got to me so quickly, but heat spread from my lips to my toes. His mouth was *inches* from mine. "I didn't mean it the way you're thinking."

"I find that hard to believe," I said, my lips grazing against his finger. He made no moves to remove it. "I wouldn't ask you to a party and then leave with some other guy."

"Do you remember last year?" he asked, his body very tense. He dropped his finger but kept standing close to me. I could smell his woodsy scent combined with the whiskey on his breath, sending tingles over my skin.

Last year... "What about it?"

"We were at the same party. You came with some girls from the dance team, and I was there with my brother. It was at the house on sixth."

The night we flirted. The night he looked at me with awe, like he thought I was worth his attention. He gave me butterflies...one of the last times I felt like that. Hopeful. But he'd left without saying a word. "Yes, I remember."

Freddie sighed, like the memory pained him. "That was my first night out after a horrible break up. My ex really shook my confidence, and here you were, this *gorgeous* bombshell flirting with me, opening up to me. I couldn't believe my luck."

"Freddie," I said, hating the longing in his voice. He *had* to know I felt the same way.

"No, wait." He gulped. "You said you'd get a drink and come right back. I waited for what felt like an hour before I saw you leave the party with another guy. You were all smiles and using the same touches with him. It...sucked. I know we only talked for a bit, but I'd thought we hit it off, and to see you leave with him," he paused, giving me a soul-crushing look that made me feel sick.

Another instance where my actions *hurt* someone unintentionally. Like Naomi all over again, only this time I remembered being disappointed when I couldn't find him to say goodbye. It all happened so fast. To think I'd caused him to doubt himself this whole time? I *hated* myself for doing that to him.

"It really set my confidence back again and solidified that I'm incredibly boring."

"Oh my god," I said, reaching over to grip his shoulders. "I didn't leave with that guy. He was the boyfriend of one of the girls on the dance team, and he was sloshed. Like, needed to get his stomach pumped sloshed. I helped get his ass into a car, and they took him to the hospital. Freddie, I felt those things too that night. I went back in to find you, but you were gone."

If there was a competition of who could best impersonate a statue, he'd win in a landslide. His face froze on an expression I could only describe as shock. I rubbed his shoulders a few times and smiled, a genuine grin that made my insides get all weird. "Is that why you always looked at me like you hated me?"

"I never hated you," he said, snapping out of his trance. He placed his hands over mine, leaving them there for a second before removing them from his body.

In a way, that felt like a rejection even though I wasn't asking for anything. It felt important to add more to the emotional firepit I was dancing in. "I was into you that night too."

Half of his mouth quirked up in a smile, the change from serious to content enough to make me want to kiss those damn lips. "That's what I meant by my comment. Even as friends…if you choose someone else when you said you'd give me time, it would hurt."

"I wouldn't do that to you."

"I know that now." The grin reached his eyes, and I wondered for a moment, what it'd be like to have Freddie as a boyfriend.

He'd be loyal, and kind, and funny. He'd probably kiss the same way he studied, and just thinking about his focus sent a shiver down my body. We had to get out of this fucking classroom.

"Now that we got it settled, bud, let's get into shenanigans."

"Ah, yes. My favorite thing. Shenanigans," he teased, making me laugh.

"Oh, you're going to regret saying that, big guy." I patted his arm and started walking toward the door. "It would be an honor to corrupt you a little, Frederick Brady the Third. Now, let's go."

CHAPTER
TEN

Freddie

I *was into you that night too.*
As Cami dragged us from bar to bar, those words were ingrained in my head like they were etched there with a damn pickaxe. We were at our third bar, and she took my hand and dragged me to the counter.

"Hydration." She patted the stool next to her and smiled up at me, showing all her teeth. "Key to surviving the parties is more water than drinks."

Another thing that surprised me about her was how intentional she was. She *never* drank anything she didn't see opened herself and always pointed out the exits.

"Is this another one of Cami's Rules?"

"Yes, in fact, it's item number two." She held up her fingers and ordered tall glasses of water from the bartender. She crossed one leg over the other so her dangling foot hit my thigh.

I didn't hate it there.

"What else is on your list?" I took a large swig of the water, unsure when or how I'd gotten a little tipsy. I could feel it in the tingles across my face and my constant urges to touch Cami. My inhibitions were weakened, loosened, gone like the wind when I drank, and there was very little holding me back from all the reasons why I shouldn't touch her.

I needed my own set of rules.

I was leaving at the semester to go on an internship in the city....working with my uncle and being close to my parents. It'd launch my career. I'd become someone. My stomach twisted thinking about living alone in one of the busiest places in the country while my *close* friends would be here. Seeing Cami like this, free and beautiful and honest... I didn't want to walk-away.

But she didn't do relationships, and that's all I did.

Oh, and the fact I was boring so she'd never be into me now.

Better. The list cooled the raging lust I had, and I downed the entire glass before looking at her.

"Big guy, you alright?" She frowned. "Should we head back?"

"Nonsense. I want to see the rest of your list. It's a must!"

She laughed, a real genuine giggle, and hit the counter. "A must, you say. Then it shall be done!"

The sparkle returned in her eyes. The one that made me want to yank her to my chest by the strap of her workout bra.

"Cami-girl!" a loud, deep voice boomed from the other side of us, like an unwanted bout of thunder. It dampened the mood and put a real cloud over me. Of *course* this would happen.

A very jacked and handsome guy headed straight toward us. He easily matched me in size, but the dude had arms strong enough to break the bar top.

"Jake! Hey!" She beamed at him, and he leaned over to give her a hug. She gripped him right back, his hands coming down on her exposed midriff, and I wished this water were vodka.

"You look good. Can't wait to see y'all dancing at the game Friday. You hitting up Jackie's after?"

"If we win, absolutely. You know I can't miss a J5 Party."

"Right on." The guy glanced at me and nodded. "Hey."

"Heya," I said, like a total idiot. I tried to say hi and hey, and that weird sound came out, and oh my Jesus. Cami was too cool for me and what was I doing here? Hanging with her? Acting like this was normal for me?

Jake laughed and hit my back before saying goodbye. There was nothing overly flirtatious about the exchange, but my neck sweat from overhearing it. The guy had to play football.

"Heya?" she said, nudging my shoulder with hers and letting out another pleased giggle. "What was that?"

"I don't know." I glanced down at the coaster on the bar, wishing I were back at the dorm and away from all of this extraness. It wasn't me. "Uh, I should—"

"Rule number three—where there is a DJ, you always request your favorite song. Come on." She slid off the stool, pressing her chest against my side as she looked up at me. "I'll request *Heya* by Outkast. Just for you."

I snorted. There was no other way to describe the sound that came out of me at the perfect timing of her joke. Her smile grew, and her eyes did that shimmering thing again, only it was all directed at me. "You little devil," I said, my voice dropping lower than intended.

She scrunched her nose, and maybe it was the sway of her hips, or the sparkle in her eyes, or the fact I just liked her that I got out of the stool and totally forgot about my horribly embarrassing moment.

Her hand closed around mine as she dragged us toward the DJ booth, and suddenly, I could picture how dating her would be. Her pushing me outside of my comfort zone and me being the support, the person she could count on. I longed for it, to be hers.

Damn beer making me imagine things.

She bent over to talk to the DJ, not once letting go of my hand, and he nodded at her. I imagined it'd be hard to say no to someone like her, so confident and beautiful. Even now, still wearing her dance gear and her hair in braids, she shone.

She said something to me, but I couldn't hear over the upbeat techno song blasting over the speakers, so she stood on her tiptoes, gripped my arm for balance, and said into my ear, "I'm having him dedicate the song to you, big guy."

I was going to hyperventilate. Her lips *touched* my ear. Her perfectly painted lips brushed against my body, making goosebumps explode down my neck and arms. I was pretty sure I nodded, but I wasn't positive. My mind was exactly on her o-shaped mouth and how good it would feel on my skin.

She yanked my hand again and started dancing in a super cool rhythmic way that made no sense to me. Her hips and stomach were mesmerizing, and at one point, she attempted to make me dance.

I did *not* dance.

"Freddie, shake your hips." She grinned up at me and placed her fingers on my waist, trying to move me from side to side. "Back and forth."

I shook my head like a petulant child. Couldn't she see I was a hot ass mess? I was still thinking about her touching my ear, not *dancing* with her when everyone around us moved in sensual ways.

She didn't listen to me. She shoved me harder, her smile growing when she pinched my waist. Cami Simpson pinched me. "Hey!" I yelped.

"Item number five: must always dance!" She did a goofy shoulder dance that almost had me smiling, but I remained strong for the rest of the song. Not letting her force me or convince me to suddenly bust a move.

I had no moves to bust, only a muscle or two. When it ended, I walked off the dance floor, unsure if I needed another water, another drink, or to slap myself in the face to snap out of the Cami-induced haze.

It wasn't like I hadn't seen her dance before. She was hard to miss on the field during football games. My attention had drifted to her quite a few times over the last year but her dancing *right* in front of me was pushing my limits.

I yawned, running my hand over my face just as Cami caught up to me. Her eyes had that sparkle, and she elbowed my side playfully. "Should we get you back? Past your bedtime?"

I checked my phone, ignoring a message from an unknown number. It was midnight.

"No, I was just up early today."

"I'm tired too. One more stop on our fun friend night then I'll make sure you get home nice and safe. I'm a real gentleman."

I smiled, charmed at her being kinda dorky with me. "So considerate."

"Thank you."

We left the bar, *not* holding hands. That seemed to be an *inside the bar* only thing which was fine with me. It was sweaty and hot anyway.

The late summer air was humid as hell, and my shirt stuck to my skin in an uncomfortable way. Despite all of the things that put me outside my comfort zone, tonight was the most fun I had in a while. Instead of the dread of heading back to the dorm, there was a lightness in my step. Didn't take a genius to know it was because of Cami, but I didn't let myself overthink as to why.

That was dangerous territory.

"I'm going to do it," she said, her voice just above a whisper and deadly serious. "I'm going to agree to be co-captain for two reasons. The first—our team needs it. It's not fair to all the girls for me to keep up this grudge with Audrey. The second—legacy. Daniella needs training on how to lead. If we work together for the year, then the team will be in great hands after I graduate."

"I think it'd be a shame if you weren't a part of something you love with your whole heart. I'm glad you came to a good decision," I said, feeling a warmth in my chest as she stopped and smiled up at the stars.

"Thanks to you."

"Me?"

She nodded and glanced up at me with gratitude swirling in her large brown eyes. "I needed this. A buddy. A friend to distract me from the emotions and let me focus on the real question: can I quit the dance team? Which the answer is no. So, thank you, Freddie."

"I didn't do anything, really."

"You were with me." She shrugged, like those four words didn't make my world rock.

Was that all she wanted? Someone there for her?

I had my parents, Camden, even Michael. Who did Cami have? We kept walking in silence back to the dorm, but I kept thinking about those words. The fact she was into me a year ago and her confession of being lonely were enough to flatten me.

We got to an intersection, and instead of going right toward the dorms, she went left.

"Where are you heading?"

"I told you, one more stop." She had that bewitching look again, like she knew an inside joke that I didn't. "It'll be worth it. Trust me."

"Is there food?" I rubbed my stomach, still feeling the drinks and damn well knowing I'd wake up feeling like crap if I didn't put something in there to soak it up.

"Guess you'll have to see. It's item six on my list—must stop at Timmy's place."

I knew better than to ask what Timmy's place was since she was almost skipping with excitement. I liked seeing this side of her, getting to learn her list and her favorite spots on campus. I wouldn't call the tunnel one of my favorites, but it was definitely a part of my story. If Timmy's was part of hers... then I was all in.

"I found this place by accident a few months ago. I'm

furious I only discovered them my final year here. But the good news is that the studio I dance at has potential for me to work more hours. If that happens, I can save up for my studio and then I can come here all the time."

"Save up for a studio?"

"Oh." She winced and lifted one shoulder in a shrug. "That's what I plan to do. Open my own dance studio for all ages and levels. I want to have team competition and have a dance therapy option too. There are so many young dancers with so few choices in town."

"You want to stay here?"

"Yes. This has been my home my whole life. I love this city." She clapped her hands and pointed to an unmarked door with just a light above it. There were two shops on either side, but this door was just black. "Here we are."

This city. Not Chicago. I shook my head, my thoughts jumping to conclusions it had no business doing. My future was set. She wasn't a part of it… right?

"Um, is this a sex club?" I asked, my beer brain being a real dingus.

She stopped walking, narrowed her eyes, and blinked. "I thought you'd be okay with it? They make you sign this NDA, but it's no big deal. We should strip out here though before going in."

She gripped the edge of her bra, and my breath caught in my throat, needing her to finish the movement and remove the tiny piece of clothing she'd been wearing all night. My mind tried telling me her tone was off and she was joking because why would there be a sex club right here? Why did I even say that?

"My god, Freddie, I'm fucking with you. You should see your face right now." She tilted her head back and laughed, deep and loud, drawing stares from others walking on the street. "Come on, big guy."

My face burned, and my palms were drenched. A sex club

with her would straight up kill me. From lust alone. A month ago, the thought of going in one wouldn't have computed, but with her? I'd do almost anything.

She took my hand in hers again and opened the unlabeled door. She had no idea why my face was twisted like that. None. It was all from her little tease.

She pulled me into a dark store that played soft jazz and smelled like chocolate perfection. Gelato and coffee and cookies covered the counter, and she glanced back at me with the light shining right behind her, giving her an angelic look. "This is my secret place. I only allow myself a small each time, but *unnnh* it's the best thing you'll have in your mouth."

She went up to the counter, pulling me with her when a familiar laugh had me turning my head. I knew that laugh. Not super loud, but it was deep and raspy. There was no way… not here though.

But when my gaze landed on the table to my left, I couldn't believe it. My ex was here.

Maddie was *here*.

CHAPTER
ELEVEN

Cami

"Hey, Cami," Timmy said, the owner and creator of the best place on campus. He was a thirty-something guy covered in tattoos with long hair he wore in a bun. He'd dropped out ten years ago and started this place because baking was his thing.

"Got a virgin for you today," I said, smiling as I glanced at Freddie, but his attention wasn't on us. He was staring at a table to his left where a pretty girl looked back at him with wide eyes.

An unwelcome shot of jealousy went through me, which was *not* something I felt often. I envied others' successes, but jealousy was more about not sharing my toys. Freddie wasn't mine, yet the thought of this girl knowing him, holding his hand, and getting his secret tunnel tours made my jaw tighten.

"Freddie?" I said, hoping he'd turn back to me. I really needed him to remember he came with me. It just seemed important.

But he didn't. He stood still as a statue and eyed the woman. She got up out of her seat, and I tugged on his arm. "Hey, do you want anything?"

"Um, no," he said, shaking his head as he barely glanced at me. He immediately dropped my hand, like he couldn't stand to be seen with me as the woman approached. My stomach soured, and the thought of eating gelato didn't seem as fun anymore.

"For you, Cami?" Timmy asked, his dark brows furrowed as he studied Freddie. I didn't blame him. The giant man drew attention, and he'd basically thrown my hand from his. It was weird. Plus, I *never* brought anyone here with me. It was my thing.

"Um, just a small vanilla, please. To go." My tongue felt too large for my mouth as my stomach churned in a horrible way. I chewed on my lip when Freddie walked away from me and met the pretty girl halfway to the small booth section. I paid for the treat, got a spoon, and tried not to feel gross inside.

It wasn't new for me to be dropped when something else came along. I was a temporary, shiny toy for people.

You're more than that. Freddie wasn't cruel, and I should give him the benefit of explaining who this girl was because from his tightened fists at his sides and bunched up shoulders, she mattered somehow.

A fling?

No, he didn't have flings.

Was he seeing someone? *Oh.* I never thought of the fact he could be dating someone. I hadn't seen anyone since we'd been at the dorms, but that didn't mean it was reality. Our places were hot as fuck. Who would want to visit?

*But the way he looks at me...*looking didn't matter. It was the actions that happened after it that did.

"What are you doing here?" he asked, his voice deep and almost angry. "At Central?"

The woman pointed to some other girls at the booth before responding. I couldn't catch her words, but Freddie didn't like her answer. He cracked his knuckles with his thumb as he shifted his weight from side to side.

"I don't know what you expect, Maddie. You can't just... spring this on me. There was a reason I didn't respond to you."

Shit. His voice had that edge of hysteria to it. I recognized the feeling and said to hell with it. Freddie was gentle and kind and never raised his voice, yet this woman made him break his character. I walked up to him and wrapped my hand around his. "Hey, sorry to interrupt this convo, but are you ready to head back?"

His gaze moved from my hand on his to my face, and I swore he took a breath and relaxed. The fact I could help Freddie settle himself gave me a bloated sense of pride. Like I could be there for him somehow. Like maybe I wasn't in complete last place for his attention.

"Cami," he said, my name on his lips like my favorite Taylor Swift song. He blinked hard. "Yes, sorry."

"I didn't know you were with anyone," the girl said, a slightly accusing tone to her words. She eyed me up and down, the narrowing of her eyes making it real clear she didn't appreciate the way I was dressed.

I flashed her a smile. I wasn't going to lie and say I was *with* Freddie, but she could create her own assumptions. "We should get back and hydrate. A little too many parties tonight, you know?"

"You party now?" the girl asked, her brows rising into her hairline.

Freddie swallowed, his throat bobbing, and I moved my hand from his wrist to his back. I gently pushed him, and he cleared his throat. "We have nothing to talk about. There's a reason I didn't respond to you."

"We had years together, babe. Please, just let me take you out and explain how sorry I am."

Okay, so she was an ex. Was she *the ex* who made Freddie lack confidence? If so, I'd like to have a few words with her. But I remained quiet.

Freddie huffed, and something snapped in him. He put an

arm around my shoulders and guided us out of Timmy's, onto the sidewalk and under the moonlight.

"Fuck," he said, releasing me the second we exited the door. He pulled on the ends of his hair and let out something between a groan and a grunt.

"You okay?"

"No." He righted his glasses and eyed the ice cream in my hand. He had that intense stare again with the tight jaw, like he was trying to see through me. That sort of look had the ability to steal my breath away. "You're dripping."

He rushed over and took some of the napkins in my hand to start wiping the ice cream spilling down my arm. "I'm so sorry, Cami. You tried to show me your place, and I wanted to hear all about it." He kept cleaning my arm and hand, bunching the used napkins in his hands. Seeing him clean me up made my stomach somersault in a warm, fuzzy way.

He clenched his jaw a few times before pointing toward a bench a few yards away. "Sit. Eat your ice cream before it melts, please."

"It's fine." I shrugged, opened the plastic spoon with my mouth, and took a bite of the ice cream. I crossed my eyes at the flavor. "So good."

He looked at the door and back to me, indecision still on his face. "Sit, please."

"Sure, but we really can go back."

"No. Not yet."

"You planning to wait for that woman to come out?"

"No, I want you to enjoy your ice cream, and I'm hoping to convince you to let me try a bite."

"That could be arranged." I winked and went to plop down on the bench. The conversation was flirting with the edge of tense, and I needed to make it light again. He followed, his large frame casting shadows on the sidewalk around me, and he sat down right next to me so our thighs touched. His thigh was twice the size of mine and so warm. My fingers itched to touch him. Would he like if I trailed a finger over his leg? Would he shudder or pull me closer against him? I cleared my throat, forcing the sexual thoughts away. We were *friends*.

"You get a bite when you answer a question."

"Using my own game against me?"

"Absolutely."

He sighed, but his lips quirked up on the sides. "Fair. Ask me anything."

"What's the most useless talent you have?" I asked, pleased with myself for using his question when it was so obvious that I wanted to know the story behind the woman.

It was the right thing to do because Freddie slapped his knee and let out a deep belly-laugh. It was ridiculous and made me chuckle too.

"Quite a cackle there."

"That was good, Cami. Thank you." He reached over and patted my knee, squeezing it for a second before letting go. It was such a *relationship* gesture, one I'd seen Michael do to Naomi all the time.

My stomach did a whole back-handspring at the motion.

"Well?" I asked, keeping my tone light to not give away the zing he just sent through my body. "What is it?"

"I can make a clover shape with my tongue." He opened his mouth and made his tongue curl into exactly that, a clover shape, and my god. I squeezed my thighs together as I thought about all the things he could do with that tongue.

If he could curl it... he had control over it.

I was going to burst soon. I just knew it.

"Wow, that is...I'm sure there are ways that's useful, Freddie." My face burned red as I stared at his lips. They were so full and inviting. *Fuck*. I was attracted to this man.

He cleared his throat. "Did you intend for that to sound dirty?"

"Yes."

"Well, I appreciate the honesty."

He didn't move away from me on the bench. If anything, he scooted closer, invading me with thoughts of cable knit sweaters and walks in the forest. He just smelled so damn good and had a comforting air about him where I felt safe.

"Do I get it now?"

"Get... what?" I asked, looking up at his face just inches from mine. His glasses reflected the moon, but his dark lashes were still visible. I could almost count each one of them.

"A bite. I answered your question."

"Yes, right, here." I handed him the cup of vanilla like we were playing an aggressive game of hot potato. It almost spilled on him at the speed of my movement, but he righted the little cup and took a bite. There was something erotic about watching the spoon that was just in my mouth go into his as he swallowed.

His tongue touched *my* spoon.

"Oh, this is good. It's sweet and creamy." He licked his lips and handed me the cup back, not giving any indication that he was as turned on as I was.

The lick of his lips, the size of his hands, the intensity of his eyes...Freddie was becoming my own version of kryptonite. He stared at me expectantly, like he was waiting for me to talk. I cleared my throat and nodded. "My favorite."

"I wouldn't have taken you for a vanilla person."

"Meaning...what?"

"You're so colorful and full of life and sass. I don't know, like rainbow sherbet or the chocolate explosion with a bunch of mystery pieces. Vanilla is so... plain compared to your personality." He sat up straighter, running a hand over his jaw. "I really meant that as a compliment. Not sure if I hit the mark."

"I took it as one." I smiled up at him, but his attention was on the sky. He yawned, and I knew it was time for our night to conclude. I hadn't been on a date—no, a night out with a friend like this in...ever. No expectations. Just fun. I didn't want it to end.

If he suggested pulling an all-nighter, I'd do it in a heartbeat. Even though I had practice in the morning and a ton of homework. Being with him like this was a vacation from my life, and a weight of sadness pulled my shoulders down.

He scrubbed his eyes, letting out a groan, and I held out my cup of ice cream again. "Help me finish so we can head back."

He leaned onto his knees and frowned at me. "We don't need to rush."

"I'm getting tired," I said, faking a yawn. "I have practice early and everything."

He was trying to be a nice guy and stay out because he knew I wasn't ready. At my words, he literally relaxed, like he was dying to return and end our night. I knew it wasn't *all* about me, but the feeling of being second place lingered.

"Right, of course." He took another large bite and handed it to me before standing up and staring at the door with longing all over his face. That girl in there mattered.

"You dated her," I said, throwing away the cup and forcing my voice to not contain an ounce of attitude or sarcasm.

"Yup. That's Maddie."

"The one who said you were boring?"

"Bingo." He shoved his hands in his pockets, sighed, and jutted his chin toward the direction of the dorms. I didn't respond, just tossed the ice cream into a trash can and started walking.

A million questions raced through my mind, all of them starting with *do you still love her?* Did it matter if he loved his ex? The guy who wanted relationship sex and was clearly a commitment type of guy? It shouldn't, but my feelings weren't always rational.

Crickets chirped and lightning bugs danced all around us, and it smelled like it might rain soon. The summer was brutally hot and humid, and a good rain would wash away the temperatures for a bit. Maybe I'd keep the windows open if it stormed.

"I don't know why she wants to talk. She texted me she missed me a few weeks ago, and I just…" He sounded exasperated and tired, which had to mean he wasn't entirely in love with *Maddie* anymore. "Getting over her was hard, and now she wants to speak to me? I don't understand."

"You don't owe her anything you're not ready to give."

"But we dated for three years."

"No amount of time demands you have to put yourself in a situation that makes you unhappy," I said, hearing the hypocrisy in my own words. I ignored the twinge in my gut about the dance team and kept going. "Seriously. It's such a trap to assume, *oh, I spent three years learning to kayak! I could never give it up! What a waste!* Life isn't about what you owe or don't owe. If you don't want to talk to her, then don't. It's that simple."

"What if I do though?"

My heart sank like a rock in the middle of a lake. I bit the inside of my cheek to keep myself from letting out a noise of dislike. I didn't care for *Maddie* for the sole reason she hurt Freddie.

The guy who wouldn't let me flirt or bully him to leave me alone. The guy who gave me Skittles. The guy who brought me to a secret tunnel because I was upset.

Fuck Maddie for hurting this gentle soul.

I opened my mouth to say something that would hopefully be positive, but he beat me to it.

He waved his hand in the air, like an animated composer. "What if it's serious? Or maybe she's going to apologize sincerely this time? I've run through a thousand conversations with her where I have all my lines ready. That makes me pathetic, doesn't it?"

"No, not at all." I hated the knowing tone of his voice, like he thought he was speaking the absolute truth. "You're not pathetic."

"She hurt me and yet I'm worried I'll upset her if I don't hear her out."

"Because you're a good person and you care about her." I couldn't stop myself from reaching out and taking his hand. It wasn't a full, fingers-intertwined type of hold, but it was a nice palm-to-palm. I squeezed his giant paw, and when he returned the gesture, my stomach did its own version of The Running Man.

"Tonight was something, huh?" he said, a new lightness to his rough voice. The dorms came into view as we crossed the street, and Freddie slowed to allow me keep pace with him. He didn't try to let go of my hand once.

"Yeah." I smiled at him, but he wasn't looking at me. He stared at our hands to the point I wondered if I had something odd on the back of mine. His gray gaze met mine for a beat, a significant shift of the air causing my heartbeat to double in speed. I knew, without a doubt, that we were both caught up in a moment together.

Then he released my hand and used a key card to open the dorm door before holding it for me. His face went back to his standard *focused* look, without the sly smile or the sparkle in his eyes.

"Please, go ahead," he said, ushering me with his hand again.

I went in and hated the shift. It was our hand holding. It'd thrown him off. Messed with him. I knew better than to do that when my usual flirtations were lost on him. Things felt different as we walked down our narrow, hot hallway. I wanted to say something to fix it, to make the fun banter come back, but nothing came to mind. I took my time putting my key in the door, fumbling with it as Freddie watched me. The lock made an awful screeching sound once the key slid in, and I turned it hard to the left. The door creaked as I pushed it open, a blast of hot hair hitting me in the face. I swore I could feel every breath Freddie took as he continued to watch me from a few feet away.

I flashed him my best smile, hiding the weird combination of regret, sadness, and want. "Good night, neighbor."

"Goodnight." He still made no moves to go into his room, but I couldn't handle the vibe anymore. I escaped into the hot-as-hell room and shut the door behind me. The stale air almost choked me, and I got all my fans running before I fell into bed.

I tried to fall asleep as I listened to the sounds on the other side of the wall, and that was when it hit me. I *liked* Freddie.

It had been so long since I had feelings for someone that the emotions were foreign to me. Content that I'd figured out why my stomach clenched, I told myself I'd worry about the implications tomorrow. Because I knew that emotional connections led to heartbreak, and I had enough going on. Too much hurt. Too much betrayal lately. Freddie had the power to crush me and risking my heart for him wasn't an option.

But then again, he'd torn down those walls and made me believe in more. For every reason I convinced myself it might work, there were a million it wouldn't, and I focused on those.

Freddie deserved the best, and that would never be me.

CHAPTER
TWELVE

Freddie

Maddie was at my school.

I knew she had friends here even after she'd moved away last summer, but her being back totally threw me off my routine. It didn't help that when I wasn't thinking about her motives, my mind drifted toward Cami and all the secrets I'd learned about her.

My gorgeous neighbor had shown me sides of herself that put a stupid smile on my face as I waited at a café for Camden. I heard her leave at the ass crack of dawn for what I assumed was dance practice, and I couldn't go back to sleep. Not with my mind running a damn marathon with different images of Maddie, then Cami, then my favorite documentaries that I always put on to relax me. It was no surprise I was listening to them more than usual. With the distraction of Cami and picking an internship, my stress level was elevated.

But food never made the situation worse.

The café was perfect, plus Camden was my guy to talk to about feelings. He wore them like accessories and wasn't afraid of them like me. He viewed every heartbreak and disappointment as an opportunity to learn while I hated them and went out of my way to avoid feeling anything less than content.

He was annoyingly positive about life.

"FB3," he said, his normal way of greeting me. He plopped down in the chair, his messy hair hanging from his face, and he flagged a waitress over. "Please, give me the biggest coffee you have. Black. Like dirt."

She nodded and took off. Then, he looked at me. "You pulled me from a morning class."

"Wait, you're missing class for this?" I asked, my voice getting all high. "Go, don't miss. Jesus."

"I'm fucking with you. I get a kick out of riling you up." He laughed and thanked the waitress as she brought the mug. "You're an angel. A beautiful, wonderful angel."

She didn't respond. Wise woman. It would only encourage him.

"Maddie's on campus."

"Why?"

"I don't know, but it's stressing me out." I scrubbed my palms over my face. "I saw her last night."

"Where? What happened? Dude, you can't go back to her. She's awful for you," Camden said, the bite to his words hitting me in the chest.

He never liked her, and it had always bothered me. He came clean after she broke my heart into pieces, but it still burned. She wasn't a horrible person. Just confused. We were allowed to be disorganized in our early twenties. How the fuck were we supposed to have it all figured out?

"We didn't talk much. I was out with Cami and—"

"Cami Simpson? You were *out* with Cami Simpson? Dude." He leaned back in his chair, his eyes wide and his smirk a little too much to deal with. "You hook up with her?"

"No." My jaw tensed at his insinuation. His tone reminded

me of how I'd misjudged her, and a rush of anger flowed through me. He didn't know her *at all*. "We're friends."

"This is the same girl you thought was into you at Kyle's party last year who left with *another* guy?"

"Misunderstanding. She's not at all how she seems," I said, ready to defend her honor to my closest confidant. "She's... more."

"Here we go." Camden rolled his eyes and leaned his elbows onto the table. "You're into her. A popular girl. A girl who is way too cool for your dorky ass. It's Maddie all over again—which, tell me how last night went. Did you flip Maddie off?"

His words were like a bucket of cold water dripping over my shoulders. I was way too nerdy for someone like Cami, but I swore I'd seen desire reflecting in her eyes. Deeper than the typical flirting I witnessed all the time. It was more an understanding, like she saw me for me and preferred me that way.

She was different. Special. Like how she intervened with Maddie and took my hand. How she let me figure my feelings out rather than demanding to know who Maddie was. *I was into you that night too.*

What am I doing?

I shook my head, like that would shove the inappropriate thoughts out of there. I shouldn't be even hoping that Cami could be into me. I would be leaving for the city. It would end poorly, and hello! Maddie all over again? I'd rather cut off my fingers.

"I didn't speak to her much. Asked her why she's here. She wanted to talk to me. To apologize, I think." I rubbed my chest a few times, my attention momentarily caught by a head of curly brown hair who just walked in. *Not Cami.* "I want to hear what she has to say."

"How could it possibly make anything better?"

"I think I need to hear her admit she regrets leaving me."

There, I put it out in the open, not caring if it made me pathetic. It might be petty, but I'd thought about her almost every day the past year, just recently feeling strong enough to admit I didn't love her anymore.

If she planned to apologize, I wanted her to work for it.

"I'm sure she does. The last guy she slept with dumped her after a week. Jude, I think was his name. She's coming back to you because all the dudes have treated her like shit. Of *course* she regrets it." He took a large sip of the coffee, hissing as he set it back down. "Hot. Hot. Hot."

"You think I shouldn't talk to her?"

He looked up, a soft expression coming over his face, and he sighed. "You need to do what feels right, but you don't owe her shit."

"That's what Cami said too."

"Cami again." His eyes flashed. "You know… having a little fling with her might be just what you need. A wild night with a wild girl."

My eye twitched at the thought of letting myself do just that —sleep with Cami. It had been so long, and I wanted to taste every inch of her skin. Feel every curve of her muscles and run my fingers through her hair. The fantasy of her had been living in my head since we moved into the dorms, but while my brother's intentions were good, she wasn't just someone I could use. I *cared* about her and wanted her to be happy.

"How's Brayden doing?" I asked, clearing my throat and changing the subject to his on again, off again boyfriend. Sorry, *fling*. Camden didn't get attached much.

"Okay, you're diverting. You called me here though, FB3, so I'm not ready to talk about me yet."

"That's a first."

"Fuck off, weirdo." He smiled through the insult though. Conversation flowed after that, but I didn't feel any more settled about Maddie.

Or Cami.

I wanted to ask her how practice was going or if she really did accept the co-captain role. Was she happy? Tired from last night? My left hand burned as I thought about the way she'd gripped it on our walk back. For whatever reason, her holding my hand had felt different than all her other over-the-top flirting.

I checked my watch. *Nine am.* Only eight more hours until we'd meet up at the library…assuming nothing had changed. It had become our thing, and I needed to get more Skittles. "Want to run errands with me?"

"Sure. I need TP anyway." Camden rolled back onto his heels, and a sad look crossed his face for just a second. "I'm gonna miss our errand runs when you're off living the dream working for Uncle Martin. Pretty sure you're dad's favorite right now, which I know is temporary, but I hate it anyway."

My stomach dropped at the mention of Chicago and the damn internship. Of *course* Dad assumed it was a done deal. Why wouldn't it be? I scratched the back of my neck and nodded. "I'm not the favorite."

"Dude, yes you are. Literally, he wouldn't shut up about how proud of you he is. I get it, you're smart and got into less trouble. Big fucking whoop." Camden was back to his usual smirk, but I sensed the underlying emotion beneath it. He'd miss me.

Which was weird because as much as I wanted to make my dad proud…I'd definitely miss living so close to Camden. I cleared my throat and picked up my keys. "Let's head out."

He nodded, letting the topic drop which was what I needed. My head wasn't on straight, and even though there was a prickle of unease about moving up north, I shoved it down because this was always the plan. Why would I let my dad down now? Because I had a crush on a girl?

Couldn't happen.

I had a new bag of Skittles and had already opened them and sorted out the yellow ones so when Cami got there she could reward herself with her favorites. She disagreed with my ranking system of putting the least best first. The fact she didn't pick them all up, throw them at my face, and call me a loser was amazing in itself, so she deserved the good ones.

5:10pm. Where was she?

I ignored Maddie's texts again and tapped my foot against the table leg. I didn't want to dive into my material if she was going to show up soon, but the more time went on, the more worried I got.

We didn't make real plans to meet at the same hour. It just happened, and she was late. She was rarely late.

5:20pm.

She's not coming.

I exhaled a large, pent-up breath and was surprised to feel so disappointed. After one night out with her as friends, I'd turned into this weird guy. Friends had things come up, and we didn't have each other's numbers, so she probably figured it was no big deal.

Totally fine.

I tried focusing on applying for the internships and submitted one application to a company in Chicago. At second glance, the place was two blocks from Maddie's place—if she still lived there. *No. Not now.* No thinking of her.

I applied to two more in the city before a familiar scent of vanilla carried my way, making my heart thump heavy in my chest. I couldn't whip my head around fast enough to see Cami walking toward me. She wore very loose jeans that went up high, above her belly button and a plaid shirt that cut off below her ribs.

Her hair was down and curly, and my breath lodged in my throat. She was beautiful. And waving at me.

"Freddie! Oh, thank god, you're still here!" She walked up toward me, not stopping until she threw her arms around my neck. I couldn't even get my brain to catch up to the fact that her body pressed against mine because I was so *happy* to see her. My skin tingled with joy.

She came. She was with me. She was *hugging* me.

She pulled back before I could return the hug, and she sat in the chair across from me with a slight blush on her cheeks. Her makeup was done up, and her lashes looked longer than normal. The dark colors around her brown eyes made everything sexier on her too.

But the biggest swoop in my gut was the happiness on her face when she said my name. Like she was equally happy to see me too.

"Hey," I said, willing my pulse to settle down before she realized I was a total fool.

"Shouldn't it be *heya?*" she teased, winking at me before getting out her laptop and firing it up. She had that mischievous look again, and I wished I could capture it in a picture.

"Rude."

"Oh, my apologies." She smirked, and her little nose scrunched. "For real though, I'm sorry I was late. I ran into my dad, and we chatted for a bit. I know we didn't plan to meet here, but it's been our thing, hasn't it?"

"Yes, it is." My face warmed like I stood staring at the sun for ten minutes. I liked having a *thing* with her. I liked it a whole lot.

"I wanted to text you but realized I didn't have your number. It's weird that I know about your secret Skittles and tunnels but don't have a way to call you." She smiled as she said it, her eyes twinkling with as much joy as I felt.

Was it because she was here with me, or had something happened? I had to know. It seemed so important. "Was practice good?"

A line appeared between her brows for a second, and she set the phone in her hand down. "Um, yeah. It was okay."

"You were so happy. I thought it might be because of

dance," I said, like that would justify why I was acting so weird. She ran her teeth over her plump bottom lip and shrugged.

"Maybe I just had a craving for Skittles."

Fuck. Was her tone extra flirty or was I reading into it because I'd thought about her all damn day? I sucked in a breath and cleared my throat, handing her my phone because I was a total caveman. She'd asked for my number, and I'd gone straight to my questioning because I wanted to know if I was the reason for her smile.

Camden was right. I was *not* the guy for her.

"Here, put your number in so we can text if we need to miss our study sessions." My voice sounded like I had an entire frog living in the back of my throat, so I took a sip of water.

She entered her number, but the line remained between her brows.

"What is it?" Was the gig up? Had she come to her senses about me?

"You got a text, that's all." She sat up straighter and pushed her hair behind her ears. I glanced at my phone.

UNKNOWN: *I know you miss me.*

Fucking Maddie.

"I still haven't talked to her."

Cami blinked before meeting my eyes, and *maybe* I was trying to read into the way her gaze might've softened, but she seemed lighter at my admission. I wasn't sure what to do about that.

"I've decided I don't like Maddie." She pursed her lips and got out her purple pen. I waited, tense as hell, wanting her to continue.

But she didn't.

"Why?"

"Because she hurt you." She made an incredulous face, her eyebrows lifting. Then, she twisted her lips into a smile. "Duh."

Her attitude caused my lips to curve up, and there we were, smiling and staring at each other. Her lips were red and full, and I fought the urge to lean over and kiss her, just to show her without words how much her smile lit me up inside.

"You brought a bag of *yellow* Skittles? For me?" she asked, breaking the weird trance she put me in by just being here.

"Shut the fuck up."

"I didn't buy a bag of them. I couldn't find just yellow, but I sorted them out of this one." I held up an extra-large bag that I set against my leg and wiggled it.

The smile froze on her face, like it was forced to stay there. I had *not* expected this reaction. Joy, sure. A cute little smirk, yes. But this…worry? No, she wasn't worried. Upset? I had no idea, so I set the bag down, feeling my entire face blush.

"Forget it," I said, needing to change the subject. "We should get started. I have a lot to get through."

I swallowed down the pins and needles and focused on my thesis. I had to turn in a rough sketch of the paper to my advisor for us to go over together in a week. Cami's touch on my hand startled me.

Her lone silver ring on her middle finger glittered in the light, and she squeezed my wrist. "Hey," she said, her voice low and dangerous. "Look at me."

I blinked a few times, feeling like an idiot. Then I glanced up.

Her face was all soft lines and happiness, a total contrast to her fake smile, and she let out a laugh before saying, "This makes me sound super lame, but this is the nicest thing anyone's done for me in a long time."

"The Skittles?" I asked, staring at the bag like this was their fault.

"You sorted out hundreds of them because they're my favorite. It's incredibly thoughtful, and I'm charmed. Really." She squeezed my wrist again, her voice thicker. "You made my entire fucking week."

My blush felt different this time. "Well, great."

"Yeah." She removed her hand, and I swore the heat

lingered there. I stared at the skin for a second, letting myself wonder what else I could do to make her week.

Ice cream. Dancing. Treats.

"I'm not following your rules today, by the way. I'm diving right into my lemon candies because I survived my co-captain meeting, passed my first biology quiz, *and* ran three miles." She wiggled her eyebrows, daring me to argue.

I remained quiet, and she tossed two into her mouth.

"Smart man. Now, stop distracting me so I can get work done."

"Me? Distracting you?"

She nudged her knee against mine under the table, humor dancing in her eyes as I realized she was teasing me. She'd joked with me numerous times and touched me twice.

I could deny it all I wanted, but I was getting feelings for Cami Simpson—which was the last thing I needed to be doing. But she was a light, and I was a moth, and I was so drawn to her. I could sketch her entire face from memory, including the dusting of freckles that lined her nose. The urge to reach over and cup her face, to see how smooth her skin was against mine was so strong I had to grip my pen tighter. I might've thought Cami had a million walls ten feet high at first, but now that I was inside those walls, I wanted to stay there, be her person for… until I left for Chicago.

I needed math. A clear chart to distance myself from her. I could totally crush on her and keep us friends.

It could be done. I had no choice because if I couldn't get it together, then she might know I was catching feels. If that happened, she'd want to stop being friends with me, and that was a reality I didn't want to think about.

If I only had a few months left with her until I moved, then I wanted to soak up every second I could.

CHAPTER
THIRTEEN

Cami

My makeup was on point, my hair almost perfect, and my uniform fit like a second skin. There were very few moments in my life where everything made perfect sense, but dancing was always one of them.

"You ready for this?" I asked Daniella a week later as we stared out at the stadium. "Our first home game."

"My stomach feels like tennis balls are beating around in there."

"Deep breaths. You know your moves, but try not to look nervous. The girls can tell." I wasn't close to liking Daniella, but in the past week, we'd come to understand each other in different ways. She wasn't a mean girl or out to get anyone, and she'd learned that I was more than my boobs and dance moves. I knew at some point the attacks on my character would stop feeling like a gut punch, but it wasn't anytime soon.

"My hair okay?"

I paused, checked out her ponytail, and clicked my tongue. "You got a loose one. Here." I dug into my bag and pulled out a bobby pin to secure it in place. "There."

Audrey chose that moment to make her entrance, and her attention moved straight to me. "Ladies, you pumped up?"

"Yes, Coach," Daniella said, straightening up and smiling.

Since her issue was learning to work with me and lead the team, she was totally on board with all things Audrey. I was not.

Growing up with a coach for a father taught me a lot of lessons. I knew better than to complain and just worked harder to achieve my goals. I also understood that coaches had their own perceptions I couldn't control. Making decisions really was up to their discretion. However, I'd worked the hardest I could for Audrey, and she still didn't see me that way. The only reason I was co-captain was because the team was suffering, and I would never forgive her for handing the captain title to Daniella.

"Cami, you look great!" she said, putting a little too much effort into saying it.

I gave her a tight smile and focused on the pre-game warm-ups. We'd stretch and prepare for our sets. We had a specific number of routines we did for certain moments in the game, but our real show was during half-time.

Before I left my bag in the dressing room, I went to check my phone. Naomi and Michael were coming to the game, and my dad often showed up for halftime to see us dance. They'd all sent texts, but the one that got my heart all weird was from Freddie.

Freddie: Hood

Freddie: GOOD. I meant good. My thumbs are too big for this. GOOD luck.

Something flowed through me like a hug and a warm blanket after a long game outside. Comforting. Wonderfully awkward.

I couldn't help but tease him back.

Cami: Spank you.

Cami: THANK. I meant THANK you.

Freddie: lmao

Seeing Freddie type *lmao* caused my lips to curve up even more. Was he laughing so hard he fell off his chair? Ehh, doubtful. He was so huge the chair would crumble under his weight if he shook at all. God, I wanted to know how it would feel to straddle his massive frame. Feel his thick thighs against mine, see what made him tremble. Imagining touching Freddie sent goosebumps down my arms in a way that was unfamiliar to me. I'd been attracted to guys before, but this?

It was more.

I didn't get time to think about it too long though. Coach had us all gather round as she gave us a pep talk. It was different to not be one hundred percent zoned in on her speech. Normally, I'd hold onto every word she said, clinging to them. But instead, I wondered what Freddie was doing. He wasn't hugely into sports, but he had school spirit. Was he at the game?

Damn, I should've asked him if he was coming. I could've looked for him or said hi. It certainly would've made it a bit more fun to know he was watching. I scanned the first couple of rows and found a couple people staring at us. Some guy waved, and I wiggled my fingers back at him. Fans did that, and it helped PR to smile or wink back.

Plus, I did like attention.

"You get that, Cami?" Coach asked, her eyes narrowing.

I shrugged, giving a noncommittal answer. Annoyance flared on her face, but Daniella leaned over and whispered, "She wants you in the back row."

"What?" I snapped, my eye twitching and my temples pounding worse than the time I hit myself in the face with a golf club. It wasn't an ego thing. It was a *we've been practicing in a certain formation for two weeks thing.* Plus, seniors were often in the front.

The best on the team stood in the front.

"I don't know why," Daniella said, her voice lacking the

conviction a real leader had. In the past, I'd pushed back on Audrey if I felt it was right.

"You agree with her? You think me being in the back is the right move?"

"Are you two listening?" Audrey asked, her tone impatient now.

"No, because I'm confused. Why do you want me in the back? We practiced *yesterday*, and you didn't say a word."

"I think it's best."

"For you or the team?" I fired back. The girls all sucked in a breath, the humid air thick with tension. Music blared over the speaker as the guys warmed up, and fans were already filling the stands. "Why would you make the change now when nothing warranted it?"

"You'll do it because it's best for the team. Unless you want to walk away?"

Daniella reached over and had a death grip on my forearm, her little squeaks of *please don't leave, please don't leave* grounding me to the spot. There was active hate on Audrey's face, and I had no idea why. None.

It just solidified that the bullshit smile from earlier was fake.

My blood boiled, and Daniella's nails dug into my skin. I glanced at her, and she looked terrified. Pale face, wide eyes, bottom lip quivering. Her eyes pleaded with me.

One game. You can quit after tonight.

With a smile that tasted like vinegar, I sounded as bitchy as possible. "Sure, I'll be in the back now because I wouldn't want to fuck the team over at the last minute. But the second the game is over, I'm done. You want real leadership? It's standing up for yourself. It's walking away when someone becomes too toxic. I'm assuming this is what you wanted from the start, so congrats, Audrey. You won."

Buzzing sounded in my ears like a million bees flew around my head. No, it was more like a train, a loud engine roaring as I headed off the field. I was going to hyperventilate. It'd be horrible and embarrassing and shit. My vision got cloudy, and I sat on the ground near the tunnel that led to the locker rooms. *Deep breath in, then out.*

In, then out.

"You're not quitting. I refuse it." Daniella ran up to me and crouched. She smelled like apples and hairspray, and her eyes had a fire in them I hadn't noticed before.

"I need to. Coach…" I swallowed down the lump in my throat. "I don't know what happened with her, but I'm not doing this."

"I'll walk away with you. She won't lose *both* captains." Daniella got onto her knees and put her hands on my arms. "You held my hair when I puked on you. You agreed to co-captain with me because I'm a mess. *You're* the leader of this squad, Cami. You're the heart of the team."

My eyes watered, and the emotions roaring through me were going to explode like a horrifying mascara-filled volcano. I had sparkles and glue on my eyes. I couldn't fucking ruin them with stupid tears. Swallowing down the horrible ball in my throat, I shook my head. "You'll stay. Our school needs a team."

"We *need* you though."

I shook my head, suddenly hating everything around me. I wanted to be alone so I could cry. I wanted to sob so hard I wouldn't have a single tear left. I wanted to punch a wall over and over. Daniella shook me a little, her wide blue eyes searching my face. A part of me wondered if she enjoyed this, seeing my world crash and burn.

But there was no indication she was happy. She looked distraught.

"Please, Cami. Get through the game, and we'll talk."

It was the hardest thing I'd done in years, pushing myself up to my full height and willing the tears away. It was pride and ego, the only reasons I would go through the game with a blinding smile on my face. My family would be there, watching me and cheering. The formation of the team depended on me. I dusted off my butt and flashed my fake-ass megawatt smile.

"Okay, I'm ready. I'll do the game."

I imagined this was heartbreak. I couldn't be sure exactly, since I'd never let myself feel enough to experience the sensation of my heart breaking, but this had to be close. Even the four shots of vodka didn't ease the pain radiating from my chest like I was hooked to an IV of liquid fire.

My brain buzzed like a million flies swarmed in it, and I moved my body from side to side, swaying with the music to not think or feel. The party was the perfect place to go to avoid everything...the fact I left my uniform on the floor, shoved my decorations from my locker into my bag, and walked out without a word.

Audrey didn't even try to stop me.

Daniella did, but I refused to look into her helpless face. I was choosing me this time. Me.

"Get it, Cami!" someone yelled, whistling at me as I danced on top of the bar. This was the perfect spot for me. On a bar, drunk, wearing little clothing. This was prime leadership right here. Moving my hips and bending low enough to show off my cleavage. If I made them all think I was this way, they couldn't hurt me.

"Want another shot, baby?" a deep voice asked, and I nodded, watching the guy pour vodka into a glass. I might've been sloshed, but I still followed my rule of making sure I knew where my drink came from. Another shot wouldn't kill me, but it could numb the lingering pain.

"Enough." A stern, angry voice had me snapping my head toward the owner. I leaned closer to him, like all the nerves in my body knew safety was near, and I reached out a hand.

Freddie.

"You're here!" I shouted, throwing my arms into the air. "Freddie is here! Another shot, please."

"No." He glared at me, his jaw working tight as he glanced around the bar. "What are you doing up there?"

"Distracting myself? What else?"

"Get down."

"No." I twirled around, shimmying at him, but I didn't do it for long before he reached up with his paw-sized hands and gripped my hips.

Then my world spun, my stomach clenching as I tried to not throw up. I somehow ended up upside down, my legs hanging over Freddie's chest with my face pressed against his back. "You're carrying me like a caveman."

"Yup." He moved through the people, curious stares following us as I felt something soft and light touch my ass... almost like his hand was there. "Sorry, I'm making sure your dress doesn't ride up."

"You apologize for that but not for hoisting me over your shoulder."

"Correct."

A part of me was furious with him for interrupting my plans to forget everything. How dare he ruin my self-pitying vibe? I was on a roll. But another part of me, a small one, wanted to sink into him. I craved his kind eyes and gentle touch and for him to tell me it would be okay. That I hadn't left my soul in the locker room.

He pushed open the bar door, and once we were outside, he set me on the ground and put his hands on his hips, glaring at me with disappointment. The idea of getting drunk seemed great at the time, but my legs felt too heavy to walk under the weight of his sadness, like I'd let him down.

It was one of the worst feelings ever. I focused on the sidewalk, trying not to spin from the shots. "Why are you here?"

"You never came back to the dorm."

I snapped my gaze to him. "Were you waiting for me?"

He swallowed, hard, and his hands clenched at his sides. "You mentioned this party last week, and I don't know… something seemed wrong at the game."

"You were there?" I asked, hope infusing my voice. I didn't know why it mattered, but if he was at the game…my chest swelled. "You don't like football."

He shuffled his feet back and forth and blushed. Even in the dim moonlight, redness painted his cheeks. "You told me you do this." He gestured to me up and down. "When you want to not feel pain. What happened?"

My bottom lip trembled, his soft tone my complete undoing. His quiet, steady gaze pulled the final thread holding my emotions in, and I cried.

The sobs came out as big gasps of air, clogging my throat and stinging my eyes rimmed with makeup. *Nothing* was how I planned it this year. Not a thing, and the boxed-up emotions I sat with for months poured out like a leak in an air mattress. I was deflating. Wetness rolled down my face, ruining my makeup, but I didn't care. My nose got stuffy, and my head spun as a cathartic, relief coursed through my body.

I didn't hear Freddie approach me, and I certainly didn't see him through the tears, but his familiar woodsy scent and comforting presence alerted me to his proximity. Utterly soundless, he wrapped his large arms around me and hoisted me up to his chest. Those large hands ran over my hair and down my back, and I swore he kissed the top of my head.

It had to be the alcohol talking.

I pressed my face into his shirt just above his collarbone and couldn't stop the tears. He rubbed an up and down pattern along my spine and let me cry. It could've been ten minutes or an hour—I wasn't sure. He held me against him, and just thinking about how nice he was had me crying all over again.

My gentle, soft-hearted giant.

"I'm taking us home."

I sniffed, looked at the ground, and tried wiggling down to walk. He shook his head, and his grip on me tightened.

"No." That was all he said.

Never in my life had a guy carried me, or held me, or let me cry on him. My dad had seen some tears but nothing like this. My breakdowns were private and in the shower without witnesses. But it didn't seem to annoy Freddie. If anything, his disappointment had turned to sadness. Like my pain *hurt* him.

Something warm and pleasant plucked in my chest, my pulse getting stronger and faster as I rested my head against his neck. He took large strides, and his movement caused the wind to hit my face just right.

People would talk about this. Him carrying me. But I didn't care. I didn't want this to ever end, and when I nuzzled against his neck, I swore he trembled too. He smelled so good.

One little lick wouldn't hurt.

I bit down on his neck, letting my tongue brush his skin, and I might as well have turned him into stone. He stopped everything. Walking, breathing, moving. His nails dug a little harder into my body before he said, "*What* was that?"

"My mouth." I did it again, and for real, his body shivered. "I wanted to taste you."

"Cami," he said, his voice strained. "No, please."

The rejection hurt, but I was so used to it that I ignored it. Instead, I went with pushing him. "Why? Does it not feel good?" I nipped his earlobe, and he sucked in a breath.

"We're almost there."

He walked faster, his strides so large that they jostled me so I couldn't keep teasing him. It was a shame, really, because he tasted great. Sweaty, but all *him*. Something in my mind was telling me to knock it off, that this wasn't the time, but I was in full self-destruction mode, and he was intent on saving me from it. Which was admirable, but I didn't want to be stopped. I craned my neck to meet his eyes, but he wouldn't look at me.

His throat bobbed with each swallow, and his jaw was tense

enough I worried he could hurt himself. Poor Freddie. He didn't have to carry me.

"Put me down, I can walk."

"Thirty more seconds." He grunted, and then without warning, he set me on the ground just outside the dorm. His chest heaved as he got out the key card and opened the door, walking a little weird.

"Did you hurt yourself carrying me? You shouldn't have done that."

"No. I'm fine."

I frowned, reaching out to touch his hip to, you know, inspect it, but he turned at the same time, and my fingers brushed a very large and rock-hard bulge. "Oh."

My stomach swooped, and I squeezed my thighs together. He was hard for *me*. My breathing became erratic, and my skin fucking tingled with want—the desire to touch him again, lick his skin, kiss him.

Time froze as my eyes locked on his. Heat and want and lust pooled in his gray gaze, but it didn't last long. He ran a hand over his face and stormed down the hall. "Go to your room, Cami."

"But—"

"No. No buts. I care about you and don't want you sabotaging yourself, okay? Go to your room and stay in there."

My temper flared. "You can't just boss me around! Being by myself is the last thing I want right now!" I yelled, not caring that everyone could hear us. We were being *those* people. The ones who should take this conversation somewhere private.

"Then what do you fucking need? I'm not letting you dance on bars and get shitfaced alone. Call your sister if you have to. Anyone."

I eyed our doors, the weight of everything hitting me hard, and the fight seeped out of me. I had no idea what I wanted. To be happy. To dance. To be chosen first at *something* in my life. Sitting in my hot ass dorm room wasn't the best plan, but he was right. I should stay in there and away from everyone else. "Thanks for getting me home, Freddie."

I got my key out and opened my door, not looking back at him once as I slipped inside. It wasn't until I leaned against the door that it really hit me.

I wanted to be with Freddie. Not just as a fling or flirting. I wanted him to be mine, a person I shared my ups and downs with. The person who cared about me despite the downs. I sniffed and let myself fall to the ground as someone pounded on my door.

It could only be one person.

CHAPTER
FOURTEEN

Freddie

Cami opened the door, her eyes rimmed with black, yet she was still the most beautiful person I had ever seen. Everything about her spoke to me in a physical, terrifying way, and my fingers itched to touch her. She might think that I carried her here because I was a gentleman. My intentions had started out that way, but once I felt her body against mine—once she fucking *kissed* my neck, it was like another person entered me.

"What?" she asked, her shoulders slumped and her voice sad and small. Her brown eyes were red, and her voice was husky from all the crying.

I party to not feel pain.

She had to be feeling a lot to dance on top of a bar and be drunk alone. Anger battled with worry, and worry won. "What happened tonight?"

"I quit the team." She took a shaky breath, wrapping her arms around herself. "My coach put me in the back for no reason and demeaned me in front of the team. I can't do it anymore. I turned in my uniform."

She looked at the ground as her lips trembled again. "I don't understand. Even when I contemplated about what to do the past month, I always knew deep down I'd stay. How could I not? But tonight…something changed. Who am I without dance, Freddie?"

"You." I walked into her room, forcing her to move to the side, and fuck, it was hot in here. She hadn't turned her fans on yet, so I went to the window, putting them all on full blast. The door shut us in, and it was just the two of us. If she hadn't been drunk or sad, the scenario was a different one I'd thought about a zillion times. But she was both, and she'd admitted she didn't want to be alone. "You're still you. One thing doesn't define you, Cami."

"It's always defined me." She moved to sit on her bed and rested her face in her hands. "Why did I fucking drink this much? My room is spinning, and I feel sick."

I grabbed a bottle of water from her mini fridge and handed it to her. I then joined her on the bed and lifted her hair from her back. It was drenched with sweat. "Let me get a washcloth to cool you down."

"No, it's fine." She shoved my hand away, but I didn't care. For every step she took opening up to me, she retreated three more.

I *hated* how she hadn't texted me that she was spiraling and wanted to do something stupid. I thought things had changed after last week, but then again, I hadn't called her either after Maddie reached out. The fragile line between us was still there, and I wanted to blast it away.

Finding a washcloth from the side of her bed, I went to the restroom and wetted it as cold as I could. By the time I returned, she had taken off her dress and was lying on her bed in just a black lacy bra thing and black panties.

Fucking hell.

"It's so hot I can't breathe. Is my skin melting off?" She didn't open her eyes at all.

"Here." I sat on the edge of her bed, letting my gaze move from her collarbone to her chest, admiring the swells of her breasts and the peek-a-boo lace giving me a hint of her nipple color. My entire body went taut with want, but I shut it down. I brought the washcloth to her face and wiped it across her cheeks, her neck, then down her cleavage, and over her stomach.

Her belly ring teased me, and my mouth watered. I wanted to *bite* the diamond there, and I'd never bitten anyone in my life. I refused to let my gaze move to her panties though because I only had so much self-control.

"You're probably sweating out the alcohol and adrenaline." I handed her the water bottle. "Take a sip."

She did, and some of it fell down her throat and onto her neck. "I just want to be chosen first for once. You know? Between my parents, my friends, the team. My sister. I'm always the second choice. Always."

The absolute pain and truth in her words caused my chest to hollow out. Words escaped me because how could I comfort her? How could I fix everything for her?

"Drink again, please." I watched her swallow two large gulps, and I wiped her face and neck again with the towel. My own shirt stuck to my skin, but it had nothing to do with the heat from the room and everything to do with her.

She rubbed her eyes with her palms and gasped when she stared down at her hands. "Oh my god. My eyes! You let me look like this?" She jumped from the bed, her stance wobbly, and glanced at a small mirror on her closet door. The muscles in her legs flexed as she stood there, the line of her panties showing almost all of her ass. "Freddie! I look like a drowned rat dressing up as a zombie!"

"I was more concerned about you, not your eye makeup. Plus, you're fucking beautiful, always." I felt my face flame at the compliment. She didn't hear it though. She groaned and pulled out a robe. "What are you doing?" I asked.

"Showering!" she yelled, her manic energy unbalanced from the alcohol and emotions. "Look at me!"

"You're drunk."

"Yes, I *know*, Frederick. I have the spinny brains, but I didn't take my makeup off, and if I don't bathe, it'll stain everything." She waved her hand toward her bed in a dramatic fashion, a little sign of the Cami I knew coming out. I liked her attitude.

"You could fall."

"I will not fall in the shower." She puffed out her chest, wrapping the robe around her as she walked to the door...barefoot.

My entire body shivered with disgust at the thought of not wearing shower shoes. It was the number one rule about communal living. "You need shoes."

"Yes, sir." She bowed, then tried opening the door. It got stuck on the lock, and I pushed myself up to not only grab shoes for her but to help her.

"I can do it," she said.

"Of course you can. But you're drunk, and I'm here."

"You are here." She stared up at me, and a flash of that raw emotion came out again. It didn't last long. She covered her face with her hands. "My face! Don't look!"

If she hadn't exposed her sadness, I'd have thought it was funny seeing her like this. I'd poke fun of her and tease her about the racoon eyes endlessly. But this wasn't amusing at all. The same thought kept repeating in my head. *What if she didn't have me?*

What would've happened to her tonight? At the party? Here? Without shower shoes?

"Are you following me into the shower, sexy, silent Freddie?" She did a spin once we got into the bathroom and let her robe drop. "Oops."

Her toned back and insanely perfect ass cupped in black lace greeted me, and I groaned into my fist. *Fuck*, she was the biggest temptation. Two dimples teased me right at the base of her back where anyone could just walk in and see her.

"Cami, get in the stall," I barked out, picking up the robe and trying not to panic. If she started stripping, I'd lose my goddamn mind. "Please, just do what you need to do."

"I'm not asking you to stand guard, big guy." She spun around, her nipples straining against the black lace, and she let out a mangled laugh. "Can't believe I'm not a dancer anymore."

Focus on helping her, not her tits. I gritted my teeth together. "You are. You still are. You're not a part of *one* team—that's the only change in you. Now, put these damn shoes on and get in the water." I held out the sandals I grabbed, and she eyed me, chewing on her very full lip.

"You're a bit bossy." She stepped into sandals and moved closer to the stall. My breath lodged at the base of my throat, not daring to escape when she unhooked her bra and set it on the side of the door.

Her back was to me, all muscles and smooth skin, and *fuck.* She slid off her panties and set them on the ledge too. My feet grew roots into the shitty tiled floor. My body gave out as she turned around, her delicious, perky tits on full display.

Her pointed nipples were dusky pink and like two gumdrops. I wanted to devour her, then and there, starting at the base of her neck and moving to the jewel on her stomach and ending between her thighs, where she was completely bare. She turned on the water and gave me a wicked grin. "You were hard earlier, Freddie. Feel free to join me in the shower."

Then, she shut the stall curtain. I took a shaky breath that rocked my entire core. Seeing her naked had been a fantasy for *years.* She blew all expectations out of the water, but I *knew* my attraction shouldn't take precedence right now. She was hurting and needed a friend, someone to put her first.

I couldn't put her needs second to my raging hard-on. I just wasn't that guy.

My cock hardened beneath my jeans, but I made no moves

to adjust it. The littlest touch could set me off, and I focused on counting the ceiling tiles. I got to eighteen when I heard it.

A sniff.

It was like a crack in my heart at the muffled sound. When she'd cried on my chest earlier, those tears were a rushed explosion. These cries were somehow sadder. Lonelier. Filled with her attempts at stopping them.

I didn't even think about what I was doing besides being there for Cami. I pulled the curtain back and stepped into the blazing hot shower. She gasped, her wide eyes blinking a few times before she opened her mouth. "What are you—"

"Come here," I said, ignoring the protectiveness coursing through my body. I noticed the way her gaze softened and her shoulders relaxed when I held out my arms. The hot water pounded over me, soaking my entire outfit, but I didn't care. My glasses fogged up as she rested her head on my chest and wrapped her wet, naked body against mine.

Her fingers dug into my shirt as she sniffed again, but this time it wasn't as sad. I kept my hands respectfully at her lower back because her skin was wet and smooth. It'd be so easy to let them fall lower, but I refused. Even as my cock stiffened and my chest heaved with each breath.

"You're wet," she said, a few minutes later, her grip unwavering. "Your clothes."

"It's okay," I croaked out, meaning it.

"What are we doing, Freddie?"

"In life, or right now?"

"Both?"

"I'm not sure to either question." I cupped the back of her head, careful to not let her body move too much against mine. She kept her face hidden, which was probably for the best because I just wanted to kiss her. "I know I hate that you're sad. Hearing you cry is my least favorite thing in the world. I also know that you'll get through this moment. Maybe it's in a week, or two, or a month, or a year, but you won't live in this ragey mess forever."

She tilted her head up to look at me, and one side of her mouth quirked up. "Ragey mess?"

My ears burned red. "I'm not sure—"

"I want to kiss you." She stood on her tiptoes and moved her attention to my mouth, her eyes heating as she leaned in. "Please, Freddie."

My insides fought with my logic, and with a strength my entire family tree would be proud of, I placed my thumb over her bottom lip. It was so plump and warm, but I shook my head. The hot water dripped down both of us, steaming between our faces. "Not now."

She blinked, not looking upset at all. More like confused. "Why?"

"When I kiss you, Cami, your eyes aren't going to be wet from tears. You're not going to be drunk or sad or *naked* in a dorm shower."

She ran her tongue over the spot on her lip that my thumb grazed, the motion sending a white-hot flash of desire through me. "Then when?"

"I don't know."

"But you *do* want to kiss me?" There was a silent plea in her question, like my answer mattered to her.

"Of fucking course I want to kiss you."

A lazy smile formed on her lips, and she closed her eyes, backing away from me so the water hit her face again. I focused on the way the water ran down her forehead, over her cute nose, and over her chin. She scrubbed at the black circles and all the makeup she wore, leaving her skin bare. I let my gaze trail over her collarbone and her nipples. Her tits were literal perfection, full and heavy, and I wanted to cherish them for *hours*. But I only let my eyes move over her. I kept my hands to myself, like I needed to.

Knowing that I got to see her like this, even in this weird in-between of more and just friends scenario, lit me up. She had freckles and a birthmark just above her right breast, and I wanted to trace a line between them with my finger.

"I'm gonna be hungovaaaa tomorrow," she sang, reminding me very much that she was intoxicated. It put a damper on my thoughts, but I was grateful for the comment.

"Let's get you dressed and in bed."

"You're staying with me, right?" she asked, those damn eyes turning to saucers meant to torture me. "Please?"

How could I say no? How could I ignore the way her face crumpled with worry? "Stay with you… how?"

"I'll sleep on the floor! You can have my bed, yes. This can work!" She gripped the collar of my shirt and smiled up at me like the first blast of morning sunshine.

"How about we get dressed and then we talk?"

She nodded and jumped out of the shower so fast I almost stumbled while trying to make sure she didn't fall. "So, it's happening! Yay!"

"I didn't say—" She was already out of the bathroom, the door swinging shut with a light squeak. Damn.

Wearing soaking wet clothes wasn't the weirdest part of my day, but it wasn't the best. Each step squished as I made it to my room. I'd barely gotten my shirt and pants off before Cami burst in through my door. "Hey!" I yelled, covering my junk with my hand. "I'm naked."

"It's only fair. You saw me, so let me see you."

"You stripped in front of me. You barging into *my* room isn't the same." My entire body flushed as she dragged her gaze from my face to my legs. Her eyes heated, and that spark between us grew. I shook my head before she could even say anything. Thank god she wore a large T-shirt this time. "Give me two minutes."

"Would being in here be better? It's your space, and I can just curl up on the ground." She got onto the floor and made a little nest for herself with one of my sweatshirts. "See? Perfect. You won't even know I'm here."

"I'll know." I grabbed my boxers and slid them on when she wasn't looking. I felt better with one small layer on. I found my athletic shorts, and once those were on, I faced her without blushing like a junior high kid. "Did you lock your door?"

"Yes! See?" She held it up and grinned at me. "And I brought water."

"Lay in my bed." I pointed to it, arching my brows and daring her to disobey. "If you're in here, you get the bed."

"But you're too large for the floor."

"I'll manage." I pointed again, and she scrambled into my bed, lying on top of the sheet because it was a stove in here. She rolled to her side and patted the spot next to her.

"No." I shook my head to bring the point home.

She frowned. "I just want to cuddle, I swear. You have this comforting presence, and you smell like Taylor Swift, and I wanted to just live in it. You know?"

I had no fucking idea, but she kept rubbing her hand on the sheet, and the floor looked horrible. One night wouldn't kill me. "Just cuddling."

She bit down on her lip, not quite hiding her smile. She pressed her back against the wall, leaving me a sliver of bed to lie on. These twins were too small for me on a good day and now with another body in there? I didn't overthink it. She wanted to cuddle with me. I turned off the light.

With the air stifling and the fans blowing, I got onto the bed, and Cami rested her head on the crook of my shoulder. To make myself more comfortable, I put my arm around her, and the motion caused her entire body to press into mine. I had to say something to break the spell, to help me not think about her legs wrapping up against mine. "So, uh, do you snore?"

"I'm not sure." Her breath hit my face. That's how close she was to me.

"You do, don't you?" I teased.

"I really don't know, Freddie. I've never slept with anyone… like this before."

Shit. My throat got all tight again with unsaid things, and I pulled her a little more toward me. "Well, then I'll let you know in the morning."

CHAPTER
FIFTEEN

Cami

My skin danced with flames of heat, sweat forming in every crevice, and I groaned into a very warm, large body. The pounding in my head doubled in pain at my increased heartrate, and last night came back to me in waves of embarrassment.

The team. Audrey.

The bar. The shots.

Freddie.

I'd stripped in front of him, and *oh my god*. I'd asked him to kiss me! And cuddle with me! I bolted upright from his bed, my face losing all its blood as he lay there, eyes closed and chest moving up and down with each breath.

One of his hands rested on his stomach, and the other sat on my hip. Something hot and heavy flowed through me. The mere sight of him touching me was enough to have my dry mouth watering.

"I can feel you staring," he said, not opening his eyes. His facial structures were so pretty--no glasses hiding the real length of his lashes and the way they fanned over his cheeks. Despite all the shame and regret boiling in my chest, I smiled.

"I'm not staring that much."

He opened his eyes, his gaze moving from the light in the window to me. The gray seemed clearer somehow. There were sleep lines all around his face, making me want to snuggle closer to him.

"How are you feeling?" he asked, his voice gravelly.

At the mention of my feelings, my head throbbed again. I winced and rubbed my forehead. "Like an idiot."

"We've all had those nights." He pushed himself up to his elbows, letting out a deep groan. I snuck a glance down his body and almost moaned at the very evident bulge in his boxers. His dick strained against the black fabric, and my fingers itched to feel him. He looked *huge*. The rumble of his yawn combined with eyeing his cock sent a blast of heat through me. I brought my fingers up to my lips, about to tell them to calm down.

When I kiss you, he'd said. Not if. WHEN. That was big.

Maybe it wasn't terrible that I'd stripped?

His movement caused his entire side to press into mine, and he stilled, muscles tensing as he reached toward the floor to put his glasses on. Everything smelled like him—like books and sweaters and trees.

He probably wanted me gone. I should get up, shower, and take stock of my life, but I couldn't move away from him. Even in the blazing heat of the dorm room, it felt better being next to him.

"I'm really sorry, Cami," he said, pushing himself up and breaking the spell he put over me.

This was the axe. He was going to tell me to get lost and pretend like last night hadn't happened. That I was too much, a hot mess. My eyes burned, and my stomach heaved, the damn shots I'd downed wanting to come up. I slowly got out of his bed and stood on the almost cold tile floor. I couldn't look at him. "I-I understand."

"Wait," he said, his tone sharper. "What do you understand?"

I glanced at him through my lashes, not quite meeting his eyes, but his face was twisted in confusion. "That *this* won't happen again. I know I'm not…" I gulped, swallowing the ball of self-pity and squeezing my fists at my sides.

"Cami, no, no, no," Freddie said, pushing up from the bed and placing his hands on my shoulders. "That's not what I meant at all. Hey, look at me." He tilted my chin up and had the same intense look that he sometimes gave me when we were at the library. Or the night I made him dance.

My stomach swooped.

"I was talking about what happened on the team. I know how much dance means to you. It makes me sick that you had to walk away." He moved his hand from my chin to my neck in what I assumed was a gesture of comfort. I leaned into it, sighing in utter relief.

Maybe he didn't think I was a failure of a human.

"Oh. Well, thanks." God, my entire face blushed, making my headache worse. I winced, and he muttered a curse.

"Sit, let me grab you water and some pills." He carefully guided me back to his bed and helped me down even though I was perfectly capable of doing it myself. If anything, I deserved to feel the pounding of my head with each movement.

I was a real masochist when the problem was my own fault. Like a hangover. Once I was seated, he went to a small table on the other side of the room and got out a bottled water and a couple of red pills. He handed them to me and waited as I swallowed them.

"Thanks."

"Of course, yeah." He shrugged, the tips of his ears burning red. I wanted to know what he was thinking. He ran a hand over his jaw a few times, shifting his weight like he was uncomfortable.

"I should go." I stood, pausing as the wave of pounding continued. "Um, thanks for—"

"What are you doing today?" he blurted out, his speech way too fast and choppy to be considered smooth.

"Honestly? Wallowing in self-pity and rethinking every horrible mistake I've ever made with a finale of eating garbage food." I forced a smile, hoping it'd fool him. None of those were lies, but I knew if left alone with my thoughts I'd spiral again. Get upset. Cry. Do the things I avoided with all my soul.

He smiled the full Freddie grin, dimples and crinkles around his eyes, and he clapped his hands. I winced at the sound.

"Shit, sorry. I know the perfect place to help with garbage food."

"I'm intrigued. Maybe not this second but…" Footsteps thudded outside in our hall. Whispers. Laughter. There had to be like ten people out there. "What time is it?"

"Nine." He frowned, going toward the door and cracking it open.

"Oh, hi," Daniella said, her wide eyes moving from Freddie to me as her lips parted into a little oh. "I found her! Cami!"

It was almost slow motion how Daniella pushed through Freddie's door, running to me and throwing her arms around my neck. She wasn't the only one either. The entire dance team entered Freddie's small ass room, each one of them hugging me or muttering something about Audrey. Freddie quickly put on shorts in the corner.

"You're not quitting. We refuse to accept it. If you do, then we'll all walk away. We had a team meeting last night, and its final," Daniella said into my neck. There were so many body parts touching me, but my heart was beating three times as fast.

They came here for me.

The team… Daniella…supporting *me*. "Uh, wow, I'm not—"

"Come on. We have a lot to discuss, and Vi's place has air,

thank Christ. It's closest." Someone patted my head, and like ants, everyone moved out of the room. Daniella still clung to me, and disbelief had my body feeling light. Weightless. It almost tingled.

I wouldn't let the girls walk away from the team on my behalf. That wouldn't do, but this? This display of support? I'd never had it in my life from any team, and it made my eyes water.

Freddie met my eyes, his own dancing with amusement and happiness. For me. He smiled, shook his head, and jutted his chin toward the door. "Go on," he said, his grin almost too large for his face.

He didn't have to say it. He knew. He knew me and what this meant.

Words were still tough to form as Daniella led me out into the hall. But as we neared the door, I realized I only wore Freddie's shirt. "Damn! Let me put clothes on."

"Only you could totally pull off a boyfriend tee. Seriously."

"Right? It's not even fair how you can make a bag look good, C."

C.

A nickname?

Me?

Naomi had all the nicknames growing up, never me.

I was going to burst into tears of ... something. Happiness. Hope. Like I maybe I had someone who picked me? It wasn't until I got into my room and put on shorts and a tank that I realized they'd called Freddie my boyfriend.

Instead of my usual freak out at the mere thought of commitment, I smiled and chewed my bottom lip. We weren't anything close to that, but still...If I was going to break my anti-relationship mindset for anyone, it'd be with him. Without a single doubt.

After I was hydrated and fed, Daniella led the team in a plan of action at Vi's apartment. They weren't going to walk away from the team—thank God. That wasn't fair to the school or to them, but we were going to stage an intervention with Audrey.

It seems I wasn't the only one who noticed her picking on me. She'd made comments to the other girls about me, isolating me from them, letting the girls think I didn't like them. My blood boiled at her actions. Truly.

I might've partied a little too much and wore a lot of makeup, but I'd never done anything wrong enough to warrant this shit.

"So, Monday, we go to her office at nine and won't leave until we hash it out. Her style is unacceptable, and I think we have a case to go to the Dean of Athletics, huh?" one of the girls said.

"Possibly. She's always been so level-headed, so that's why this is so weird. Did you do something to piss her off? Even if it was small?" Vi asked, tapping her fingers along her jaw.

"Not that I know of." I met Daniella's eyes, and a rush of gratitude went through me. She was the reason the girls were here for me. She'd told them about how I helped her and took care of her, and *that* was why they started talking about Audrey.

Daniella had set them all straight, and it was crazy how every negative thought I had about her disappeared. She was being a real leader right now, speaking up for what was right and standing by her teammate.

Shit. My eyes were going to maybe sting again.

"This won't happen. Not anymore. You're one of us, Cami. You have been since you were a freshman. We'll get this figured out, okay? I promise." Daniella put her hand on my shoulder and squeezed, the fierce look in her eyes making her seem older. I nodded, and someone ordered pizza.

Then Vi put on Real Housewives.

An hour went by, then another one, and soon enough, it was evening. In all four years I had been on the team, at Central

State, we'd never had a full-day bonding that wasn't scheduled or part of camp. There were cliques within the team who hung out constantly, but that wasn't something I'd experienced before. It was unsettling and weird and wonderful.

"So, Cami, how long have you been with that Henry Cavill look-alike?" Vi asked.

"Freddie?" I choked on the water and wiped my mouth with the back of my hand. "Oh, we're not… together."

"Okay, okay, okay, I get it," Vi said, smiling. "You were wearing his shirt and looked mighty comfortable with him. You had the geef vibe going on."

"Geef?"

"Girlfriend. GF. Geef. Sorry, my partner and I use that lingo all the time, and I forgot other people don't." She shrugged, and someone else called her name, distracting her from our conversation.

Was she right? Did I have a *girlfriend* vibe? My skin warmed, and I chewed my lip, loving the hell out of this hangout but secretly wishing I was able to get garbage food with Freddie.

I twirled my phone on my palm, trying to think of something clever to text him. It wasn't like I could just say hey…well, I guess I could? But he could be busy. He could be studying at our spot, and ugh. A pang hit my chest.

It had only been eight hours, but I missed seeing him already. This was becoming too much, and I needed to step back. I had a team supporting me for the first time, and I was thinking about some guy when I had no idea where I stood with him.

I shook my head, set my phone down, and pretended to be invested in the TV show. It lasted thirty minutes before my phone buzzed, and my heart leapt in my throat. *Freddie!*

Naomi: Hey, hey! I know you're probs going to a party already but we're having a movie night if you wanna head over!

Cami: Damn. I'm with the dance team. We're bonding and shit?

Naomi: I love that!

Naomi: Okay, well, what do I have to do to get you to come to trivia with us Tuesday? Mona backed out. Plus, I miss your face.

Cami: You have the same one. Look in the mirror.

Naomi: Ha. Don't leave me hanging. Michael and his buddy Freddie are coming, and they know way too much random shit. It's fun. I SWEAR.

My heart lurched in my chest at the thought of hanging out with Freddie with my sister and her boyfriend. It'd be almost like a date? A double-date? No. A friend hangout. That was it. My thumb paused over the screen just as a text came through of a large cheeseburger.

Freddie: I have a sympathy hangover for you and am eating this burger in your honor.

My smile almost hurt my face. Keeping my distance was impossible, and I'd just figure out what to do about these feelings later.

CHAPTER **SIXTEEN**

Freddie

My left leg bounced up and down so much it made the condiments on the top of the table clink together at the small sandwich shop. The ketchup kept hitting the salt, so I moved them two inches apart. It didn't prevent the nerves, but at least the annoying sound stopped.

Maddie is coming.

It had to be done. It wasn't fair to myself or Cami if I continued down whatever path we were on without closing this one. Because one thing I knew, without a doubt, was that I had feelings for Cami. Large ones. Slightly terrifying ones if I were honest with myself. Her spending time with the dance team yesterday was probably for the best. It gave me space to get my head on straight and set up this meeting with Maddie.

"Freddie, hey," a familiar voice pulled my attention to the right just before a warm hand landed on my neck. Maddie grazed her fingers over the back of my head, sending uncomfortable goosebumps down my body.

I didn't want her touching me.

My jaw tensed, and I gestured to the spot in front of me,

ignoring the heavy beat of my pulse that seemed to radiate all the way to my fingertips. Sweat beaded on my forehead, and I used a napkin to wipe it and adjust my glasses as she sat. Confrontation was in my top three least favorite things in the world, and this one was long overdue.

Even when she'd dumped me and broke my heart, I'd let her walk away because she made it clear that she was out of my league from the start.

"I'm so glad you called me, babe. I've *missed* you." Her face crumpled into a million soft lines as she reached over and placed her palm on the top of my hand. Her touch made me squirm, and I pulled my hand away.

"You look good. How are your classes? And Camden? We have so much to catch up on."

She laughed and smiled at the waitress. "I'll have an iced tea. An Arnold Palmer for you, babe?"

"Um, no, I'm okay." I already had a drink on the table, and even though she ordered my favorite drink, I didn't want to give her the satisfaction of remembering that. "My water is fine."

The waitress left, meaning Maddie and I were alone in the back corner. *Why* did I choose somewhere so secluded? I ran a hand over my jaw and cleared my throat, unsure of where to begin. She wanted to chat, and I needed to say all the things I'd held back. But how did I start?

"Maddie," I said, my voice coming out more in control than I felt. "What is your goal here?"

"To talk to you." She frowned. "To talk about *us*."

Anger flared under my skin, causing my grip on the table to tighten. "There is no *us*. Stop acting like there is."

"Freddie," she said, her voice a little chastising. "I know I messed up, okay? I've thought about my mistake a million times this past year, and I want to rectify it."

"You told me I was *boring* and then you dated four different guys? How am I supposed to believe you?"

"You've been keeping tabs on me, huh?" She smiled, a triumphant look in her eyes that was nothing like the expression Cami had. When Cami had a mischievous expression, it was amusing and fun. Like she had a secret she wanted to tell me.

Maddie was manipulative.

"No." I put the palms of my hands on the table and kept them still. "Camden has, and he made sure I knew about all the times you were dumped. I'm not a consolation prize, alright? I'm not the guy who waits around for you to figure your shit out."

Her cheeks turned red just as the waitress returned, and she gave her a tight smile. The tension in the air was thick enough to cut with a knife. "I didn't know what I wanted! I thought I needed danger, excitement, I don't know! You had your routines and your weeks planned. I felt… Now I do. I want the safety we had and your weird little Skittles thing." She gripped my hands hard as she leaned over the table. "We talked about life after school. Living together. I still think about that. If there is even a small part of you that wants this…please, give me another chance."

Two months ago, this conversation might've gone an entirely different way. Dating was hard for me, and for three years, I'd thought Maddie was the one. I ignored all the red flags because I loved her. But with distance, those flags grew larger and large until they were huge yellow targets I couldn't avoid.

I took a deep breath, letting go of the resentment, and spoke straight from the heart. "You hurt me, Mads. You pulled the rug out from under me and hit every insecurity I ever had. I've gone over all the things I wanted to say to you this past year, but after seeing you now, none of it matters."

"What are you saying?"

"That I'm over you. Us. What we used to be." I leaned back in my chair, the tightness around my shoulders loosening as the conversation wore on. My pulse raced, sure, but this felt right. Overdue.

"Is it cause you're with someone else?" she asked, her posture going straight and the soft lines around her eyes tightening.

"No. It doesn't matter if I'm seeing anyone at all. I met you here today because I need this chapter closed."

She swallowed hard, and her eyes misted as she played with the straw in her drink. I used to do whatever I could to make her smile when she was sad, but her pouting seemed different this time. Performative. I adjusted my glasses and scooted the chair back. It caused a terribly loud scraping sound, and her gaze darted to me. "You're *leaving*? I just got here!"

"We're not going to be friends, and I said everything I had to. What's the point in staying? My mind isn't changing." I stood up, made sure my clothes were smooth, and pushed the chair back in.

"You're... different." Her eyes flashed with interest, and she rubbed her collarbone with her forefinger. That was always her *tell* when she was attracted to someone, and irritation prickled my skin.

"Goodbye, Maddie." I didn't look back as I left the sandwich shop, excitement making me walk with a little skip to my step. No more baggage with Maddie. No more knots forming in my chest when I heard her name or thought about seeing her again.

Camden had always pushed me to confront her, but that was more his style. I was quiet, calm, and passive. Yelling and big showdowns weren't my thing. The conversation with her put an end to all that garbage, and my soul seemed lighter.

While having that talk with Maddie wasn't entirely because I wanted to kiss Cami, it definitely sped up the process. With the purpose of visiting my neighbor, I walked fast back to the dorms, ignoring the way my shirt stuck to my skin the second I entered the hallway. I knocked on her door and waited.

I didn't have a plan besides seeing her...which was very

anti-me. Plans were who I was, my kink. My breath lodged in my throat as her footsteps padded toward the door and the handle twisted. Every muscle I had tensed as I froze, desperately wanting to see her with an unexplainable pull.

She wore a red dress with a tie on the side, and her entire face lit up when she opened the door. Those two seconds of witnessing the joy *I* brought her was one of the best feelings. Her lips were bare as they curved up, but it was her eyes that reeled me in. The dark brown gaze teased me. "Freddie," she said, her tone going higher than normal, and without thinking, I closed the distance between us and cupped her face.

She sucked in a breath as I ran my thumb over her bottom lip, the softness of it almost enough to ruin me. Such a strong, sassy woman who was so misunderstood. But I knew her.

"What are you…" she whispered, her pulse racing at the base of her neck as we entered her room and the door shut.

"Have you been crying?" I asked, my skin getting way too tight for my body as need prickled all over me from being near her. Cami's vanilla and peaches scent made my mouth water, and I took a deep breath as I waited for her answer.

"Um, no?" She blinked a lot, her hands coming up to grip my t-shirt. She looked back and forth between my eyes, her breathing getting heavier as I moved my hand to her neck.

"Are you drunk?"

"No."

"Sad?"

She shook her head, chewing her lip as confusion clouded her eyes. "Why are you asking—"

"Then I can kiss you now. No wait," I said, my face burning. "Can I? I mean, can I kiss you now?"

Cami wet her bottom lip with her tongue before she nodded. "Yes."

My body trembled as I ran my hand over her neck, throat, then back up to her cheek. Her skin was smooth and warm, and I could stare at each freckle and eyelash for hours, just studying the way her expressions told a story. Nerves twisted my spine, and my stomach ached with want and uncertainty, but I shoved it all to the back of my mind and focused on this beautiful woman.

"Freddie, stop staring at me and do it."

I fought a grin and finally brought my lips to hers.

The second our mouths touched, liquid fire flowed through my veins. My heart threatened to jump out of my chest to join hers, and I couldn't get enough of her.

I wrapped my arm around her back, pulling her trim body against mine so I could feel each beat of her heart, and I moaned against her lips. Her tongue greeted mine hungrily, and she tilted her head back, giving me more access. I nipped at her pillow-soft lips, wanting to savor the cherry flavor of them for the rest of my life. Her mouth was delicious and enticing, and my body trembled as our mouths meshed together. Cami kissed how she lived, boldly, with fire, and I was putty in her hands.

"My god," I said, my voice shaky as I rested my forehead against hers. Her minty breath hit my face, and she let out a tiny sound of pleasure.

There wasn't even any touching and all my blood was heading south.

I craved *more.*

I kept one hand on her lower back and brought the other to the cup her head to tip it back, giving me the angle I wanted. She looked up at with me, heat swirling in her eyes, before I kissed her again, holding her gaze.

She opened her mouth and teased the outside of my lip with her tongue, sending a shudder through me, and I snapped. Instead of being gentle, I devoured her. She tasted like mint and cherry, and every stroke of her tongue got me hotter.

This wasn't a slow, sexy kiss. It was messy with teeth and tongue and desperate sounds escaping my throat. "Cami," I said, unsure if I was begging or thanking her. She didn't respond though.

She pushed me backward until I sat on her bed, her warm, tight body sliding onto my lap. My cock twitched as she straddled me.

"The amount of times I envisioned you in my bed… this doesn't come close."

"Yeah?" I grinned, running my fingers up her bare thighs and almost combusting at feeling her skin. She was just as hungry too. She rubbed her hands all over my shoulders, my chest, up my head and through my hair. Her swollen lips teased me, and I groaned when she lowered her head and kissed my neck. "Shit," I hissed.

"You smell so fucking good, Freddie." She brought my earlobe into her mouth and bit it, sending a jolt through my body.

"Behave," I said, pulling her back up so her face was inches from mine. She had her mischievous expression again, but this time, her reddened cheeks were from our kiss. From me. "Look at you." I ran a finger over her mouth, neck, and down the center of her chest where her dress dipped low. "So pretty. So perfect."

She shuddered on my lap, the movement causing her to rock against my erection. She panted as I undid one button on her dress, right at the top. She squirmed as I stared at the way her collarbone stuck out and how she had a cluster of freckles right below her shoulder.

If she thought this was going to be quick, she had no idea. I'd waited over a year to taste her, and I wanted this to last. I undid another button, bending lower to kiss her neck, down her shoulder, and just above her chest.

"Wh-what are you doing?"

"Getting to know your body."

"Get to know other places first, please." Her voice was husky, and the fact she was so turned on made me grin against her skin. Me. The boring giant had Cami Simpson turned on.

"Mm, I'll take my time." I undid another button and sucked

in a breath at the red lacy bra she wore. She wiggled on top of me as I slowly ran my hand up her spine and pulled her in for another deep kiss. This time she relaxed into me, sucking my tongue into her mouth and full on grinding her hips. I gripped her waist, enjoying the fact she was sitting on my lap, when she reached for the hem of my shirt and pulled.

"Need to feel you."

The urgency in her voice just made me harder and made my patience thin. I took of my shirt and tossed it to the side, hellbent on feeling her skin against mine. It was more important than breathing, and I undid the rest of her buttons with shaky fingers. I wasn't sure how to remove her dress with the bow and everything, and I must've paused too long because Cami had it off in two seconds.

All she wore was a red bra and the tiniest pair of matching panties.

"Fuck," I said, groaning into my fist as I stared at her. Her thighs were spread wide, giving me the perfect glimpse of the dampening fabric. Her nipples strained against the lace, and my dick actually hurt in my jeans. My head went fuzzy, and I realized I wasn't breathing when someone knocked on her door, stilling us both.

"Cami, you there?" a male voice said, the lilt unfamiliar, but it rang with authority. "Open up right now."

CHAPTER
SEVENTEEN

Cami

NO. Not now.

Not with my body a desperate mess and my mouth swollen from Freddie's kisses. Freddie paled at the interruption, but my dad could wait.

He wanted to talk about the dance team, I was sure, but there was no way I was letting Freddie go. I leaned forward and whispered straight into his ear. "Shh, he'll leave."

Goosebumps broke down his neck, and it gave me such a thrill to see Freddie's body react to mine. He was so goddamn genuine and intent on taking his time. Did he have any idea I was going to burst? My pulse pounded between my thighs, and I needed him to *touch me.*

I expected him to argue or at least push me off him until my dad went away, but he picked me up and set me on the bed. Freddie knelt between my legs with a hand on each thigh. His gray eyes were like a thunderstorm, heated and intense as his chest heaved. My breath caught in my throat at the sheer desire on his face as he eyed me with a slack jaw. His dark hair was ruffled from my fingers earlier, and his lips were red and wet—from me. I got looked at a lot but never like *this*. Like he really was studying every square inch of me and loving it. Like he could see every good, bad, and weird part of me, and he wasn't afraid. It made me feel special... Like I mattered to him.

"Freddie?" I whispered.

He snapped his gaze to mine and flashed a grin before leaning close again. His breath tickled my inner thighs, and I shivered. "Can you be quiet?"

Oh, fucking fuck. My body flushed, and I almost let out a moan at how *hot* that statement was. My dad pounded on the door again, but Freddie paid him no attention. His hands were at my chest, his fingers circling around my pebbled nipples. The sensation caused my hips to arch up, creating a rustling noise.

Freddie clicked his tongue. "Shh, Cami."

My insides were melting. I was completely putty for a bossy Freddie. He could command me to do just about anything and I would. He held my gaze as he lowered his lips and covered my nipple through the bra. His warm mouth soaked the fabric, and he gently bit down, still holding eye contact. I was going to die from lust. This was so hot and intimate my body didn't know what to do.

He alternated between using his mouth to kiss my nipples or his fingers to tweak them lightly, and each movement had me wetter. Embarrassingly wet.

"Freddie—" I begged, my voice louder than a whisper.

"He could still be out there." He licked the valley between my breasts. "You want me to stop kissing you and find out?"

I shook my head, absolutely sure I wouldn't make it if he stopped.

"Then stay quiet." His eyes flashed with amusement as he reached behind my back to try and undo my bra. One second went by, then another. "Damnit."

"Need help? Or am I not allowed to ask?"

He growled at my response, sending a flurry of excited butterflies through my stomach as he *finally* got the clasp undone. The material tickled my skin as he slid it off and set it on the bed. With his hands still around my back and our bodies close enough to feel the warmth, he stared at my tits, and his nostrils flared. Then, oh so slowly, he cupped each of them and let out a deep, satisfying sound.

He teased my nipples with his thumbs, and each flick sent a white-hot burst of lust straight to my core. And when he licked the tip of one torturously slow, I thought I could legit come. My pulse pounded in my ears, rushing like waves in the ocean as Freddie took his time tasting and sucking and teasing my breasts. It didn't matter how much I begged or squirmed on the bed—he didn't pick up the pace.

"Are you trying to kill me?" I whispered, pulling his chin up so he had to look at me. He wore a drunken smile, his lips wet and his glasses almost fogged up. "Oh, honey," I said, smiling as I took his glasses off and set them to the side. He squinted a few times before he slammed his mouth to mine, kissing me with a new energy.

He pushed me back onto the bed entirely, crawling over my body and propping himself up on his elbows as he ground his hips against mine. *Yes!* I wanted to fucking scream at feeling his incredibly hard cock rub right where I needed it, but he only did it a few times before his kisses moved toward my chest, then my stomach, then below my belly button. He brought my belly ring into his mouth for a second, groaning before sliding his hands on the edge of my panties and pulling them down.

"Freddie, you don't have—"

"It's been a *long* time," he said, his gaze like a caress all over my body. He didn't even have to touch every part of me for goosebumps to break out and desperate shivers of lust to take over. "I want to taste you."

"You don't have to do that." My face burned redder than the

dress I wore, and I shook my head. "Seriously. It's not my favorite thing."

He raised his eyebrows. "You don't like it when someone goes down on you? Why?"

He kneeled awkwardly on the end of my bed, his large frame looking so silly with the angles of his knees and arms. If it weren't for our position and the way he kept looking at my panties, I could've laughed. His breath hit my pussy just enough for me to squirm, and I wanted to bury myself in the blankets with embarrassment. Why couldn't he be like other guys and just fuck me already?

Because it's Freddie.

My thought rebelled against the guy in front of me, and the embarrassment washed away. He wasn't judging me.

"It's always so...uncomfortable."

"How?" He tilted his head to the side, glancing between my bare pussy and my face, his breaths becoming faster as he chewed his lip. "Does it not feel good?"

"No, I don't know." I covered my eyes with my hands, groaning at the intimacy of this all. My hook-ups were fast, lights off, quick. This wasn't like anything I had experienced, but how did I put that into words? That despite this being the best, it was terrifying in its own way?

"Hey," he said, his voice soft and filled with a kindness that made my chest feel all squishy. He moved around and gently tugged my hand from my face. "We don't have to do anything you don't want to, okay? Kissing you, seeing you like this? It's enough for me."

"Why are you so fucking sweet?" I asked, annoyed that *I* was the one stalling everything between us. Not him, the nice guy who liked relationships. Me. "I'm ruining this."

"No, no, you're not. You're being honest. I prefer that, always." He ran his fingers over my jawline and pressed his lips softly against my mouth. "You being yourself, unafraid or worried. This is my *favorite* Cami. Like I get a special part of you that no one else does."

My throat got tight as he said the words right against my lips, and a different wave of heat went through me. One that felt like a string connected our hearts and pulled me closer to me. I wanted to feel all of him inside me, where he bared his soul. Like that would balance the scales and appease the insatiable hunger I had for him and his body. I arched up, trying to get that closeness with him. Our tongues met, and our hands explored each other with a new fervor. Sweat covered our chests as we kissed deeper and faster.

His delicious woodsy scent mixed with the sweat, and *unnnh,* he smelled good. Heat danced along my spine, and I reached for his belt, undoing it with a jerky movement.

He covered my hands with his and stopped. "We don't have to do anything, I swear."

"Freddie," I said, panting as my skin was about to fall off my body with how turned on I was. It was painful at this point. "You're *killing* me."

"Can't have that, huh?" He grinned at me before sliding his pants and boxers off in one swift motion. His cock looked rock hard and thick, just like the rest of him. His long, massive thighs were covered with a light dusting of hair. His flat stomach wasn't covered with muscles or lines, but it was *perfect.* I wanted to bite along the happy trail that led to his cock. His broad shoulders and chest were so fucking sexy that I wanted to lick from his collarbone down to his cock.

"Uh, do you have a condom? I do in my room, I think. It's been so long," he said, gulping and running his hand through his hair. "Shit."

"I do, yes." I got up, went through my small toiletry bag in the closet, and held up a wrapper. "It's been a while for me too."

He nodded in understanding, the unspoken agreement that this meant something to both us in the air. He might've been used to slow sex with a buildup and exploring each other. I wasn't. I handed him the wrapper, my movement awkward as hell, and a smile tugged at his lips.

He ripped it open and sheathed his cock, then pulled me back onto his lap. I thought he'd immediately go for it, thrusting up into me, but he didn't. Of course he didn't. He kissed me deeply, without any rush, and brought his fingers between my legs. He sucked in a breath when he ran one down my slit. "You're so *wet*."

"Your fault," I said, panting when he swirled around my clit with his thumb. He did it again, maintaining eye contact before he inserted one finger into me. "Mm," I moaned, my eyes closing as I arched my hips.

"I don't want to hurt you with my size." His voice was gruff and deep, like he was barely hanging on. I wanted to see him snap again. Be the bossy Freddie. He didn't answer. He slid another finger in, curling them up the ends and sending a flurry of pleasure along my nerves. "You need to be ready for me."

"Are you... are you always so considerate?" I heaved out, biting my lip and grinding against his hand. He was being so sweet and vastly different than any previous hook-up. He was a special kind of dangerous because my poor heart wouldn't survive this.

He arranged his palm so each time I rocked against him my clit got the perfect pressure. My orgasm was *right* there, just out of reach.

"I want this to feel good for you too," he said, kissing my shoulder as he increased his movements. My thighs tensed as the orgasm neared, and I held onto him harder, grounding myself.

"Look at me when you come," he said, an air of command in his voice. The air seemed to still as my orgasm started at my core and spread through my veins like fire, making me cry out and shake around him.

I never once closed my eyes. Seeing his pleasure from

watching me made it more powerful. My ears rang, and sweat dripped down my chest, but I didn't stop rocking my hips against his hand, desperate to hold onto the feeling. It was such a vulnerable state to be, putty in his hands, but instead of freaking out, I relished it. I trusted him completely, and while I could worry about that later, it amplified my orgasm. "Oh my god."

He bit my neck and lifted my hips, pumping his cock a few times before he positioned himself right at my entrance. "You're sure?"

"Freddie!" I yelled in protest, making him chuckle against my skin. Then, finally, after a million years, he thrusted into me. The air left my lungs, and I held on tight to his shoulders. He was large, and it took a few seconds to adjust to the size of him.

"Fuck, you feel good." He slowly rocked his hips, going in and out of me as his eyes searched mine for something. I got lost in his gray stare and his intense way of looking at me, like I mattered to him. His jaw tensed as he went a little faster. "You okay?"

"More than," I said, not caring if that sounded cheesy. It was the truth. I felt safe and cared for and sexy with him. With me on his lap, he held tight onto my hips and went faster. I had to kiss him.

He groaned deep into my mouth as I rode him. At some point, he stopped moving, and it was all me. Me setting the pace, me taking him as deep as I wanted. Me finding the right position to feel the best. My eyes stung at his selflessness, and I tried to tell him without words what it meant.

Each stroke of my tongue was a silent thanks, and soon enough, sweat dripped down my body as my movements increased. My pussy throbbed with the familiar tingle of an orgasm. My stomach tensed, but I couldn't get the right angle.

"What is it?" he asked, his lips hitting mine. "Tell me what you need."

"My clit."

His hand was there the next second, stroking me in slow circles, and *fuck*. White spots danced behind my eyelids as the orgasm hit me. I rode it out, moaning his name as he held tighter onto me, his movements harder than before. His thick legs turned to stone, and he groaned, deep and satisfying.

"I'm coming, shit," he said into my neck, one hand on the back of my head and the other on my waist. He thrusted two more times before he stilled. Both our breaths came out in pants, our bodies sticky with sweat. My world was rocked from the strength of the orgasm.

My heart raced as the post-sex high faded to uncertainty. I had no frame of reference for what happened next. It wasn't the middle of the night, dark, and with the absolute knowledge it was a one-time thing. He kissed my shoulder once, then twice. Then he put his glasses on. My pulse fluttered at the tenderness in his eyes when he looked at me. "Hi."

Oh, my soul wanted to live inside of his at how fucking cute he was. My lips curved up, his dick still inside me, and I replied, "Hey."

"I didn't come over here to do this." He blushed and glanced at the ground for a second. "Not *specifically* this."

"But you were kinda thinking about it?" I teased, loving how his hands continued to rub down my spine. He kept touching me.

"God, yes." He lifted me up so he could slide out of me, and after a quick toss of the condom into the trash, he put me back in his lap. "I had all these things I wanted to tell you, but then I got a taste of you."

"What things?" My smile was annoying. I couldn't stop it.

"I talked to Maddie today. Now, I know you don't do relationships, and I *only* do them, but I'm willing to bend my own rules for you." He cupped my face, joy radiating from his eyes. "No relationship talk, ever. Let's just take this one day at a time. What do you think?"

My throat got tight, the back of my eyes stinging as the truth of his words hit me. *I'm the exception.* I'm the girl who he was willing to have a *fling* with because I wasn't like Maddie. I voiced none of it though. I nodded.

He took that as my agreement and had the biggest smile on his face. Who was I to ruin his happiness because I all of a sudden wanted more?

I should've known better. I wasn't ever chosen first.

CHAPTER
EIGHTEEN

Freddie

Michael Reiner wore too many items of clothing that had our school logo on it. A hat, a shirt, his shorts, socks, and shoes. They weren't all the same color, but I couldn't help my laugh. "The season doesn't start for a while, right?"

"I'm representing." He shoved my shoulder and had a huge grin. "Thanks so much for noticing my school spirit."

"Did you visit the team store before coming here?"

"Maybe. Speaking of, I got you one of these." He held out a white hockey tee with the hockey team on the front. "You *will* attend at least one game. It's a rule of our friendship, just like how I can't touch your Skittles."

My lips twitched as we walked toward the trivia bar. It was slightly cooler and less humid that the last two days, so the air felt nice. "Fine. One game."

"I knew we were friends for a reason."

Our footsteps fell into a rhythm, and while it was weird going to trivia without Camden, Michael said his girlfriend found someone else to attend. Even though so damn much had happened since my conversation with Maddie—mainly Cami—

the thought of putting myself out there more seemed appealing. I didn't want to be the boring guy *all* the time.

So here I was, going to trivia instead of trying to convince Cami to hang out with me. Just thinking about her had my entire body blushing a horrible shade of red. We'd only studied Monday night for an hour or so, the rest of her day being a blur of school and dance team stuff. She kept her explanation short, not quite detailing what was going on with their coach, but that was fine with me. She'd tell me when she was ready. Until then, I'd just wear this goofy ass smile.

"How are the shoebox-sized rooms going? Naomi swears you can have the couch if you need it."

"I don't mind." *Yeah, because of my neighbor.* "I've only got a few weeks left."

"You're a real hero. I couldn't do it. I'd be begging to sleep on a couch, hell, on a doormat. This humidity is a real bitch." He fanned his shirt as the trivia bar came into view. While socializing in public for a few hours wasn't my ideal night, seeing who stood in front of the bar made me change my mind.

Cami was next to her sister, her hair down and hanging over her shoulder. She wore big earrings and bright red lipstick. Her hunter green dress flirted with being indecent, and my mouth watered.

"Dude, you alright?" Michael asked, frowning at me.

I didn't even realize I'd stopped walking. Cami made all my rules disappear with her beauty and fierce independence, and apparently, she made my legs forget how to move. Clearing my throat, I nodded. "Yeah, I'm good."

"You know Cami, yeah? Naomi's sister. They've gone through some rough patches, but they've gotten close again. I was glad she invited her tonight to fill in. She's your neighbor too, huh?"

"Yes." Now Michael had to pick up his pace to keep up with me. I wanted to know if her reaction to seeing me was the same as mine was—excitement, joy, and the insane urge to kiss her then and there.

She laughed at something Naomi said before her gaze landed on me, all teasing and twinkling like she couldn't wait to share a story with me. Her red lips curved up, and she waved her hand in the air way too fast. It was *adorable.*

"Hey!" She moved toward me a bit, and Naomi's knowing stare hit my face before her own smile snuck out. Normally, I'd overanalyze her look and replay every interaction I had with her the past year. Instead, I was so focused on Cami my brain didn't do the normal social anxiety routine.

While they were clearly sisters, they were very different. From how they stood, dressed, and talked. Naomi was subtle and pretty where Cami literally made my pulse race.

"You don't look surprised," I said, unsure of what to do with my hands. Did I touch her? Hug her? Kiss her? I kept them at my side, safe and behaved.

She leaned closer to me as Michael pulled Naomi in for a kiss, and Cami pinched my ribs. Her head went to my shoulder, and she touched my bicep to stand on her tippy-toes. "Naomi invited me a few days ago."

Her breath tickled my ear, and I shivered. "You could've told me."

She placed her hand on my waist, positioning herself closer so our hips touched. She smelled so damn good and looked so pleased with her bright eyes and the light blush on her face. I hadn't seen her since last night, and it was strange to *miss* her. A distant warning bell went off in my mind, telling me I was falling too hard and too fast, but it disappeared just as quickly as it occurred.

It was hard to be rational when Cami seemed so happy just to see me.

"What would've been the fun in that?" She grinned up at me, scrunching her nose as her gaze moved to my mouth, and my muscles tensed. Were we supposed to kiss? God, I wanted to. This was her sister, but we hadn't talked about *us* once.

Was there an us?

Were we just a one-time thing? I was cautiously optimistic that wasn't true... not when she leaned into me and kept looking at my lips.

"I hope everyone is ready for trivia!" Naomi said, holding Michael's hand and opening the door. A little bell rang, and after Michael went in, Cami followed. I sucked in a breath at the back of her dress.

Or lack thereof.

The dress was entirely see-through. Not quite lace, but sheer? She didn't wear a bra, that was clear, and her back muscles moved under the neon bar lights. *Fuck.* The same magnetic pull took hold of me, the one where I forgot everything besides her, and I gently yanked her back outside by her wrist.

"What—"

I crushed my mouth against hers, pulling her tight against my chest and wrapping my arm around the back of her waist. She tasted like mint and coffee, and she nipped my bottom lip as I grazed her spine with my other hand.

"You're killing me," I said, staring down at her. She licked her lips and used her thumb to wipe my mouth.

"A kiss blitz, hm?" she teased, her chest heaving as she removed lipstick from my face. "That was...something."

"A good something?"

"Oh, yes. I don't know what caused this, but I liked it."

"Your back." I sounded like a caveman, not using sentences to convey my emotions. My cock stirred at our proximity, but I forced myself to take a deep breath. We were out with her sister. I needed to *behave.* "Sorry."

"Wait, why are you sorry?" She squinted up at me as she stepped back, smoothing down her dress as her very pointed and very visible nipples strained against the fabric.

"Cami," I said, groaning into my fist. "How do we... what do we..." I stopped, her smile growing as she ate this up. "You enjoy torturing me."

"A bit, yes." She bit her lip and cupped my chin, her damn eyes sucking me in like she had magic powers. "I told Naomi about us, so if you're worried about how to act, don't. That cool?"

Naomi knows.

"So that means I can touch you?"

Say yes, say yes, say yes.

"It means you *better.*" Her face got that wickedly playful look again, and I yanked her toward me for a quick kiss. Something about her stirred my blood and turned me into this horny bastard where I wanted to rip off this dress and lick every inch of her.

I *never* had urges like this before. Never with Maddie and not even as a hormonal teenager. It was as terrifying as it was wild, and she gasped when I bit her bottom lip. All the worry about us being a one-time thing evaporated like water in the dead of summer, and a new, confident feeling surged through me. "I'm gonna need to taste you tonight, Cami. All of you."

She gulped and nodded as a bright red blush painted her cheeks. "I-I'd like that."

"Good, now try and behave so I can survive trivia night. Please." She turned to head inside, and I stopped her by putting my hand on her shoulder. "Hold still for a second."

"Wondering if I'm wearing anything underneath?"

"Christ, now I am." I sucked in a breath and tried to find evidence that she wasn't bare under the dress, but nothing showed besides the smooth curve of her ass. "I need to adjust myself before going in, but with you looking like this, what's the point?"

She giggled, the sound like a happy little bell, and my chest puffed out. I loved knowing I made the ice queen giggle. The thought made me frown though. She wasn't the flirty ice princess everyone thought she was, and I knew better than to cater to those falsehoods. With a mission to survive the night, I forced myself to think about my schoolwork, insects, and cutting grass--anything and everything that wasn't even remotely sexy.

By the time we joined Michael and Naomi at the table, my dick seemed more in control. It didn't even twitch when Cami moved her hair over her shoulder, her vanilla scent wrapping around my lungs.

"Is there a theme tonight, or is it all random?" Cami asked, searching around the bar with a cute line between her brows. "I need to be honest and upfront. I suck at trivia. All of it. I came for the drinks and company."

"Hey, that's okay!" Naomi said, a little too fast. "I don't care if we win or lose, really. Ever since Mona got in a legit fight with another player, we've eased back some."

"Mona got in a fight? Shut up."

"For real. Punched the dude in the face over a baseball answer." Naomi's eyes got all wide, and Cami slapped the table with her palm and laughed.

"Fucking hilarious."

"Best part is, they're kinda dating now. It's wild."

Cami and her sister continued talking back and forth, almost like a verbal ping pong game. I glanced at Michael who seemed content as hell with a light beer and his entire Central State outfit.

"Are they always like this?"

His face softened, and he grinned at his girlfriend before answering me. "Yes, for the past six months at least. You need to be prepared though."

I watched as Cami spoke loudly with her hands in the air. Naomi leaned in with a grin already on her face. They were in their own little world, and after everything Cami shared with me, it thrilled me that she had her sister. "Be prepared for what?"

"Settle the debate, boys." Naomi pointed to us, her brown eyes wide and a little scary. Cami followed suit and leaned onto the table, crossing her arms on the surface. "Is chemistry better if you hate someone? Like, I think indifference would be the worst, but Mona and this guy Patrick…they were nemeses who now sleep together?"

"Yeah, because all that competitiveness, the tension…. chef's kiss." Cami even kissed her fingers in the air. "Enemies with benefits has its purpose."

"Sleeping with the devil…. To what, attack them at night?" Michael said, clearly amused as he leaned back in his chair with a thoughtful expression—brows drawn close together and one finger tapping his chin. "To weaken them? You could totally use powers of sex to spy on your enemy."

"Exactly," Cami said. "Getting your rocks off *and* having a mission. I see no harm."

"Nor do I," Michael said, holding out his fist for a bump. "So, what do you think Frederick?"

"I mean," I said, clearing my throat and feeling my face flush. I certainly didn't *hate* Cami when we became reluctant neighbors. I did think about her body a lot though. My entire body heated, and something warm rested on my upper thigh. *Cami's hand.* I wasn't sure why her touch reassured me. "I get it."

"See that, Fletcher? Three to one. Let me know when you need another sample of answers, nerd."

Naomi narrowed her eyes at Michael, the two of them fitting together in every way possible. Michael had been through some shit, I knew that, and seeing him so happy made *me* happy. That was the thing I didn't understand about mean people—happiness wasn't a competition, and there wasn't a race of *who* got to be happier first. We should be lifting each other up and enjoying each other's wins.

"Okay nerd-alerts, the game is starting. Come get some paper and a pen and we're getting this 2000s trivia game started!" The trivia master wore a Jimmy Buffet shirt with a straw hat, and my blood pumped with excitement. This wasn't the same as when Camden dragged me here with his friends or latest fling.

This was with people who I could totally be myself with. I didn't dare jinx anything, but it felt damn good to be this content. I didn't even worry about what was going on with Cami. I just played the game with my friends and counted down the seconds until Cami and I could be alone again.

CHAPTER
NINETEEN

Cami

Naomi and I stood at the sink in the bar bathroom, each of us washing our hands. I reapplied my lipstick, and she met my eyes in the mirror and widened them dramatically. "Cami."

"Nana," I said back, unable to hide my grin. There was so much to be fucking pleased about that it seemed like a dream, unreal almost. The girls having my back. Not just in theory. Like, legit set up a meeting with Audrey tomorrow.

Then, Freddie. *Ugh.* I was worse than all the girls in high school who swore they found real love for ever and ever and ever. My heart was like a damn hummingbird in a sugar water buffet from the way he kissed me hard, fast, and desperate.

My face reddened, and Naomi's smile turned maniacal.

"You *like* him! Oh, hell yes. I love it! You! Him!" She gripped my forearm and let out a sound that kinda reminded me of a cartoon fox. "Oh, I'm so pumped for you."

I wasn't prepared for Naomi's arms to come around my waist, her head resting on my neck and her citrusy scent tickling my nose.

"Thank you."

"Seriously, Cami. I know things haven't been the best for you, and I haven't been there as much as I should've. But this?" She pulled back and gave me a fierce look, the same one she wore when someone told her math was useless. She was *for real*. "You deserve this. Don't downplay it or think it's not for you."

A nervous laugh escaped me. "Are you in my head or something?"

"I know you." She still had her arms around me as she spoke, and someone else walked into the bathroom and frowned at us. Naomi didn't care though. She kept her grip and waited for me to meet her eyes. "Freddie is a nice guy. He'll be so good to you."

"Don't think he's too good for me?" I asked, a sliver of insecurity flowing from me like air leaking out of a popped tire. I couldn't stop the comment from slipping out.

Naomi frowned hard. "No one is."

I gave her a grateful smile, the flutters of butterflies growing as we headed back toward the table where the guys stood chatting. Freddie wore dark black jeans and a gray and white striped shirt with his Chucks, and I wanted to climb him like a tree. The broad shoulders and height, the complete lack of athletic skill, and those damn glasses. I never would've picked all those attributes to describe the perfect guy, but now? It seemed weird to picture anyone else. He was *perfect* as is.

"Thank you both for tonight! I need my trivia fix until Mona can return." Naomi looped her arm with Michael's and gave me a long look that I interpreted as *you better tell me every detail next time we're together.*

I nodded. "Thanks for the invite. This was fun."

Freddie put his arm around my shoulders as Michael and Naomi headed out, and his clean, woodsy scent made me lean a little closer to him. Without saying anything, we walked out of the bar, and he moved his arm to my hand, interlocking our fingers as the evening air swirled around us. "Thank god you wore flip-flops."

"Why?" I looked at my feet, confused by his comment.

"Walk fast, Cami. Walk *fast*." He grunted a bit, and his meaning was clear. Very clear. We headed down Center Street where bricked walls and bars lined each side. It was the best part of campus, and normally, I'd hop between place to place to distract myself from going back alone. Tonight though? I just wanted Freddie.

But... I had to tease him. It was only fair.

"Don't you want to stop and stare at the stars? Maybe do a tour of campus?" I stopped walking, and he narrowed his eyes at me.

"You devil."

I winked at him, then he pounced. For a big guy, he made little sound as he backed me up against a wall and kissed me hard. His hand wrapped around my throat as he slid his tongue into my mouth without waiting for permission. He *devoured* me right there in public as he groaned.

It was so fucking hot to see him unravel like this. I matched his passion, stroke for stroke, and he ran one hand up my side to pinch my nipple *hard.*

"You know we're in public, right?" I said, my voice breathy and deep. My decision to go sans underwear was a mistake as moisture pooled between my thighs. "How unseemly of you."

I swore he growled as he looked down at me, his thumb rubbing my lip as his nostrils flared. His gray eyes seemed darker and more intense through his lenses, like he had to catalogue every part of my face this second.

"You confuse me in the *best* fucking way, Cami." His jaw tightened, and he swallowed hard, still keeping his hand around my throat. The raw emotion in his voice was enough for my heart to skip a beat.

It was totally, without a doubt, a compliment from him. I wanted to wrap my arms and legs around him and not let go, assuring him he confused me in a million good ways too. Like, maybe I did want to be monogamous and in a relationship. To be the person he told everything to and shared his Skittles with. To know what it was like to really be with someone through good and bad.

"I know this tall fucker," a voice said, making Freddie jump off me.

"Camden." He turned around, his voice still carrying a hint of lust.

"Dude, you're out? I love it." Camden threw his arm around Freddie and patted his chest before introducing a very tall and very skinny blond dude. "This is Peter. Peter, my brother Frederick and his…"

"Cami." I finished for him, not wanting Freddie to try and fill in that blank. I knew it'd stress him out. "Nice to meet you both."

Peter was polite and looked as unsure as I did, but Camden took the lead. "We're heading to a house party at Gallagher's. Join us. You're down for it, right, Cami?"

I wasn't sure if it was a challenge or a dare in his eyes as Camden moved his gaze from me, to Freddie, then back to me. Like… did Camden want me to bring his brother? I totally could, but *why?* "I'm always up for party, but weren't you saying you were tired?"

"He's always tired or has a test or something." Camden pursed his lips. "Did he tell you that I force him to come out with me twice a month just so he's social? I planned to do a stamp card for it. After ten, he'd get a free night away from me, but—"

"Shut up, Cam. We'll go." Freddie tensed, and I wanted to rub the worry from his muscles away. His jaw flexed a couple of times and then he held out his hand. I took it without question, and Camden and Peter kept walking.

"I'm so sorry," Freddie said, whispering to me as his face paled. "We don't have to go. I didn't even ask you."

"No, it's okay." I smiled up at him, wanting to kiss the frown off his face. "I don't mind. Hanging out with *you* is perfect."

A few of his worry lines disappeared, but his grip on my hand tightened. Was it his brother? Peter? The place we were going? I wasn't sure, but I was game for whatever. Sure, I was horny, but at some point, Freddie and I would make our way back to the dorms.

Freddie's body was tense the entire walk to Gallagher's—which, I wasn't sure was a place or a name. Maybe both. That detail didn't bother me though. It was Freddie's demeanor. I let go of his hand and smacked his ass, making him slide me a look. "What was that?"

"For fun."

"Do I get to return the favor?"

"If it helps your mood, then yes."

He sighed, did *not* smack my ass, and ran a hand over his face. "It's just—"

"Here we are!" Camden said, pulling Peter in for a very loud, wet kiss. "You know where the drinks are, FB3. Peter, follow me to the porch. I plan to sit on a hammock and do dirty things with you."

Peter shrugged and went with Camden, leaving Freddie and me outside on a big porch. Gallagher's seemed to be a white house on the edge of campus and east of Center street.

Freddie eyed the door like they had a history. "Do you need a drink?"

"Um, maybe?" I tugged his hand and made him look at me. "Are you going to tell me what's going on?"

"Maddie and I used to hang out here all the time, so I don't know why Camden is doing this to me." He pulled his shirt from his chest a few times. "I'm over her. I need you to know that, but this also wouldn't be a place I'd ever willingly take you? Does that make sense?"

Every time he mentioned Maddie, I got the urge to fight this woman who hurt him. Even now, a year later, Freddie was sad or at least down because of her. "It makes perfect sense, but I have an idea. A really, really good idea. If you're up for it, that is."

The hurt in his eyes shifted to curiosity as his eyes trailed down my body. "What kind of idea?"

"I can't tell you, *but* it involves making new memories at this house."

He licked his bottom lip, the lines around his face softening as he took a deep breath. "How would we make new memories?"

I wiggled my eyebrows and held out my hand. He intertwined our fingers, and I led us into the house. It smelled like old carpet and over-the-top air freshener. There were probably ten, fifteen people scatted in what looked to be the living room to the right and ten near the kitchen. Camden and Peter leaned against a doorframe that led into the back, and I eyed the place for what I needed.

A small room for just us.

I flashed my *smile, the fake one,* as I drew lots of stares. The dress I wore specifically for Freddie definitely showed way too much of my tits. But it worked right now because people stared at them and moved out of our way.

Music pumped from somewhere below, and I found stairs that went up. *Perfect.*

"Where are we going?"

Great question, Freddie. I still didn't know, and the first two doors were locked. Then, like a miracle, the third one was open. *Bingo.* The room had a small desk in the corner, a chair, and a laptop charging off to the side.

This was a small ass room that had to have been a closet at some point but now served as an office? One without decorations?

It didn't matter.

I propped myself up on the desk and jutted my chin toward the door. "Lock it."

Freddie did, the pulse at the base of his neck racing. He wouldn't stop looking at me up and down, his hand forming a fist against his thigh.

"Like what you see, Freddie?" I said, biting my lip as I spread my legs a bit. I didn't show a thing *yet,* but I wanted him distracted like he'd been against the wall. I needed him unraveled. Plus, fuck Maddie. I planned to replace all his memories of her here.

"What are you doing to me, Cami?" He walked toward me, placing a hand on either side of my thighs. He pushed them apart and sucked in a breath. "This dress is lethal. The things I want to do with you…"

"Tell me," I said, sitting up to get closer to him. "Tell me what you want to do to me."

He oh-so-slowly dragged the hem of the dress up my thighs, the delicate fabric tickling my skin as he stilled. "You're bare."

"I told you I might've been naked under here."

Freddie licked his fucking lips before getting onto his knees, his gray eyes almost black with lust. He spread my legs even more and blew on my pussy. I shivered and leaned back on my elbows to watch. The thought of *him* going down on me wasn't as weird anymore. Not with the way he looked at me and treated me. He wasn't the only one who needed new memories, and I couldn't think of a better person to try things with.

"This is what I want. To lick, suck, and taste every part of you. You turn me into this…" He stopped, brought his tongue to my inner thigh just shy of my core, and bit down. "I can't stop thinking about you."

He kissed my other thigh. Then, he spread my pussy apart and brought the flat of his tongue against my clit. He licked me slowly, like we had hours in this room. Heat blasted every nerve ending in my body as he teased the swollen bud. "You're a dangerous woman, Cami."

"H-how so?" Words were getting more difficult now. With the deep tone of his voice and hungry eyes, each flick of his tongue brought me closer to orgasm. He moaned into my pussy, sending a vibration through my body, and I shuddered.

"Addicting." He made repetitive, swirling motions with his tongue as he slid one finger inside me. "Your sounds. Your taste."

"Y-you too," I mumbled, sounding like an idiot. The sensations were too much. He inserted a second finger as he quickened the use of his tongue, and with his one free hand, he held my lower stomach down, keeping me in place.

He hummed into me as my thighs started clenching. I was so close. The pressure built in my core, and I thrashed around, but he didn't stop. He continued eating me like I was his favorite dish, patient and with purpose, and his eyes found mine right before I came.

"*Oh*, oh shit!"

He never broke eye contact as my orgasm consumed me, my nerves, and my body. Sweat covered my chest, and my pussy was uncomfortably wet, but he didn't stop. Not until I rested my head against the desk and sighed. "Wow."

"Yes, wow." He kept pulling my dress up my body, kissing up my stomach, and swirling his magical tongue over my belly ring. "You are…I'm struggling with how to express what I'm feeling with you right now."

"Words are also hard for me," I said, laughing because the weight of his tone seemed a bit too heavy.

"No, more than sex." He lifted the fabric over my tits, and he groaned. "I could tease and suck these all day." He didn't wait before doing just that, bringing my nipple into his mouth and pulling on the end. "Thank you."

"Thank you?" I asked, confused as he moved to my other breast. It was wild to feel the start of another orgasm from nipple play alone, but the tingle was there. "Freddie, hey—"

He lifted his head and looked down at me with complete seriousness. "You spread out like this, on this desk, is the best memory."

"This isn't even half of my plan," I said, the ball in my throat growing a little too large. It was the way he spoke, in deep bursts of truth. The heaviness of each syllable, like each sound took a lot of effort.

He kissed my nipples, then the center of my chest. "What could be better than finally tasting you?"

"You on this desk as I taste *you*."

He flashed a grin but shook his head. "Another time, please. You're sitting here so pretty and wet—I need to be inside you."

I sucked in a breath and nodded. This aggressive side of him was hot as hell. All that feisty energy tucked in a cute package, and *fuck*. Freddie undid his belt and took off his pants and boxers, tossing his wallet at me as he stroked himself.

His fist barely covered his shaft as he worked it up and down, the look in his eyes making me hot all over again.

"Get a condom out."

"Freddie," I said, my throat scratchy. Seeing him touch himself was enough to set me on fire. I practically panted with the desperation to have him. My fingers shook as I opened his wallet and found a packet. His strokes got faster, and he jutted his chin toward my hands, as in *put it on*.

I pulled out the rubber, and he stopped stroking long enough for me to cover his cock with it. He throbbed in my palm, thick and ready, and he cupped my face with both hands, kissing me hard as he edged my legs apart.

This kiss felt different than all the others. Those were exploratory, savoring even. This one was messy and almost painful. His tip nudged my center, and slowly, he thrust into me, stealing my breath and sending explosions of pleasure through me. He felt *so* fucking good. He pulled me to the edge of the desk and held a leg over each shoulder, the angle absolutely incredible.

"So fucking perfect," he said, grunting with each word. "Damn, Cami."

I could feel every inch of him as he pounded into me, his

fingers digging into my calves as he held on tight. The pulse at the base of his neck went haywire, and his lips parted as he continued fucking me.

That was what this was—a primal, aggressive fuck mixed with errant feelings, and it was the hottest sex of my life. I didn't care about the way the wood dug into my ass underneath me or the sounds of the party that carried through the door. My focus was on Freddie's deep gaze never leaving mine as he slowed his pace and ground into me.

"*Yes*," I moaned, arching my back and taking him even deeper. Pleasure swirled around my spine and soul as he reached down with one hand to rub my clit.

"I love watching you fall apart," he said, his voice a low rumble. He applied just the right amount of pressure on my swollen nerve. He thrusted harder as the orgasm took me, my pussy clenching around him, and I cried out.

I didn't care if anyone could hear us or if someone tried to walk in. I was with Freddie, out of my mind with bliss, and he furrowed his brows, biting his bottom lip as I rode out my orgasm.

His muscles twitched in his thighs, and he gripped both legs even harder as he released a deep, satisfying groan that went right to my heart.

"Oh, hell," he said, slowing his thrusts as he came. A vein popped on his forehead, and his dark eyes dilated as he continued to stare at me like I mattered.

Sweat pooled down the side of his face, and he pulled out, quickly discarding the condom and buttoning his jeans. Then, he fixed my dress with the same face he wore when he studied before kissing me softly on the forehead. "My mind is a bit fuzzy right now but that was...I've never done something like this before, and I'm so glad it was with you."

I wanted to ask what he meant, even though deep down, I knew. He never lost control like this with anyone, and that knowledge lit me up inside. "This is a first for me too," I said, brushing my fingers through his thick hair. He had the best head of hair, all dark and full with a little curl.

He closed his eyes and let out a sigh, like my touch did something to him, and I knew right then that when it came to my feelings for Freddie, I was in deep trouble.

CHAPTER
TWENTY

Freddie

Cami popped into the restroom for a minute, leaving me with my thoughts, and holy shit. My life wasn't made up of multiple incredible moments ingrained in my mind, but that was definitely one of them. The sounds she made, the way trust swirled in her eyes as she looked at me... yeah, best memory ever. I swallowed hard, trying to cool down. I hadn't stopped sweating since we went into that small room, and even fanning myself did no good. Even stepping out to get us some drinks in the kitchen didn't cool me down.

"Dude, Freddie." Someone patted my back, and Gallagher O'Brien grinned at me. "I haven't seen you in a year!"

"Yeah, it's been a while." I forced a tight smile, the memories of Maddie and me hanging out with him flashing through my mind like a montage from a movie. Us drinking, going to dinner, sitting at this house as Maddie complained about how bored she was. The long looks she'd given him always had me wondering if she was into him.

"You hear Mads is back? Y'all going to reconcile or what,

cause she's fine. She might be stopping by tonight, and if you two are done—"

"We're done, for good."

Gallagher didn't get a chance to respond before the doorknob twisted.

Cami walked out, looking like a dream, and flashed a smile my way. Her face glowed, and some of her makeup was still messy, and my God, my heart hammered in my ribcage. A slight line formed between her eyebrows as she gazed at me, then Gallagher. She waltzed right up to my side, slid her arm around my waist, and smiled her performative one at him.

I knew I was in trouble when I could tell the difference between her real smiles and the fakes. Plus, she rarely showed others the real one. Just me. It made my fucking heart soar to know that.

"Hey, I'm Cami."

Gallagher blinked a few times, his eyes wide, then he smiled so big it worried me. "Dude, *dude.*"

"Your name is dude or…what?" She wrinkled her nose, making me like her even more. She damn well knew the tension was thick with something, and she busted through it.

"Gallagher." He held out a hand, his eyes roaming her body and stopping at her chest. A strong, almost frantic urge demanded I yank her away, out of his sight. How dare he ogle her in front of me when it was clear we were together?

Had he always been this way and I didn't realize it or had I not cared?

"So, you're the infamous one." Cami shook his hand quick, letting go and tucking herself deeper into my side.

"Talking about me already, Brady? I love it!" Gallagher rocked back on his heels, his gaze never quite leaving Cami's body.

"We're heading out." I didn't even bother to be polite. I had a feeling he'd hooked up with Maddie either right after we ended or while there was still overlap. There wasn't proof, but his blatant flirtations weren't sitting right with me.

"Don't wanna stay to see Mads?"

"No."

I led us down the hallway toward the stairs when some guy threw his hands up in the air, shouting Cami's name.

"Oh my God, Jarod." She broke free from my arm, and she let the guy pull her into a huge bear hug. She embraced him and kept her hands on his face when he grinned down at her. "It's been how long?"

"I don't know, years? You look good."

"You too. What are with all these muscles?" She gripped his bicep and squeezed, laughing as he flexed and struck a pose. "I'm surprised we're both alive at this point."

He cringed. "I know, do you remember that night with the body shots?"

"And the fire?" She tossed her head back and cackled. "Or those guys with the blindfolds?"

"You got up on stage with the *band*. I still see you dancing up there with that damn boa."

"Remember Ricky? That random bartender who quit and joined us?"

"Fuckin' wild. Highlight of my undergraduate years." His face softened at her before his gaze moved to me.

My insides were a blazing storm of envy. It was clear Cami knew this guy well, well enough to hug and give her real smile to. Plus, the body shots? Did he take them off her? The thought of his tongue on her body made me want to rip my hair out, and I wasn't a violent person.

"I'm Jarod, once a friend to this crazy creature." He held out his hand, and I shook it, unable to quite form words. My throat filled with invisible cotton balls, and all I could do was grunt.

This guy was attractive and clearly an athlete. If not now, at one point he had been. He was cooler than me, clearly, and

Cami had done all sorts of wild things with him. God, was I ever that fun or crazy?

No.

She's too popular for me. I'm too boring.

She'd prefer to be with a guy like *Jarod*. Doing shots and dancing on stages. Goddamn Gallagher for bringing up Maddie and making me question everything.

With my lack of answer, Cami gave me a knowing smile and introduced me. "This is Freddie. He's with me."

"Ah, lucky man." Jarod hit my arm like we were old pals. "She's a good one."

I nodded, wishing I could acknowledge that I already realized she was a good one. "Nice to meet you." I croaked the words out, honestly hating myself a little bit for acting so boorish. Cami had a past.

She was *allowed* a past.

But that didn't take away the doubt that one day I'd be like Jarod, reminiscing about my time with Cami while she'd be with a guy way more exciting than me.

Someone shouted his name, and he nodded before pulling Cami into another hug. "I'm in town for a week. We're getting dinner one night. It's a must."

"Absolutely."

She watched as he walked further into the party before she gripped my forearm. "I can't believe he's back! I loved that guy before he transferred to a better university for basketball. We tore it up for a while."

"Sounded like it."

She took my hand and interwove our fingers, tilting her head up to look at me with a twinkle in her eye before she frowned. "Whoa, hey, what's wrong?"

Shit. I wasn't good at hiding my issues from her. I ran my free hand over my face and tried but failed to come up with a rational reason for why my stomach was in knots and dread weighed my shoulders down. We'd had an amazing time upstairs, and she tried so hard to help me get rid of my own baggage, yet here I was, pouting because some guy she knew years ago did fun stuff with her.

"Freddie." She tugged me outside and onto the front porch. It smelled like weed, and she dragged me until we stood on the sidewalk. She pressed her lips together hard, a clear sign of her annoyance, and my stomach bottomed out.

I'd upset her by acting like a dumbass. "I'm sorry."

"Why are you sorry? You're not telling me what's going on, which leaves me to create a million scenarios in my own head that snowball." Red covered her cheeks, and she put her hands on her hips. "I'm not… I'm not like that anymore, okay?"

She spoke so softly and blinked a few times, my entire body tightening with regret. *She thinks she's the problem.*

Oh, no, no, no.

"It isn't you, fuck." I'd messed this up so badly. I could punch my own teeth out. She chewed on the side of her lip, waiting, watching with her large brown eyes as I figured my shit out. "Hearing your friend Jarod talk about your past… made me think of Maddie and why she left. You have to realize how *boring* I really am."

"You're not boring at all." She snapped her head back and frowned, like what I said made no sense to her. "With all the respect in the world to you, you need to let go of Maddie's words. You've let them live too long in your beautiful mind. Stop thinking you're not enough for anyone and be yourself."

I blinked, absolutely silent.

She wasn't done either. She rammed her finger into my chest and spoke with such conviction I wouldn't dare to argue with her. "Would you call what we just did upstairs *boring?*"

I shook my head.

"Then please, for me, stop thinking badly about yourself." She moved to cup my face with her soft hands. Her perfume tickled my nose, and it was now my favorite smell in the world.

"I know I need to work on that too, for fuck's sake, but it upsets me to see you doubt your worth."

I swallowed, *hard*, as nerves took over. We agreed to take things easy, but I'd passed that at some point. It was more now and fuck if I couldn't stop my damn mouth from moving. "I'm falling for you, Cami. Fast. It terrifies me, and I keep trying to put up roadblocks to slow down. You can say all of this to me, but I have baggage. I thought I was over it, but I guess I'm not."

"That's okay." She stood closer to me, our toes touching as she looked up at me with her *real* smile that went all the way to her eyes. "Don't rush the process. Just know that it's the same for me, too."

"What's the same? No one has ever called you boring a day in your life."

She shook her head, then bit her bottom lip as she glanced at the ground. "I meant... I'm falling for you too. It's new for me, but I'm happy when we're together."

"Yeah, I am too." I covered her hands with mine and let out a deep sigh, pushing all the negative thoughts away and focusing on her. Self-sabotaging was *not* in the plans, and with this beautiful, wonderful woman in my arms telling me she liked me? I better chill the hell out and enjoy it.

"Then let's just be happy and not let our minds get the best of us, okay?" There was a plea in her voice, like she was battling her own demons too, and I made a promise to myself that I would do whatever I could to slay her personal misconceptions. Was it her reputation? The dance team?

Suddenly, I had to know what made her frown so I could form a plan to fix it. But I didn't ask because she stood on her tippy-toes and pressed her lips against mine in a soft, short kiss that still sent a ripple of lust through my body.

"Promise me you'll tell me the next time you start to break us up?"

"Oh, are we together?" I laughed, teasing her to lighten the mood. "Would that make me your first real boyfriend then?"

The second the words escaped my lips, I wished I could take them back. Cami paled whiter than the moon, and her grip on my shoulder loosened as she took a step back. Then another. Fuck. I was internally panicking. Why the hell did I say that? I ruined it all. I totally did.

I could almost hear her mind swirling and her heart pounding. Her lips parted, and I mumbled a curse. "Shit, no, I'm sorry. I didn't mean it."

She crossed her arms and gulped, so loud it clicked the back of her throat, and I felt like a piece of trash. The worst kind.

I dealt her my emotional baggage and then said one of the triggers that unleashed hers? Awesome. Just fucking awesome. "*Please* say something."

"I get it. It's fine. We're not really together." She played with the ends of her hair and spoke with less warmth than normal, distance even. Like she was trying to put actual distance between us which was the last thing I wanted.

Before she could say more, I walked toward her and put my hands on her shoulders. "I want this with you, to be really together. If you're doubting that right now, please know I'd love to be your boyfriend."

Boyfriend? Jesus. It was like a bell chimed in my soul, the countdown until Chicago getting louder. I shoved it all away, intent on fixing whatever I broke between us. Even if I only had a few months with her, I wanted that time. I could explain the internship later...as soon as the light went back into her eyes and she smiled *that* smile at me again.

"It sounds so lame." She shielded her face from mine. "I'm in my early twenties, and the word *boyfriend* has me spiraling after I gave you a whole speech on baggage." She snort-laughed, and I pulled her against me in a hug, hoping the embrace would help right things between us. Her laugh eased a few of my worries, but it wasn't enough.

The scales were tipped and our vulnerabilities bared to each other. It was horrifying to know that our insecurities were a part of us. But I did want to get through this. She rested her forehead on my shoulder, sighing as I ran my fingers up and down her back.

"It would be a fucking honor to be with you, boyfriend label or not. I want to try this with you. All of it. The messy parts too because I have this deep feeling the good is really gonna outweigh the bad." *Like moving away...*

She nodded against me, still not looking up, but her body didn't seem as tense anymore. "We're a beautiful fucking mess."

"Maybe." I grinned, even though she couldn't see me. "We're two of those weirdly shaped puzzle pieces that don't fit the standard size or angle. You know what I'm talking about? The ones with the sharp triangle type shape?"

"I've never done a puzzle in my life, Freddie."

My face flushed. "Right, well, you get the idea. Maybe we're those pieces that when paired together, they fit."

"Yeah, maybe."

We stood like that for a few more minutes, our breaths matching up before we started walking back toward the dorm. It wasn't until we both got undressed and into her room that she kissed me softly with half-closed eyes and declared that I was her boyfriend.

Me. The nerd. The dorky Skittle dude was Cami Simpson's *first* boyfriend.

CHAPTER
TWENTY-ONE

Cami

This had to be either the worst or boldest thing I had ever done. Maybe not worst. There was a list of regrets fueled by alcohol that made the top three, but confronting Audrey? With Daniella by my side?

Watch out, world.

What was next--me solving inequality in the workplace?

My phone buzzed with a text from my dad agreeing to get lunch soon, but I didn't have the mental strength to deal with him right now. Confronting someone who'd once been my mentor was all I had room for.

"The girls are upset they aren't here, but from my leadership classes, it's best not to come across like an ambush. This is going to be hard enough." Daniella looped her arm through mine, pushing her sunglasses up on her nose and her head up higher.

She put the plan in place. Audrey was meeting *her* at her office while I snuck in. The rest of the girls would all wait at the juice cafe in the student union, and I would miss my morning class to do this.

The showdown. The confrontation to the coach I had the last

three years. The level of betrayal from her was worse than an ulcer. It had me questioning the entirety of our three-year relationship. All the conversations, the laughter, the support... had it been fake? She'd helped fill the absent mom, not-close sister gap I went through, so for her to treat me like this? It hurt, inside out. My stomach churned with nausea—this was a blitz. I rubbed my palms over my simple black shirt. I'd paired it with dark green jeans and even wore a knotted headband, hoping to look non-threatening.

Freddie had held my hand all morning, hyping me up that this was the right move. Fighting for something that mattered so much to me was important. It'd be hard but worth it.

After all, if I could *finally* have a boyfriend at twenty-two, then I could have a tough conversation with a coach.

As we neared her office, my throat lost all its moisture. It was like I'd spent a week at Burning Man without drinking any water. My head was feverish, and even though Daniella chatted my ear off, I tuned her out. Dealing with anger wasn't new for me, but raw vulnerability? Asking what I did to deserve this treatment from someone I once respected?

Here it goes.

Daniella opened a set of glass doors, humming as she redid her messy bun. She strutted, head held high, and I admired how she'd grown into this leadership role. She had a ways to go, but she'd be an excellent captain.

"I'm gonna knock and walk in, then you follow after three seconds. Got it?"

I nodded.

Daniella tapped on the faded wooden door that said *Coach Audrey*. Light footsteps approached on the other side, then Coach swung it open. Dark circles formed under her eyes, and her outfit was nothing like the put-together woman I knew. It was like she'd just gotten out of bed... or maybe like she'd slept in her office?

Daniella walked straight into the office, but Coach's gaze

landed on me. Something wicked crossed her face, her lip curling up on the side as she stared me up and down. "*What* are you doing here?"

I opened my mouth to answer, but Daniella spoke faster. "To chat about your behavior, Coach. You're not really demonstrating *leadership* qualities with your treatment of Cami at the game and as captain, I've been chosen to talk to you."

"Voted?" Coach snorted. "The girls *chose* you?"

Daniella's cheeks pinkened, and she lost the temporary swagger she wore walking in. Seeing her shoulders slump snapped me into action.

"Audrey." My tone left no room for argument. "The team is threating to walk because of your bullshit. Every single one of them."

"They wouldn't dare." She shook her head, swallowing so hard her throat moved.

"Oh, they would." Daniella met my gaze, puffing her chest out as the three of us stood in Audrey's small office. It was clear she'd slept there with the blanket on the chair and food wrappers everywhere. I didn't have it in me to feel bad.

I shut the door, standing in front of it in case she bolted. The angry look in her eyes shifted to something like panic. Wide-eyed, worried.

"I wouldn't let them."

"How noble of you." Audrey rolled her eyes and fell onto her desk chair. "Such a people pleaser, aren't you, Cami? Everyone just *loves* you. Are you proud of what you did? Do the girls know?"

"What are you talking about?" My throat tightened. The evil expression on her face made zero sense to me.

"Your bimbo act never fooled me. Not once these past three years. You're smart for being so damn pretty." Audrey leaned in the chair, the wheels squeaking with her weight. She looked maniacal. Lost, even.

"If you're trying to insult me, it's not working. Now, what the fuck are you talking about?"

"The day I named Daniella captain to try to get you to step up." She bit her lip, her eyes flashing red. "You had to sleep with him. Well, congrats. You won."

"Again, you're not making any sense. Sleep with *who*?"

"My boyfriend, Cami. Jesus. Do you enjoy making me say it?" Her eyes bugged out, spit flying from her mouth. "That's who you are, right? Coach made a bad choice, so I'll fuck her boyfriend. You won. Happy?"

Ice flooded my veins, my feet growing roots into the shitty hardwood floor. The pure hatred and genuine truth she believed in her words took hold of my heart and squeezed. She actually thought I did that. Slept with her boyfriend.

That I was capable of doing it.

Daniella sucked in a breath, taking a step toward me and placing a hand on my shoulder. "Cami was with *me* that night."

"You're lying for her." Audrey rolled her eyes before rubbing her palms across her face. "I don't know what she has over your head, but there's no point in covering—"

"I'm not covering for her. I got blackout drunk at a party, and Cami brought me home, Coach. She took care of me." Daniella's eyes watered, and her voice shook. "She wouldn't sleep with *your* boyfriend."

"Yes, she would."

"You're a terrible person." Daniella's shoulders tensed as she eyed Audrey up and down. "I'll be reporting this to the Dean of Athletics. You don't deserve to coach us."

"Jeff's not gonna believe you, sweetie." She pushed herself up from the chair, placing her palms on the desk with a groan. She narrowed her eyes at me, a small flicker of doubt entering them.

"Good thing I recorded it then." Daniella held up her phone, shocking the shit out of me. What a sneaky move. "Also, your boyfriend might be a piece of shit, but there's photos of that party all over social media. Take a look. Cami was there alone."

Audrey stared at me, a showdown of sorts happening between us, and I could only glare back. The woman I once admired had become a broken mess because of a guy.

"Please." Her voice cracked. "Did you have sex with him?"

"No. I don't even know who your boyfriend is."

"You waved to him at the game though!" She almost shouted, her barely-held façade of decorum shattering. "I saw it!"

"I wave at fans all the time. It's part of our job." I stepped toward her, and she flinched. "It's clear you misjudged me. Many have. But it's a shame you let your beef with me affect the team."

That broke her. She sobbed, her entire body shaking as she hung her head. Parts of me felt bad for Audrey—isolating herself from the team *and* dealing with a prick of a boyfriend. But Daniella didn't show an ounce of sympathy on her face. She looped her arm with mine and guided us out the office.

"I'll set up a time with the dean to get this taken care of. This was such a poor example of being a leader. God, did you know she sent me YouTube videos on how to step it up? To be better for the team?"

"No." My mind still reeled from what happened, and my stomach somersaulted at the future. Would Audrey get fired? Should she? *Yes.*

"Bullshit. I'm so fucking mad. You want to go let the girls know what went down? I might march into the Athletic office right now. Yes, I'm gonna do that." She let go of me and turned right, not looking back and leaving me alone. A horrible combination of confusion and sadness made my chest ache. Audrey was hurting, but that didn't make anything that just happened right.

With heavy footsteps, I walked toward the student union where the entire team waited for me. It was the second time ever that they felt like home, a real family. I blamed my watery eyes on what Audrey said, but in reality, it was from the fact that in the process of my world falling apart, I'd found my team.

Freddie met me at Timmy's place. He arrived before me, his massive body hunched over on the bench we sat at those nights ago. Before we were *together*. My face flushed as I stared at him, my pulse racing.

Boyfriend.

Freddie was my boyfriend, and while the term was juvenile, I didn't seem to care. My pace increased with a need to touch him, and he glanced up, worry lines spreading along his face.

He jumped up and met me halfway. "How'd it go?"

His cupped my face, assessing my eyes with a furrowed brow. My skin tingled from his touch, and I placed my hands over his. "Weird. Good, but weird."

"You seem okay." He pressed a soft kiss on my forehead, and my knees almost buckled. The gesture was so damn sweet, so *Freddie,* and I threw myself against him.

"Uh." He stumbled back from my force but soon wrapped his large arms around me and squeezed tight. "This is a good hug, right?"

"Uh huh." My voice came out muffled. He promised me ice cream after the meeting like a good boyfriend, and all I wanted to do was hold onto him. He'd never be like Audrey's guy, shady enough to make her lose her mind.

He cupped the back of my head, running his fingers over my scalp and lightly massaging me. All the years of being alone and struggling were worth it to find this bliss—Freddie and the team. I clutched the back of his white and grey striped shirt and tilted my head all the way to look up at him. "Hey." I pinched his side.

He glanced down with his lips slightly parted. I stood on my tiptoes and kissed him. He let out a satisfied groan and kissed me right back. He placed his hand on my neck, the sheer size of it covering part of my collarbone. Then he squeezed.

"I like you." I kissed the corner of his lips, then his cheek.

The tips of his ears reddened, and he cleared his throat. "Well, I like you too. But you knew that."

I winked, patting his chest a few times and smoothing down the wrinkles my face had created. "You promised me ice cream, big guy."

"That I did." He grinned, flashing his straight white teeth. "My treat."

We entered Timmy's place with his hand on my lower back. I appreciated that he touched me all the time, like he couldn't stop himself. It made me giddy, like I was on the verge of giggles constantly. It was almost maddening.

Timmy's cousin Presley scooped for us, giving me vanilla and Freddie mint chocolate chip. We thanked them, and I chose a secluded booth in the back. Our knees knocked together under the small table, and I fought a grin. I loved how awkward and large he was, all those strong limbs without knowing how to use them.

"You're staring at me with this twinkle in your eye. Should I be nervous?" He ran a hand over his chest.

"Not one bit." I took a bite of vanilla and sighed. "I never knew it could be like this."

"What could?" He tilted his head to the side, a little ice cream dripping from the side of his mouth.

He was so fucking cute.

"Being with someone." I reached over with my thumb and swiped it from his chin. Our gazes met, and his flared with heat when I brought my finger to my mouth to lick it off. "Being with *you*."

He blushed. "I'm glad you think so."

"Is it always like this?" I meant the question with sincerity, truly wondering if this was how everyone felt. If so, why wasn't everyone with a person like Freddie? But he frowned and blinked a few times.

"Um, well." He chewed on his lip, studying me through his glasses. "There are parts of being in a relationship that I imagine are similar. The comfort, the trust, the looking forward to seeing your person. But." He set his cup of ice cream down and balanced the spoon on the side before leaning closer. "There's a spark with us I haven't experienced before. It's part chemistry, part trust, part... I'm not sure yet, actually."

His words lit me up inside out, and I beamed at him. "I know exactly what you mean. The spark. I feel it."

His answering smile turned me into complete goo. He leaned back into his chair and picked up the cup again. "I've been patient, and I don't want to push you if you're not ready to talk about it yet. But I'm dying to ask how it went with your coach."

Oh shit. I was so into him, engrossed with his movements, that I'd forgotten about the shitshow that went down. I caught him up on everything, sparing no detail, and shrugged. "Daniella will text me once she talks to the dean. Then, I don't know what happens."

Freddie ran his finger over his eyebrow quite a few times as I spoke and stilled it. His jaw flexed. "I'm so fucking sorry your coach said that to you."

His blatant anger on my behalf just made me lo—like him more. I took another bite of the ice cream and lifted my shoulders in acknowledgement.

"Don't downplay it, Cami. No adult in a leadership position should act that way. I'm so disappointed." He sucked his teeth, a dangerous glint in his eyes. "I hope she loses her job and apologizes to you."

"I doubt it." My gut tightened. The possibility of her getting fired was very real. I had no idea Daniella recorded her, and the evidence was stacked against her. But apologizing? Yeah, it'd be great. But my sister's words from last year still weighed on me. I projected a certain *scandalous* vibe into the world, and people believed it. My own sister had thought I'd intentionally stolen guys from her.

Freddie had assumed I went home with someone else at a party.

My coach had thought I fucked her boyfriend to get back at her.

None of those rumors were true, but it was what my ice princess attitude had created for the past four years. I wouldn't be getting an apology, and I'd have to live with it. I could feel Freddie's stare, the intensity radiating off him like sunlight. It'd be easy to brush the hurt away and focus on the good—the team, Daniella, our relationship. But I owed him the truth.

"I respected her, looked up to her. This betrayal stings. Now that the adrenaline wore off, my soul hurts." That was the heart of the matter. I'd gained a team but lost a mentor.

"People can disappoint you, but you *know* your worth." His tone went deeper and more aggressive. "I had to learn that. Still am. Thanks to you."

Suddenly, we were that couple. Our fingers intertwined with one hand while the other held the spoon. Instead of feeling silly or self-conscious, I focused on him. My boyfriend.

Then our phones buzzed at the same time with a notification.

THE APARTMENTS WILL BE READY IN A WEEK. WELCOME BACK.

CHAPTER
TWENTY-TWO

Freddie

"Dude, why are you *sad*?" Camden eyed the dorm room, his lips curling in disgust. He scrunched his nose as he fanned himself with his shirt. "It smells like Satan farted into an old pair of socks."

"Way too specific of a smell."

"Gross. I can't believe you guilted me into helping you." He put his hands on his hips and faced me. "I only agreed because I don't know where your ass will end up in a few months."

The internship. The heavy rock in my gut I tried not thinking about. I had eight weeks left on campus before holiday break and then…I could be in Chicago with my uncle. I was supposed to find out next week where I was accepted. Which, I knew deep down there was no way my Uncle Martin wasn't going to accept me. My dad texted me about it three times a week. But that didn't make my choice any easier. It was either here or three hours north.

Away from Cami.

The thought of letting my dad down? It made my stomach

tighten with worry. My uncle's text was a lead weight dragging me down.

Uncle Martin: I couldn't be prouder of you, Fred, nor could your dad. You working here with me? Dream come true for both of us. I never wanted kids of my own but if I did? I'd want one just like you.

God, why couldn't he be an asshole or something?

I set the final items from my desk into a bag, pushing all thoughts of the internship to the back of my mind. Things were so good with her, even thinking about me moving sent my heart into hyperdrive. "You're saying you'll miss me."

"Ten percent, yes." The dick even separated his thumb and pointer by an inch.

My lips quirked up though, which I welcomed. There was a heavy melancholic mood following me since we got that text message. Of course, I wanted to live in the nice place with air conditioning. I wanted my own shower and to not hear every sound echoing down the hall.

However, I was going to miss sharing a wall with Cami. The coed bathroom, the showers, the way her laugh carried into my room. What if things changed when we weren't right next door to each other? What if the past few weeks were an illusion and reality would set in, making her realize we didn't match? That she was way too cool for me? I gripped the back of my neck, hoping to ease the self-doubt when a familiar voice sounded in the hall.

Michael Reiner.

"Jesus Christ on a cracker." He fanned his face with his hat. "Cami, this is disgusting."

"Seriously. You turned down our couch for this?" Her sister joined them, and I stepped into the doorframe.

"Hey, Freddie." Michael grinned at me. He wore a school outfit again, and Naomi even had on a Central State Hockey shirt. Dorks. "You all should get an award or a sticker or something for surviving this."

"It wasn't that bad." I searched Cami's gaze, and her brown

eyes had that flirty look again, like she knew exactly what I meant by my statement.

"Yeah, you get used to it." She walked by her sister and Michael, right up to me and kissed me. She tasted like strawberries and sin, her bright red lips curving against mine when I yanked her harder into me. She'd hung out with the team the past two nights, which she needed to do. But I missed her.

She pinched my side, beaming at me. "The heat wasn't so bad. I have some good memories here."

"Okay, settle down, please." Camden blanched. "I don't need to hear about my brother having sex."

"Camden." My face burned while Michael, Naomi, *and* my girlfriend laughed. She tugged my shirt and gave me a little shake of her head. I could read her expressions now, and she told me *let it go*.

Why couldn't we be neighbors, again?

"I gotta head back to meet Coach Simpson in thirty minutes, so start loading the car, people. Some of us have jobs."

"Okay, calm your tits, big shot. You have a lunch meeting with *my dad*. Not that cool."

"We're talking about scouting new talent. That is the literal definition of being cool as hell."

Naomi rolled her eyes, and Cami snorted. This seemed so easy—Michael, my brother, the twins. I'd built it up so much in my head about how different Cami and I were, and yet... our worlds meshed so well together.

Cami broke apart from our embrace, taking her vanilla scent with her. She winked over her shoulder before the three of them went into her room. Their laughter and constant jabbering carried into mine, and I turned to find Camden staring at me with bug eyes.

"Dude."

"What?"

"You love her."

I blinked at the way his words comforted me. Was it too soon? Probably. Did it scare me? Yeah. But was he wrong…? No. I knew it in the way my mood lightened every time she smiled. In the way she opened up with just me, showing her vulnerabilities. The way she pushed me to be better. The fierceness to her that made me want to do anything.

Admitting to loving Maddie had been a whole thing. I'd sweated like crazy and couldn't sleep. Cami though? It was like taking a deep breath.

"Yeah, I do."

"Alright then, let's hope she's not Maddie 2.0." His eyes went all wide, and he wrung his fingers together as he rocked back on his heels.

I growled, and he held up his hands in surrender. "Don't talk about her like that. I'll tolerate your teasing, but *don't* say a word about Cami."

Camden's nerves shifted to amusement, and he smiled. God, why did I like my brother again?

"Message received. Now, what do I get for helping you? Dinner? Drinks?"

"You put two things into a basket. You get nothing." I stacked my bags in a pile and set them in the hall. Michael had brought a wheelie, and we'd load all of my and Cami's bags before putting it into the truck. The plan was simple.

The ache in my chest wasn't.

If anyone picked up on my mood, they didn't show it. Not while we loaded our stuff or in the car ride over. Michael and Naomi left us with our bags right at the front desk where a line of people in front of us tried to get their keys again.

Cami tilted her head up at the air vent and moaned. "Hello, beautiful. I missed you." She scrunched her nose at me. "I'll never take it for granted again."

I nodded, still not quite sure *why* I was grumpy. My insecurities annoyed me, and we'd already communicated so much about being together that I didn't want to irritate her with more worry. *Four more people to go.*

"First thing I'm doing is showering without shoes. Then, I'm strutting around my place naked. You?" She elbowed my side playfully, but her brows came together. "Hey, what is it?"

"Anxious, that's all."

"Why? I'm sure the apartments are safe, or we wouldn't be back. They couldn't handle the bad press." She put her hand on my forearm. "Have you heard about your internship yet?"

It was a normal thing to assume. It would've been easier to talk about that then this weird weight that told me everything was going to change. I shook my head. She didn't need to know it was with my uncle or that his encouraging text weighed a million pounds on my phone. It was easier to just bite my cheek. "Not a word."

She pursed her lips as another woman joined the desk. The line moved faster so I never had to explain myself. Cami had her key in hand, I had mine, and there was nothing left to do besides go to our own places on different floors of the building.

"Do you have plans after you unpack? We could have an unpacking party together if you want. I don't have to meet Daniella for a bit." Cami and I carried our stuff into the elevator. She hit floor six, and I hit floor seven.

"That sounds fine."

She frowned, clearly not buying my bullshit. "Or not. We could always catch up later. I missed you last night, so I wanted to spend time with you, but if you need some alone time, tell me. I won't be upset."

She didn't demand answers from me like Maddie would've. She gave me an out. *This fucking girl.* The urge to kiss her overwhelmed me, making my senses go into Cami-overdrive. The sweet smell of her lotion, the way her hair hung over her bare shoulders. The black shirt hugging her tits and her high waisted shorts that showed off her trim waist. She was beautiful and so kind. My throat filled with emotion, and I reached for her just as a loud clunk sounded.

Her eyes went wide. "What was that?"

The sound repeated, like metal grinding on metal. Then, we stopped.

"Freddie." She paled as the lights dimmed. She had a death grip on my forearm. "The elevator."

Her voice shook with fear, and I took my own calming breath. It'd be fine. This happened to people. Not me, but people. *Be strong.* "It's okay. Hey, come here."

I pulled her back against my chest. She trembled head to toe, so I wrapped an arm around her middle. "I'm pressing the button to let them know."

She nodded, her breathing coming out in pants.

"What's your emergency?" A voice crackled through the speaker.

"We're stuck in an elevator in the new apartments on Center. There's two of us here, and the car made a loud grinding sound."

"Someone will be there in a few minutes. Is anyone hurt?"

"No. We're okay. Just scared." Cami shook harder now, and I slid to the floor with her in my arms. She tucked her head under my chin, and I shielded her entire body.

"I-I-I don't want to die."

"We won't. This happens more than you'd think." I ran my hands over her face, her hair, and her shoulders. She clung to me even more. "I promise."

I kissed the top of her head, hating her pain. I was worried but not like her, not with my whole body on the verge of breaking down. I had to distract her, to help her. Trailing my fingers over her smooth skin, I wrote letters on her.

I spelled out 'I love you' a few times, then all the things I loved about her. Her breathing slowed, and her muscles weren't as tense. My gut said it'd been about two minutes. *Almost safe.*

The dimmed lights, the close proximity of the elevator, and

the fact she wasn't staring at me with her large eyes made this the perfect setting to confess. "I'm afraid things are going to shift with us not living next door."

She lifted her head an inch but stopped. She adjusted her position so she was cradled in my lap. "What would change?"

"I don't know. Routines matter to me. I liked seeing you all the time, and this place is huge."

"Freddie." She dug her fingers into my chest. "We'll still see each other as much as we want."

"I know." I sighed and rested my chin on her head. "I'm sorry I keep having moments of insecurity."

"I have them." She squeezed me tighter, her voice low. "I'm worried you'll realize I'm too much work."

How could she think that? Did she not realize how she'd changed my whole world?

"Cami, I—"

"Everyone okay in there?" A voice boomed through the doors, and we jumped.

"Yes!" Cami stood and looked at me with wide eyes. "We're rescued! Thank fucking God."

The firemen propped the door open and helped us out along with our bags. We gave some statements, and after twenty minutes, we were on our way toward our own units.

I'd almost told her I loved her. After weeks.

Was I insane? Partially.

Even though my shoulders sagged and my muscles strained, I walked her to her door. She unlocked it with a click and pushed inside. Paint fumes flooded my senses.

"So much better than the dorms." She dropped her bags on the floor and spun in a circle. Her hair went everywhere as she closed her eyes, and I couldn't stop watching her. She was so beautiful.

She stilled, her brown eyes finding mine. They softened, and she waltzed toward me. She pushed the straps of my bags off my shoulders and fisted my shirt. "Kiss me, Freddie. Kiss me like you mean it."

How could I not do what she asked? Not when my heart sped up at the tender look in her eyes. Things might be different, but that didn't mean anything had to change. Not between us.

I backed her up until she hit the counter, and I kissed her *hard.* Taking my time and telling her without words how I felt. With the internship looming over my head, I planned to make every second count with her. She was unlike anyone I knew, the most special person who lit me up inside. She soothed me and when her fingers found my neck, pulling me closer, I was done for. I wanted this girl for…ever.

The girl I loved.

CHAPTER
TWENTY-THREE

Cami

My dad stood in my apartment two days later, his hands on his hips and his signature frown ingrained on his face. He paced the kitchen, huffing out a breath every two seconds. After a few breaths, he'd stare at me, shake his head, and repeat the process.

This started five minutes ago.

"Dad, come on." I sat on the counter, my legs dangling over the cabinet as Daniella sat at the kitchen table. "Please?"

He grumbled something under his breath, and Daniella and I shared a look. It was a big ask—having him be interim coach for three weeks until the school could refill Audrey's place.

Yeah, she resigned before Daniella ever had to show the nonexistent video. The girl had balls of steel and totally faked it. We'd agreed to do all the work, but there had to be a certified coach on the field with us.

"There's no one else?"

"Correct."

"And she quit?"

I chewed my lip, not quite telling him the whole story. I was embarrassed. Mortified, even though the whole dilemma was on her. Daniella narrowed her eyes at me, but I shrugged her off. "She crossed a line and realized she had to resign."

"What did she do?"

"Doesn't matter. The fact we don't have a team is more important."

"Please, Coach Simpson. It won't take long. I know a few people interested, and they just have to interview with the dean." Daniella stood up, looking so much older than she did a few months ago. This whole experience had aged her but in a really good way.

"Two games. That's it. But you'll tell me the *whole* fucking story, Cami. I know you're keeping something from me." He pointed at my face. "Alright?"

"Thank you, thank you!" I hugged him and jumped up and down. "You're the best!"

He patted my back and eventually leaned into the hug. "Okay, okay."

"This means a lot, Dad. Seriously." I gave him another quick squeeze before releasing him. He stepped away and ran a hand down his face.

"I'm going to regret this."

"No, you won't, Coach Simpson! Thank you so much!" Daniella smiled so sweetly at him that I had to do a double take. Who was this girl?

He waved and walked out, leaving Daniella and I alone. She wiggled her ass and spun around. "This is gonna be dope! Your dad the coach. How fun."

"We better find someone soon. He means it when he says two games." I pushed my hair out of my face, the weight lifting off my shoulders. We still had a team. Daniella and I were still co-captains. "We fucking did it."

"Yeah, we did!" She threw herself at me, and I caught her in a hug. She laughed. "This is unreal. Seriously. We need to celebrate!"

"For sure." I matched her grin, already thinking about Freddie's face when I told him the news. "We could invite them here?"

"Hell yeah! I'll send out the text. I'm gonna run home and change. Then I'll be back!"

"Sounds good." I waved as she left. A party with the girls. Interesting. No more getting ready to party alone…where I'd drink just enough to be safe and surround myself with people so I wouldn't feel like it was just me. I had a team. A group of girls who supported me. It was amazing.

I opened up the patio doors and smiled as the sun hit my face. There was only room for two chairs and a small table on the wired patio, but it was perfect after living in the shoebox. I breathed in the fresh air just as a familiar voice came from above me.

"Hi, yes, it's Frederick Brady. Uh huh. Thank you. Of course. Sure thing."

Freddie?

He lived *right* above me? My stomach fluttered as I stole glances of the large body. It was definitely him.

A wild idea hit me. Our windows faced an empty alley so the chances of anyone seeing me doing this was slim. It was still a risk, but imagining his face would be worth it.

I undid my bra, sliding it through my armhole, and tossed it up. First try, I missed. But the second…it landed near his feet.

Feeling daring and excited from all the adrenaline, I removed my shirt and sat on the chair with my feet on the table. I stretched my arms above my head, thrusting my breasts out. A part of me would always be wild, and I hoped Freddie liked that little streak.

He shifted in his chair, his head peeking over the railing. "*Cami.*"

"Hey, upstairs neighbor."

"What are you *doing*?" His voice cracked, and his gaze stayed on my tits. Hot and intense. "Your shirt!"

"I seemed to have lost it. Want to help me find it?"

He licked his bottom lip and then he was out of sight. Maybe I imagined it, but I swore I heard heavy stomps from the ceiling above me. I couldn't stop smiling at the possessive face he'd made and how we were floor neighbors.

Freddie was so worried about not sharing a wall with me, but look at us now. I had no idea he was right above me. Our units didn't match in number or letter, so this was a fun coincidence.

Bam, bam, bam.

I pushed myself up, still shirtless, and opened the front door. "Oh, hello." I wiggled my brows as he barged inside. He wore a dark black shirt and ripped jeans, the fabric stretching across his body in a marvelous way.

"You little tease." He backed me up against a wall and held my hands above my head. His chest heaved as he took his time eyeing my face, neck, and breasts. My nipples were pointed out toward him, hungry for his mouth, but he didn't touch me.

He just looked and stared.

"Tell me, Cami." He nipped my neck.

Heat flooded between my thighs, and I slammed my head against the wall in pleasure. "Hm?"

"Do you enjoy flashing your tits for everyone to see? Does it turn you on?" He sucked my earlobe for a second before dragging his nose over my collarbone. I straight-up whimpered now.

Freddie unhinged was my second favorite Freddie.

"What if I said yes?"

He snapped his head back, his gaze dropping to my mouth as his lips parted. His jaw went slack, and he carefully set my arms down. Without warning, he hoisted me up and brought me closer toward the patio door.

"Does the thought of someone seeing you naked get you hot?" He captured my hands again, this time holding them behind my back.

"A little, yes."

"Liar. It does *a lot*." He finally bent down and sucked one nipple into his mouth in a hungry kiss. I bucked against it, loving how his jaw rubbed on my skin. "Is this what you hoped would happen when you threw me your bra?"

"Maybe."

"Mm." He sucked my other nipple harder, humming against my sensitive flesh. My body was amped up, an orgasm just seconds away.

He stopped sucking and pulled my thin bra out of his pocket. He wrapped it around my hands and pushed my arms above my head again. "Don't move them."

Holy shit.

I was going to combust. Freddie. Soft, sweet Freddie basically handcuffed me with my bra. It was so fucking hot.

He cupped my neck and seared me with a white-hot kiss before he spun me around so my nipples pressed against the glass. I shook with a desperate need. Every fantasy I ever had… this was *so much* better. "Freddie." My voice cracked.

He slid my athletic shorts and panties down. Then he spread my legs apart and ran his fingers through my slit. "So wet for me."

My ears buzzed, and my pussy ached from all the sensations. The cold window on my nipples, the clean woodsy scent he brought with him. He kissed the back of my neck before he spread my ass cheeks. I whimpered as he kneaded my globes.

"Someday, I want to taste you there."

"O-okay." I panted and could barely stand up. "Please, I want—"

"You're waiting this out, baby. You teased me with your perfect tits. Your fucking body is a dream. Your strong muscles. God, I want to bite them." Something shuffled, and he bit my thigh.

"Oh, shit." My hands slipped on the glass, and he righted them.

"When I'm with you, I want to do *everything* with you. It's addicting. *You're* addicting."

Something soft thudded on the ground. Then a buckle. Something warm pressed against my back, and Freddie moved his hand around my front to play with my clit. "I want you to come like this, against your window so anyone could see."

Who was my boyfriend?

He swirled his fingers around my swollen nerves, fast, hard. Like he knew it would only take seconds. His other hand held my stomach, and he sucked *hard* on my neck. "I fucking love your body."

I fucking love you, I wanted to say. How could I not? Look at the shy guy doing dirty and crazy things for me. I held those words in just as the orgasm started at my core. The pleasure exploded through my veins, making me cry out in a scream. He kept massaging my clit, holding me against him as I rode it out.

"That's my girl," he kept saying. Each time had me falling for him a bit more.

When the pleasure subsided, my arms fell, and he undid the restraint. He spun me around, lifted my chin, and assessed me. "Are you okay? Was that too much? I lost my mind—"

"It was perfect." I smashed my lips against his, jumping onto his body, hungry for more. "You're perfect."

He laughed against my mouth and walked us toward the couch before pulling me onto his lap. I knew just what to do. How to even the score, how to repay the favor of letting me be wild.

He moaned in protest when I slid off him and went to grab my bra. His gaze trailed my every move as his chest heaved. "What are you doing?"

"Returning the pleasure, big guy." I flashed my best smile and motioned for him to lift his arms. He held them above his head, and I tied the fabric around them. "No touching."

"How's that fair?" He pouted. His glasses almost fogged up, and I took them off. "No, leave them. I want to see every inch of you, Cami."

I could feel the truth of his words too. I placed them back on his nose, letting my nipple graze the outside of his lips. I arched back before he captured it, and he hissed. "See? Isn't this fun?"

"You're killing me."

I moved between his thighs and dragged off his boxers and jeans. His massive, thick cock slapped against his stomach, and I clenched my thighs. *My turn.* I licked the shaft, base to the top, took him into my mouth, and sucked.

He almost erupted from the couch. "Cami! Fuck."

I pushed him back down and swirled my tongue around him. He shook when I cupped his balls. I wanted him to feel even a small amount of the pleasure I did earlier. The build-up was just as important as the release, and I needed him to feel it all.

"I love having you in my mouth." I found a rhythm he liked and noted all his reactions. The way his muscles flexed, the groans escaping from his mouth. The heavy breaths. Sweat formed on his stomach, and I rubbed my hand over it.

"Cami, stop, I'm gonna come."

I stopped. "Don't you want to?"

"With you, not like this." His face softened, and something shifted. My own heart beat erratically against my ribs, and suddenly, I couldn't get close enough to him. I crawled up his body, undoing the bra from his hands and kissed him.

He cupped the back of my head, slowly thrusting his tongue into my mouth as he trembled. He held me like he loved me, all close and intimate. I mirrored the embrace, and instead of a roaring fire of lust, an emotional need filled me.

"I want to feel you, all of you." I pulled back just to meet his eyes. "I'm clean and on the pill."

His eyes searched mine. "I'm clean too."

Then, he lifted my hips and rested his cock at my entrance.

He waited for me to finish the connection, and I slid onto him. God, he felt good. He held my gaze as I slowly arched my hips. He gripped my sides, urging me to go even slower.

We'd had sex a lot since that first night, but *nothing* had felt like this. Each movement was slow, deliberate. He ran a hand down my neck and over my chest until it rested over my heart. My breath caught in my throat at his tender expression.

"Freddie," I said, my voice breaking from the onslaught of *everything*.

"I know, baby." He kissed me again, our heavy breathing matching the pace of me riding him.

We stayed like that forever, his mouth on mine and his cock filling me up. But after a while, a hot tingle teased in my lower gut. He sensed it too because he reached between my legs and rubbed my clit, somehow not breaking our kiss. "Come for me again."

I arched my back, took him deeper, and *oh my god*. It was the best orgasm I'd ever had, making the top of my head tingle with pleasure. I barely caught my breath before Freddie's movements became jerky. Tight. He kneaded my ass as his face twisted. "*Fuck.*"

He spilled into me, his eyes never leaving mine. I'd never had sex with anyone without a condom and the sensation—the closeness I felt to him, was unparalleled. "Whoa."

I giggled, moving off him and collapsing on the couch. He sat there, legs spread, eyes wild, and chest heaving, and I couldn't imagine *not* being with him. "Freddie, this is the hottest thing I've ever experienced."

"Yeah?" He gave me a lazy grin. "Me too."

"That wasn't… too wild for you?"

His face tightened with understanding before his eyes warmed. "You make me want to try everything. So no, this wasn't too wild for me. Nothing is when I'm with you."

My face heated, and I scooted closer to kiss him again. The words were *right* there, but I couldn't say them. Not yet. "I'm having a party tonight with the dance girls. We're celebrating the fact my dad will be our temporary coach."

"No way!" He pulled me into his arms, his chest still sweaty. I didn't care though.

"Yeah, how fun is that? Anyway, do you want to come over? It'll probably be a lot of music, dancing, and beer pong."

"Are you sure you don't need to bond with just the team? I don't mind."

"Meet my team." Damn, nerves hit me out of nowhere. After all that we did, *now* I got nervous. "If you want."

He seemed to read me though. He nodded in understanding. "I'd love to meet the other part of your life. Of course I'll come."

CHAPTER
TWENTY-FOUR

Freddie

Dad: *Today's the day, son! You'll be working with your Uncle Martin soon enough. Proud of you. Can't wait to stop by for lunches twice a week!*

I pressed my palms into my eyes, not responding to my dad. He meant well, I knew that, but each text or call just made the guilt more painful. Like he couldn't fathom the fact that maybe… I didn't *want* to work with Uncle Martin. That *maybe* staying in town was a better choice for me.

Because of Cami.

My computer hissed from overheating, and my jaw tightened at the forced restart. My knee hit the table over and over, causing my coffee to spill over my mug. *Damnit.* The text on my phone read YOUR STATUS FOR INTERNSHIP IS UPDATED. CHECK PORTAL.

Check the fucking portal? I'd *love* to if my laptop would function. I rubbed the back of my neck as my future waited until the damn device would work. I'd find out if I got into the local businesses or if I'd have to move to the city with my uncle.

Moving hours away. My stomach ached.

Camden would give me shit for worrying about something before it happened, but I was that kinda person—imagining all the ways it could go wrong before it did. I cracked my knuckles as my laptop finally started, and then I typed the incorrect passwords three times in my hurry to log in.

Finally. The portal loaded.

Urbana Associates: Declined
Urbana LLC: Accepted, Pending
Chicago Associates: Accepted
Chicago LLC: Declined
Northern Chicago: Declined

My pulse flooded my ears at the *Accepted, Pending*. What did that even mean? I clicked the more information button and scanned the small font. *Acceptance pending paperwork.*

What paperwork?

I researched immediately what that meant. It seemed there could be a delay in a form or application—which, phew.

Pending... that signified there was still a chance, and it wasn't a no. If it was a no, that meant I had to move to Chicago with my uncle. I gulped, *hating* the unfairness of it all. I was excited for the internship, looking forward to learning more and applying my skills to be a legit environmental engineer. If Cami wasn't in the picture, I'd be thrilled I got into Chicago Associates and working close to my dad. I grew up hearing about all the lunches and networking they did in the city. My future always ended there, in the city with them. Plus, they had a great reputation and would pave the way for more opportunities.

But Urbana LLC...that was in town. Nearby. I'd still get to see Cami and Camden and Michael...I lied to myself. I'd miss my brother and friends, but it was her that came to the forefront of my mind. I *loved* her. Some would say it was too soon, but I knew what love felt like, and this was so much more than what I had with Maddie. There was trust and a vulnerability in the way we communicated.

When I thought about the future a year from now, I pictured Cami with me. It was that simple. But would she be with me if I moved hours away so soon? Before we had a chance to see if we could survive it?

My fingers tapped against my thigh, and I paced the living room. Cami was sitting in on interviews with Daniella for a new dance coach, and Camden was with his current fling. I needed to talk to someone about what was going on in my mind. My dad gave great advice, even if he always pictured me working for his brother. He'd be able to give me an unbiased opinion. Content with my decision, I called him.

"Hey, son."

"Got a minute?"

"Sure thing." He shuffled some papers around. "Your mom and I are looking forward to parents' weekend in two weeks. We already got our outfits and everything."

I fought a smile. They were so dorky, but I appreciated their effort. They cared about us and went all in. Also, Camden hated their school spirit, so it made the whole weekend more enjoyable for me. "Can't wait."

"But more importantly… Martin already texted me the good news! You're in, Freds! You're gonna be working in the city like we always talked about!"

"Right, yeah." My throat closed up tight, making me sound like a dehydrated frog. "About that."

"What about it? Were you nervous you wouldn't get in? Come on, Martin thinks the world of you. He already told his staff about all the innovative ideas you'd bring and how including the next generation in projects is the way to go."

God, the pride in my dad's voice almost broke my resolve. How could I disappoint him? Uncle Martin? My mom? I could almost hear the displeasure in his voice, the change of how he used vowels if I didn't take the one in the city.

"You think you'll live at home or get a place? I keep telling your mom to not ask you, but since I have you on the phone…"

he paused, clearly waiting for me to respond. My poor brain started fritzing.

"I'm seeing someone," I blurted out, awkward and unsure. Dad and I didn't have relationship talks besides the whole *wear a condom* speech I got in junior high. Plus, they'd really disliked Maddie. "It's... intense."

"Okay." He swallowed, and silence greeted me for a few seconds. "That's great, Freddie. I can't wait to meet her."

That made me smile. Cami would love my parents, but I refocused. The October air chilled a little, and I slid the patio door open, letting the breeze cool me off. *Ask him. Do it.* "It's about my internship."

"What about it? Did you *not* get accepted? I'll kill Martin."

"No, no. I got into Chicago Associates." I cleared my throat. "And one here in Urbana pending paperwork."

"See? Two places saw your potential. That's great, son. It'll be hard to tell Urbana no since it's your college town, but just think of the city! All the Cubs games, the food, the movie festivals? It's your dream come true."

Is it though? Or yours? I wouldn't dare say the words.

"I'm worried about what to do."

"About what? The woman you're seeing?" His voice was laced with apprehension.

"If it weren't for Cami, I'd be thrilled for the Chicago acceptance." While I loved her, a small, tiny part of me wanted to preserve my heart. The *what if she changed her mind* part of my brain was getting smaller and smaller each day we were together, but was I being a total idiot to turn down an internship in Chicago after being with her for a month?

"Hmm, well." He took a sip of water, the sounds coming through the phone. "This thing with Cami...it's new and exciting. I'm happy for you. You deserve all the love and happiness after what Maddie put you through, but I'd be a fool to not advise you to put yourself first. You always worry about others—Maddie, your brother. You bent over backwards for that girl, and she played you like a fool. If you think Cami's worth it ... distance for a few months won't kill you."

"Meaning I should take the Chicago internship?"

He sighed, the sound weighing me down with guilt. "Freddie, of course you'll take this one. It's a huge opportunity for your career, your future. You've worked so hard the past five years. Don't throw it away because you're seeing someone new. Choose yourself *first*."

Doubt still plagued me. I did always worry about others and catered to them. I didn't mind being that guy, but could I let it compromise my future? Five years in college and my final semester? I sighed, closing my eyes as the sun warmed my face. "I have two weeks to choose."

"We'll celebrate when we're there in a few weekends and we can get your head on straight. Working with Martin was what you always wanted, kid. Don't let a temporary distraction ruin your future for you. I say that with love. Remember that."

"Sure, yeah, bye, Dad."

We hung up and pocketed my phone. Fuck. That didn't help at all. He couldn't even fathom a reality where I chose staying here. *Why* couldn't this year be normal so I could spend it with her without worrying? Moving from the dorms to the apartments had made me nervous, and the thought of living three hours away?

Fuck.

My phone buzzed.

Cami: Hey, you! I've been dying to hear from you. Any news?

My stomach tightened. Of course, she remembered today was *the* day. Her text wasn't any reason to worry--she was curious. That was it. Plus, I'd told her I would check this morning and that I'd let her know.

Freddie: Yes—

I hit send before I could type anything else. Dots appeared, disappeared, and reappeared before her response came through.

Cami: Well?
Freddie: We'll chat when you get back.

I brushed my hair out of my face, hating myself for acting so weird. Yesterday, we'd talked about her dreams of owning a studio and all the things she was doing to make it come true. I told her about working for a good cause. We'd shared everything and yet *this* held me up.

It was a horrible idea to put all the feelings and uncertainty in a text message. She'd understand. I couldn't tell her I got into Chicago and possibly the one in town in text. She could misread it and worry. Plus, was I capable of standing up to my dad? Could I actually turn down Chicago?

Just imagining that conversation made my palms sweat.
Freddie: Not bad news!

She didn't respond, and I chewed my lip. Fuck, this was already making me act different. She'd know it too. She could see right through me.

Knock, knock.

Damn, Cami must've run back here from the admin offices.

I adjusted my glasses and opened the door, frowning at the expression on her face--her mouth turned down at the sides, her chin lacking the normally defiant determination I loved. Her cheeks were pink, her lips bare of any lip gloss, and her braided hair had a bunch of flyaways. Despite the way my heart beat faster around her, doubt seeped in.

Would she stick with me if we did long distance? I was her first *boyfriend* of a few weeks. Three hours away was asking too much. It was hard for couples who'd been together for ages.

Emotion lodged in my throat, and my hands weighed a million pounds. I couldn't lift them to comfort her or pull her toward me. She sensed the change. I knew she did. Her posture stiffened, reminding me of the first few days of living by each other in the dorms.

"Uh, how did the interview thing go?" My voice came out gruff and uncomfortable. The words didn't fit the mood, and she still stood outside my door. Like she was unwanted. "Come in, please." I forced myself to guide her in, everything feeling out of sorts.

We normally kissed. She'd wrap her arms around my neck, and I'd pull her chest against mine. I'd breath her in, and she'd let out a little sigh that made my heart get tight. None of that this time.

She crossed her arms and dragged her teeth over her bottom lip. "They went okay, but I'm not here to talk about that. You're tense as hell, Freddie. What happened?"

"Right." I gripped the back of my neck and squeezed. My shoulders ached like I'd tried working out for the first time ever, and no matter how I stood, everything hurt. She looked up at me with her big brown eyes, uncertainty and worry leaking out of them.

She arched a brow, still not touching me. I wasn't sure why it mattered to me that she made the first move, but it did. So, I kept my space.

I should tell her everything. All the worry and fear and choices bothering me. We could talk about them and come to a solution together, but no matter how much I tried to do that, my mind wanted me to see her reaction to distance. To test her? Maybe. To ensure she wasn't Maddie? It wasn't fair. I *knew* that. Yet, I couldn't stop myself from saying, "I was accepted into the program in Chicago."

She closed her eyes and nodded curtly. Then, she stared at me, her nostrils flaring as she made fists against her stomach. "Any here in town?"

I shook my head. Things were too tense to mention the *pending paperwork.* The way her face crumpled made my stomach fall to the ground. She looked *shattered.*

Her jaw tightened, and she blinked a lot. "That's... are you excited?"

"I don't know."

"Freddie." She scrunched her brows and stepped toward

me. "You need to *talk* to me." She ran her fingers over my forehead, smoothing down my wrinkles. Her freckles were more pronounced with the lighting, and everything seemed so stupid.

Why was I acting like this?

I cupped her face and pressed my lips softly against hers. "I'm sorry. I assumed you wouldn't want to do distance and created all this shit in my head. You're not like that. I know. I *know*."

She wrapped her arms around my waist and patted my back as she kissed me back. "I thought you were going to break up with me when I walked in."

"What? No. *No*." My throat ached from holding everything in. I needed her closer to me. More of her. I rested my chin on her head, still confused about the future but content in the moment. "I see a future with you."

"I want one with you, too, Freddie. If that means we do distance for a semester, then we do that. You living in Chicago doesn't mean we're over… unless you want it to be."

"I don't. I really don't."

"Then it's settled." She squeezed me again, sighing into my chest. "I'm proud of you." She spoke so quietly I almost didn't catch it.

"Me?"

"Yeah. You applied for an internship. You're moving away to live alone. That scares me, and you're just doing it like it's no big deal. That's amazing. I'm proud of you."

"I'm… well, thanks. I'm not alone… my family is close. But yeah." My ears burned at her compliment, and another wave of gratitude washed over me. How did I think this would end? That she wouldn't support me? "You're… I just love being with you."

"I love being with you too."

The unsaid words hung between us. It wasn't the right time. I doubted her, us, ten minutes ago, and to say I loved her now would be an insult. I'd wait and make it special. If she'd never had a boyfriend, she might not have heard those words before, and I wanted to make it something she'd never forget. Cami deserved the world, and even though going to Chicago wasn't *for sure*, the fact she didn't run off secured everything.

I loved her, and we'd be okay.

CHAPTER **TWENTY-FIVE**

Cami

My hair was curled to perfection. My makeup was ten out of ten, and I wore the cutest school spirited shirt and my black cutoff jeans to go meet Freddie's parents. Instead of coming in on Friday before the football game, they'd arrived Thursday afternoon.

Which was fine with me. Meeting them after dancing at the game would've been fine, but this was easier. Nervous was an understatement. My stomach did ten backhand springs and cartwheels as I locked my apartment door. My phone buzzed, Daniella's name popping up.

Daniella: Good luck with the rents tonight!
Cami: Check on me in an hour. Might need CPR.

God, my life was so different than it had been a few weeks ago. Freddie., our new coach, and my friendship with Daniella. I wasn't sure what I'd done, but the girl had declared herself my new best friend. I even liked her? Trusted her? The feelings were weird and scary, but her text made me smile.

Naomi already FaceTimed me, wishing me luck.

Now, it was just my first time ever meeting the parents of the guy I really fucking liked. My palms sweated an embarrassing amount. *I can do this.*

I got to his unit, wiped my hands on my jeans, checked my teeth in my camera, and knocked. *Gametime.*

Freddie opened the door, a huge smile on his lips. "Cami, hey." Happy lines appeared around his eyes, and he tucked me under his arm. "I missed you."

"You saw me yesterday." My face hurt from smiling so much.

"Yeah, but you didn't sleep over." He kissed the top of my head before shutting the door. Last night was another team dinner where we stayed at a diner way too late laughing.

Bizarre experience, but also amazing?

"Gotta keep you on your toes, big guy." As I said the words, two older people who were carbon copies of Freddie grinned at me from the living room. His mom was petite and had the same dark hair and thick glasses while his dad was built like a bus and had Freddie's easy smile.

He held out his hand first. "It's wonderful to meet you, Cami. I'm Frederick."

"You too." I smiled, turning to his mom. She had a twinkle in her eyes as she shook my hand and said pleasantries. They were so pleasant and kind, and I didn't pick up even a spark of judgement on their part.

I was looking for it too.

"Freddie was going on about you, so it's so wonderful to meet you. Tell us all about yourself. You dance? Minoring in business? What a tough combination. I was a cheerleader all through college."

Oh my God, I love her. "That's tough work."

"I know. Dance is too. I can't wait to see you tomorrow. Dancing and cheer are way more fun than football. I go to support the school? Honestly, I'm not sure. Mainly because our family goes. Fred, why do I go to football games?"

"Because I like watching, and you love me?"

"Right. That." His mom rolled her eyes and hit my forearm like we were friends. All my nerves zapped out of me. She was so easy to be around.

His dad too.

"Guys, come on. We're having a drink and be *cool*."

"Freddie, dear. If she's with you, she knows you're not *cool*. You don't come from *cool* no matter how much Camden tries."

I snorted, absolutely adoring this family. The comforting atmosphere, the obvious love between all of them was so strange, but in a wonderful way. They loved each other. It was so clear. I couldn't recall a single time Naomi, my parents, and I were in a room with an openness like this. The divorce was the right move for them, but this sort of ease? It was fascinating to know it existed, and to be a part of it even for a short time felt special. Like maybe... with the right person, this was what life was like.

Freddie led me to the couch and got me a beer while his parents sat on the love seat. They asked about my dad, what I thought about hockey, and even my twin sister.

"The thought of twins makes my heart freeze up. Two of Camden. Boy howdy. No thank you." His mom put a palm over her heart. "Fred, it's like a nightmare."

His dad ran a hand over his face just as someone walked into the place. Camden.

"You must've known we were talking about you." His dad got up and gave his second son a hug. "Good to see you, Cam."

"Talking shit already?"

"Always." His mom beamed at him, pulling him into a hug next. "Just imagining the horror of having two of you. I can't believe Cami is a twin."

"Ah, the fun I could've had with another me. We would've made Freddie's life hell."

"You do that well all on your own," Freddie said.

Everyone laughed, and Camden grabbed a drink before sitting on the couch. Everything seemed so simple. So nice.

Freddie rested his arm around the back of the sofa, occasionally dragging his fingers through my hair. Each time, goosebumps broke out down my neck. I almost laughed at how worked up I'd been before meeting them. They were so sweet and down to earth. Was this how normal people felt? Secure and safe and welcomed in a relationship?

"Have you made up your damned mind about what you're doing next semester yet?" Camden asked, whistling as he eyed the living room. "If you want to sublet this place and keep it in the fam, I could try and break out of my other lease. I could live here. Be lavish and shit."

"Of course you're subleasing it. What do you mean *made up your mind yet?*" his dad asked, his gaze on Freddie. His voice was stern and then he narrowed his eyes at Camden.

"Shit. Didn't mean to walk into an awkward-sauce convo. Bro, you chose Chicago then? Swore you said you were considering here?"

Camden furrowed his brows and looked to me, then his brother.

The hairs on my neck prickled as the air shifted. His dad sat up straighter, and his mom tightened her grip on his knee. My pulse raced, and I wasn't sure why. The growing silence became so loud I heard my own breaths coming in and out like I'd done fifty burpees in a row. The tension made no sense. The question was simple enough, and yet my shoulders slumped like they understood something I didn't. The weighted secrets reminded me of my parents splitting up, the looks, the concerns, the obvious fact I was kept in the dark intentionally.

"Yes. Yes. I'm moving, uh, to the city, right." Freddie cleared his throat and crossed one leg over the other so his ankle rested on his knee.

"Okay," Camden said, his voice lacking the usual swagger he seemed to ooze. "I thought you said you were accepted into a business down here. My b." Camden leaned back into the La-Z-Boy and spoke to the ceiling. "I know this ruins my rep, but with the parental units here I might as well play up my soft side. Dude, I'm gonna miss you. I hoped for a hot second you'd stay in town but at least give me your place."

"Should we head out for dinner?" Freddie said, almost shouting. My throat hurt to swallow, and my chest heaved as my mind caught up to the conversation.

"Yes, we should. I agree." His mom stood up too fast.

Camden and I shared a look, and something gross twisted in my stomach.

I thought you said you got into a place down here.

I wouldn't have thought twice about him saying that if it weren't for Freddie's weird reaction. Or his mom's...like they wanted to avoid the comment and act like it wasn't said. Even now, as they all bustled around me, talking about where to go, the pieces clicked together.

The last two weeks, when I asked Freddie about the internship, he'd been really vague. *Working out the details. Still in progress.*

When I'd asked if they gave him a reason why he didn't get into the programs here, he'd changed the subject.

That day I'd come up here and he looked at me like we were over...*what if* he had gotten into a program here and didn't want to tell me? What if he chose not to stay here?

"I need to use the restroom really quick." I ducked my head and went to the one in Freddie's room, needing some space from what had just happened. Freddie said something, but I waved him off, shutting the door and locking it.

Deep breath.

"*Why the fuck did you say that in front of her?*" Freddie's angry voice carried through the door, solidifying my dread.

In front of me.

My *boyfriend* had lied to me. He'd gotten into a program in town and said he didn't. He *chose* to go to Chicago instead of staying here. All without telling me. All with lying to me.

His whole family knew the truth. Just not me. They probably thought I was a distraction, a tease, someone not worth his time.

He could've chosen here, this town, *me,* but didn't.

Fuck. I ran a hand over my face, careful not to smear any makeup. I knew better than to get comfortable with him. My life didn't have moments like his—where everything was peaceful and everyone loved each other. No one chose me. Not my parents, my coach, my sister.

We'd talked about distance, but was I so agreeable because I'd thought that was the only option? That he didn't *choose* to leave this town? Leave…me?

Shit. My eyes got that prickly feeling in the back of them. I took a few breaths, but it didn't stop the sting from growing to full tears. My eyes filled with moisture, and I blinked them away. My fingers shook as I texted Naomi.

Cami: call me, sos.

She rang the next second. "What happened?"

"Give me an emergency." My voice cracked with emotion. "Invent one."

"I got in a car accident then. Where are you? Do you need me to come there?"

"No. I need to get out of this dinner." I sniffed and rubbed my forehead. "Fuck."

"With Freddie's family? What happened?"

"Cami?" Freddie knocked on the bathroom door, his voice nervous and tight. Sadness masquerading as anger made me snap.

"*What?"*

"Open the door."

"I'll be at your place in ten," I whispered to Naomi, hanging up and pocketing my phone. My *boyfriend* wanted to talk? Fine. We'd talk.

I unlocked the handle, flung it open, and faced him. All six and a million feet of him filled with self-doubt and half-truths. "You lied to me."

"Yes. I did." His jaw flexed, and he glanced over his shoulder. "Camden shouldn't have said that."

"Don't blame him for something that was your doing."

"My fault?" His brows disappeared into his hairline. "Cami, it's my decision where I go next semester. Not yours."

The second he said the words, he winced and blinked. "Wait, no, that came out wrong. Shit, I'm sorry. I'm so sorry. Could we—"

"I gotta go." I sniffed, not caring that he could see me being weak. His words were a truthful slap in the face. *Of fucking course* it was his choice, but lying to me about it was shitty. Boyfriends didn't lie. Not to the people who loved them.

"Cami, wait."

"No." He reached for my arm, and I yanked it away. "Naomi got in a car accident."

"You're lying." He frowned, the muscles in his jaw flexing every other second.

"Hm, not so fun when the game is turned around, huh?" I brushed past him, marched into the living room, and avoided his parents' gaze. Shame and embarrassment covered me head to toe, but they had nothing on the shattering of my heart.

My insides felt twisted around, like they'd been misplaced, and my throat throbbed with my pulse. My vision blurred as I ran down the hall toward the staircase. Freddie hurt me. He'd lied to me. He hadn't told me the full truth.

I would've accepted him choosing his future over me, but *keeping* it from me intentionally? God, this betrayal hurt. He didn't trust me or us enough to be honest, so what was the fucking point?

Heavy footsteps followed me in the stairwell, and I went faster. Tripping on a step. "Fuck!"

"Shit, are you alright?" Freddie was right there. His damn

large frame took up half the staircase, and I inched away from him. "Did you hurt your ankle?"

I half-sat, half-crouched on the bottom step, ready to bolt again before I stood to my full height. "I'll be fine. My ankle will be fine."

"Please don't run away. Can we discuss this?"

"Now? No. Last week? Yes. Any other day this week when we were together, talking about our wants and dreams? Yes." I sniffed, tears rolling down my face. "We d-don't have anything else to say, okay?"

"What do you mean?" His face crumpled, his voice getting shaky.

"Answer me this. Did you get into a program in town?"

He hung his head before he nodded. "Yes."

"Were you ever going to tell me? Wait." I held up my hand. "I don't care. I wouldn't have known unless your family accidentally spilled it. This? You and I? We're done. There's no trust here."

"You don't mean that. Please." He stepped toward me, his face shattering. "I fucked up, but I can explain. I got in my head, thinking about my dad and uncle, letting them down and you, and my future—"

"Freddie. I need a partner who includes me in their thought processes and *trusts me enough* for it to be real. I need someone to *choose* trusting me." My voice broke on the last word, the utter weight of the truth causing my heart to crack.

He plopped onto the stairs, holding his head in his hands and pulling his hair. "I messed up. I really did, just… how can I fix it? How can I make this better? I love you, Cami."

"You don't *love* me." I laughed, a bitter, horrible sound filling the air. I saw what love did to people who didn't want the same things. This wasn't *love*.

My chest heaved, and even though the anger still vibrated through me, I still fought the urge to crawl to him. While he might not love me, I loved him with my whole soul. That was what made the next part so hard.

"Please, leave me alone."

With that, I continued down the stairs, but this time, he didn't follow me.

CHAPTER
TWENTY-SIX

Freddie

With Maddie, it had been so easy to blame everything on her. She was the villain in our breakup story, and now that I experienced the other side of it, my stomach ached like I had the flu. It was a miracle I hadn't thrown up from the pure panic and pain coursing through my body. I did this. I'd broken us.

I'd hurt Cami.

It'd been twelve hours since she left me on the stairs, and I didn't know what to do. The finality in her voice, the way she looked at me with so much disappointment. She didn't even believe me when I told her I *loved* her.

And I did. How could she not realize that?

Oh, because you lied about getting into a program in town. Kept it from her. Told your family and blamed her for it.

My life was spiraling. Today was the due date to make a decision for the internship too. The one that had been sitting on my shoulders all week, the worry of choosing one for the wrong motivations. Did I pick here for Cami or Chicago because... it would make my dad and uncle happy?

The one here wasn't just pending anymore—I was fully accepted. And it was pretty great and even had more of an environmental focus. I rubbed my palms over my eyes until white spots danced in my vision. My parents had spoken like I'd already made my choice, like working for Uncle Martin was the only option. Even bringing up staying here was shot down. Especially after Cami ran out.

You want to throw away the future you've been building for her?

Was I a fool for staying here to try and resolve things with her?

My phone buzzed, and my dad's name popped up.

Dad: breakfast?

Freddie: sure.

Maybe some coffee and fresh air would clear my head and help me stand up to him because that was the root of my issue—Chicago was only on the table because it had always been *his dream.*

I showered, put on a black shirt and jeans, and made my way to a breakfast diner near the hotel, letting my mind wander to when Chicago started being a frequent topic of conversation. High school? Countless dinners talking about my future where Camden would chat about having fun, going on adventures. They'd laugh at him while my future talk was serious, matter of fact.

My dad said I needed to put myself first, but relocating to a city...living with my parents at twenty-four? I didn't make friends easily, and moving away to live in my childhood home sounded horrible.

I'd been fighting it the entire time, but I knew what I wanted, and it was to stay here. My body hummed with how right the choice was. But letting my dad down? My Uncle Martin? I was the damn kid who wrote apology notes to teachers if my lab-mate acted rude. I never disappointed anyone and yet... I'd hurt Cami.

If I was going to pick myself, then I was going to do it right, damn it.

Determined to finally make a choice about my future, I headed to meet my dad. My parents loved this hole-in-the-wall joint, and we ate here whenever they visited.

Usually, it was the four of us, but this time, it was just my dad waiting for me. He had his hands in his pockets, and his face was lined with worry. I didn't blame him. I'd forced them all out after the incident with Cami, and I might've said some things I regretted, accusing them over actions that were only my own.

"Hey, Freddie." He smiled, but the lines didn't reach his eyes. "You alright?"

"Not really." I shrugged. I'd waited outside Cami's door for a couple hours that night, but she never came home. She'd probably gone to her sister's, and I didn't have it in me to text Michael. He'd call me a dumbass, and disappointing him would make it worse.

"Let's eat. Then we can talk." He squeezed my shoulder a few times, the gesture almost causing my eyes to sting. Then he opened the door and ushered me inside.

The smell of greasy hashbrowns washed over me, and we sat at a booth in the back. We both ordered the special--eggs, sausage, toast, and hashbrowns with a large cup of coffee.

My dad leaned back in his chair, sighed, and arched one brow. I swore he saw right through me, into my soul, and was about to call me out. But instead, he leaned forward and asked, "Why did you apply to your uncle's company in Chicago?"

"Because it was always the plan. We've talked about it for years." I swallowed down the harsh truth that it was his insistence all these years, but ultimately, I'd applied on my own. "Why?"

He frowned. "What makes you happy, son?"

"Wait, what?"

"What do you enjoy doing? Is it hanging with your moron

brother? Your bud Michael? Cami? Or is it exploring new places on your own?"

Where was this coming from?

I sipped the bland coffee, his question running circles in my mind. I hated new places. I was an introvert and liked routines. Hell, I went to the same spot in the library every day because it was familiar.

Michael's future was here coaching.

Cami's future was here with her dad and sister and her connections to dance.

Camden would probably be in school forever—here.

When I thought about *the future,* I thought of trivia nights and study dates with Cami. I wanted Camden and Cami to give each other crap. I set the mug down and rubbed my temples hard. This was it. My chance. "I'd be happier staying here." I tensed, waiting for his disappointment and remarks about how it was a mistake.

Silence greeted me. I snuck a glance at him, but his face remained unchanged. Curious, almost.

"Why?" he asked, his voice neutral.

I cleared my throat. "My friends. Cami. Camden. The things I like doing." I swallowed the bitter pill that I'd let my fear about standing up for myself potentially ruin what I had with Cami. "I was so afraid of letting you and Uncle Martin down, I kept going with the plan even though my heart wasn't in it. You've talked about it for so long that I didn't realize I had another option."

"You choosing what you want is *never* letting me down. I'll admit I pushed it a lot, and for that, I'm sorry. I thought you were on board with it, but after last night… I could see your face. Your indecision. Freddie, I'm with you no matter where you live. Your mom too. Tell me you know that."

I exhaled a shaky breath, relief flooding my senses and almost making me smile. "Thank god."

He cringed. "Please speak up when it comes to your

happiness. I love having two kids who are total opposites, but no more of the suffering in silence, okay?"

I nodded, my body relaxing against the chair. This conversation was almost unreal. Never did I think it would be this easy, but then again, too much had happened up to this point. "I should've talked to Cami about everything."

He clicked his tongue. "You should've, yes. It's a big decision, and while I agree it's *yours* to make alone, if she's your partner, she deserves to be a part of the conversation."

"She said we're done. There's no trust anymore." My throat tightened, and the smell of the food made me sick. "I saw her face…she meant it."

"She met your family for the first time, and everyone knew the truth but her. How do you think she felt? Humiliated? Played? Son, she's probably embarrassed too."

"Fuck." I scrubbed my face as panic fluttered through my chest. This pain was so much worse than when Maddie and I broke up. That had been like a stab wound. Sharp, aggressive, quick. This was like constant drip of pain, reminding me that I'd ruined it. There was no relief.

"It's clear you two care about each other. I saw the way she looked at you. Now, I can't speak for her, obviously, but maybe this isn't the end."

"She said it was."

"She was hurt. Can you blame her?"

"No. I can't. I told her I loved her though, and she didn't believe me. I do though, so much."

"Then show her. Plus, if you stay here, you don't have to give up. Keep trying with her."

The waitress brought our food, and our conversation stopped. I forced myself to eat as I thought of what I could do to show her how much I cared. How much I wanted a future with her.

Hearing her laugh and seeing her smile were my favorite parts of the day. How could I have been so stupid to not fight for that? I could send her flowers, notes, candy. I could apologize in person again and make her one of her favorite meals. Yeah, that might work.

But would she agree to come over? Or let me inside?

Probably not.

I spun my phone around on the table, the four messages I sent her still sitting there without a response. The game. I could wait for her after the game. I blew out a breath, forced a tight smile at my dad, and said, "Thanks for all the advice and for understanding my decision."

"Of course." He nodded. "Know what you're gonna do?"

"Not really, but I gotta try."

"Relationships are hard, and everyone has their own baggage. It's figuring out how to work through the baggage and trusting each other that will really open everything up. She's not Maddie. That's very clear."

"No, she's not."

"You'll figure it out, I have no doubt."

I sure fucking hoped so.

Attending the football game with my parents and Camden was the original plan, but instead of easy conversation and laughter, there was a bit of a dark cloud. Camden felt bad for mentioning the internship, but I couldn't blame him. It wasn't his fault. It was mine and mine alone.

Before, I'd attended games and secretly admired Cami Simpson from the stands. She was so fucking pretty, and she dazzled me. Now though? Her beauty was somehow painful. She smiled and radiated grace and joy, even though she had to be hurting. She was amazing and had been through so much, yet still did such a good job. She impressed me constantly with her dedication and hard work. And her mind! God, she was so creative and brilliant, and I'd gotten to know all sides of her, parts no one else did.

I *had* to get her back, to prove to her we were worth it.

"You alright, man?" Camden hit my shoulder as concern filled his eyes.

"I guess." I gestured toward Cami and the dance team. They all wore two-pieced outfits, orange and blue shiny sparkles covering them. Her long legs and her toned stomach were on display. God, she was beautiful and talented. The way she trained each muscle to do what she wanted, how her body felt against mine, the sounds she made when we hugged. "Just trying to figure out how to make it better."

"Even the game. That's what I think."

"What do you mean?"

"She was probably embarrassed as hell, you lying to her and her figuring it out in front of your family. What's something you could do that'd even it out?"

"I don't know."

He left me alone after that, and instead of watching the game against our school rival, I stared at Cami. The way she kicked in the air, dazzling everyone with her smile. The way she laughed with the other girls on her team. She seemed so perfectly content, and while my gut ached, it made me so happy to see her happy with her team. That was where she belonged, and she had a place now.

I scratched my chest and counted down the minutes until the game was over. She told me once that they'd shower and leave the stadium through the south entrance, away from the players. I'd wait for her there and beg for forgiveness. It'd be step one.

We won with a last-minute touchdown, and the whole place went wild. Camden hollered, and my parents jumped up and down, hugging each other like it was the Superbowl. People went bonkers over college football. I didn't get it. I liked the school spirit and the entertainment, but the tears? It was too much.

I had to be the worst student in attendance since I was so glad the game was over. That meant I could go find to Cami and try to fix this. It'd been too long without talking to her, and if I knew her...she'd want to go out after the game, and if she was feeling too much...she'd do something stupid.

I couldn't have that. Things were going so well for her now.

"I'm going to wait for Cami. See if she'll speak to me. You all go on." I waved at my parents and brother and took off. I had no idea what I'd say, but I sure as hell hoped the words formed when I saw her.

My pulse raced as I wove through people. I had time, but I was so afraid she'd sneak out, like she'd know I was waiting for her. My size helped me navigate through the crowds, so I didn't stress out with how many people there were. They were like ants, just everywhere.

After ten minutes of dodging and creatively moving through the crowd, I arrived at the southern part of the stadium where the girls would leave. I leaned against the wall and got out my phone.

Bullet point list, here I come.

1. I was so afraid of getting hurt that I ended up hurting you in the process.
2. I'm happiest when I'm with you
3. I'm staying here because my life is here
4. I love you

Jesus, what a dumb list. I had to do more to earn her trust back. I refused to be another person who let her down. She deserved the world, and I wanted to give it to her. The crowd thinned out, and some girls I recognized exited, one by one. Daniella, the redhead, briefly glanced my way, her face hardening before she moved past me. *Shit.*

This wasn't good.

Another couple of girls glared at me. I rubbed the back of my neck as someone else leaned against the wall on the opposite side. She wore a navy-blue outfit and seemed familiar. I'd definitely seen her before, and I frowned, trying to place her.

Another girl came out, gasped when they saw the woman, and shook her head. The woman tried talking to her, but the dancer moved faster. What the hell was going on?

Time came to a stop when Cami walked out of the double-doors. Her hair was down, her face clear of all the show makeup, and her dark brown eyes landed on me. Her lips twisted as she took a deep breath. She stepped my way, and my mind betrayed me.

Words disappeared. I couldn't say a word to her. My feet grew roots into the ground, and my mouth glued shut. *Fuck!*

"Cami?" The woman pushed off the wall and approached her. She had dark circles under her eyes and the posture of someone guilty. She hunched forward and looked at the ground. "Can we please talk?"

Cami moved her gaze from me to the woman, slowly. Whatever emotion she had on her face shifted into anger. Her features hardened, and she gripped the strap of her bag tighter. "Why?"

"Because I owe you an apology in person. That's all I need to do."

Cami swallowed hard. "Coach--Audrey, you shouldn't be here."

"I know, I just…" The woman ran a hand through her hair, leaving it sticking up in every direction. She looked like a mess, and everything pieced together.

Cami's old coach. The one who'd accused her of sleeping with her boyfriend. The coach who'd hurt Cami more than she cared to admit. I'd gauged that from the way she talked about what happened with a lilt to her voice.

Cami sneered at the older woman, and without thinking, I said, "She owes you an apology and then some."

Cami chewed on her bottom lip, questions swirling in her chocolate eyes as she stared at me. I wanted to kiss and hold her, but this was more important. Dance had been a part of her life way longer than I had, and she'd earned this closure. "Talk to her," I whispered, nodding like she needed encouragement.

Her knuckles were white, but she steeled her shoulders back and faced her old coach. "Okay. Five minutes. Then I have a party to go to."

A party. A weight formed in the base of my gut as I watched the two of them walk away. She could go wild and... do whatever she wanted. She was free to do that, and there was nothing I could do.

She deserved this time with her former coach, that I knew. So, I texted her.

Freddie: If you need to talk after, I'm here for you. I'm always here for you, Cami. I hope you know that. Have fun tonight.

I'd let her go today and try again in the morning. Because even though there was a chance there was nothing to save, I had to keep trying. Cami was a gift, the person I wanted a future with, and I'd just have to earn her trust back...no matter what it took.

CHAPTER
TWENTY-SEVEN

Cami

Audrey looked like hell. She'd always been put together and cute AF, but she was a hot ass mess. She'd lost weight and let herself go. A part of me felt like she deserved this, a little *what goes around comes around.* But it didn't last long.

We walked shoulder to shoulder, and with one more look to my right, I found Freddie watching us. He nodded, his lips forming a tight smile before he shoved his hands in his pockets and headed in the opposite direction. God, my body was in overdrive with him being here, the look on his face when he saw me... like he *cared* for me. I had some time away from our argument, and we had some things to discuss. But... later. Audrey wanted to apologize?

It was all too much.

I needed to focus on one thing at a time. Audrey. Then Daniella's party. Then... Freddie. I exhaled and kept my face neutral. Audrey had been a good coach for three years, but that didn't excuse her irrational behavior that harmed me and the team. I wasn't sure if I could forgive her, but I would hear her out.

I wouldn't admit it to anyone, but her apology meant a lot. Closure of sorts. I cleared my throat once we left the stadium. There was a black bench donated by a sorority house, and I gestured to it.

She sat down first and crossed her legs. She tapped her fingers against her knees as I joined her. I wrapped my arms around my bag, grounding myself. I wasn't going to make this easier. She'd have to speak first.

"Cami," she said, her voice breaking. "I'm so sorry."

She cried, putting her face in her hands and leaving me completely unsure of what to do. I refused to comfort her. I locked my fingers. "Why?"

She sucked in a breath, wiped her nose on the back of her arm, and faced me. "You're so…perfect, Cami. You're beautiful —you have the face, the body, the moves. You had an attitude on your shoulders that I didn't like. I wanted to knock you down to see what you'd do."

"Then you don't know me at all." My words came out sharp and jaded. "Kinda fucked up that you, as a coach, wanted to *knock me down*."

"I don't regret naming Daniella captain. You two as co-captains is the best thing for the team. With you graduating next year, you could guide her and the team's future." She bounced her knee up and down, grimacing. "I'm so sorry I blamed you, accused you, and treated you how I did. It's the lowest moment of my life. I should've never let my personal life infiltrate into my coaching."

Hearing her say the words didn't make everything better, but I didn't feel unsettled anymore. "Thank you for apologizing."

"I can't sleep, eat. I broke it off with my piece-of-shit boyfriend who was cheating on me with my roommate." She pulled on the ends of her hair. "That doesn't matter to you though."

"I want you happy, Audrey. You were good to me for three years." I sighed and patted her shoulder. "You gotta get your life together."

"I know. I moved in with my parents again, and I'm going to a therapist. I have a long way to go, but I trusted the wrong guy. Let him overtake my life." She leaned back and wiped under her eyes. "I said things to you that are unforgiveable, and I understand that. I was in a position of power and abused it. My biggest regret is hurting you. I need you to know that."

I nodded, feeling the conversation coming to an end. "I'm glad you're talking to someone. Really."

She sniffed, stood up, and gave me a watery smile. "Seeing the girls rally behind you was amazing. I hope you found your place now. There are always silver linings in the low moments."

She waved and headed off toward the parking lot, leaving me alone. I took a few seconds to digest our conversation, the knot in my stomach loosening just a bit. This was good—closure. With her and the senior year that took a million left turns. I brushed off my shirt and jeans and kept my head up.

I needed to stay busy, or I'd think about Freddie. While Audrey had done something more extreme, Freddie essentially did the same thing. Judged me and assumed I was someone I wasn't. The sort of person who'd sleep with my coach's boyfriend as revenge.

A person who couldn't handle the truth that my *boyfriend* wanted to leave town. I would've supported him either way. I understood it was his choice *and* that Maddie fucked him up, but I was so goddamn sick of people not trusting me. I put my headphones on and marched past the busy road toward the quad when a familiar, tall figure raised a hand in a wave.

My breath caught in my throat. *Freddie.*

"Hey, hi, uh," he said, frowning and rubbing the back of his neck. "This isn't what it seems like."

"What does it seem like?" My heart pitter-pattered against

my ribs like a downpour, and I couldn't stop staring at him. His gorgeous face, laced with worry. His glasses and jawline. He looked tired and torn up. Despite being put together, the turmoil in his eyes matched Audrey's.

"I saw your coach walk by crying, and it's late and dark, and I didn't know if you'd be upset or alone. I'm... I can walk you? To be safe? Wherever you're going? I can follow behind you or across the block." His throat bobbed, and he scrubbed a hand over his face. "Are you okay?"

He was so charmingly awkward, and I so badly wanted to leap into his arms. My feet twitched with movement. I wasn't done being upset or mad at him, and Audrey had solidified it. "I'm fine. Just another case of someone making judgements about me without talking about it *with me*."

"Cami." He closed his eyes tight. "I did the wrong thing and said the wrong words. Can I please just make sure you're safe?"

"You don't want to hash this out?" My adrenaline pumped through my veins, and I had that wild streak in my blood, the energy that made me do dumb things. Sneaking around, drinking tickets, dancing on bar tops, and doing body shots. The crazy girl already had so many opinions about her, so why bother trying to change my reputation?

"Of *course*, I do. God, I miss you, and it's been a day. My whole body hurts thinking about how upset you were...are. But you probably had a tough conversation with your coach and want to have fun?" He blinked fast and kept looking between my eyes.

"What if I do?"

"What if you do, what? Want to talk or want to have fun?"

"I'm not sure, Freddie. You hurt me, and I don't know what I want, alright? I have this... uncomfortable urge inside me to do something dumb. I mean, what's the point? I try to be better and change everyone's perception of me, but it didn't fucking matter. You, my sister, my coach... everyone already made judgements. So *why* bother?"

"Stop. This isn't you. This isn't my Cami." He shook his head back and forth, hard. "You can be mad at me, your sister, and your coach. Be mad at all of us, but don't for one fucking second put yourself down."

"Your Cami?" I shoved his chest. "You don't get to say that. If I was *your* Cami, then you would've told me the truth. Included me."

He exhaled, his nostrils flaring, and he put his hands on his hips. "You're right. Now, what do you need to do?"

"Wait, what?"

"Tonight. You want to do something dumb? Name it. I'm in. I'll do it all with you."

"That's not how this works."

"How what works, exactly?" He stepped closer to me, his intense gaze moving to my mouth. "I'm going to fight for you, every second of every day. I need you to understand that. I fucked up, and I'll own it. I fell so hard for you but was so afraid of disappointing my dad that I hurt you."

What? Disappoint his dad? This was new. He couldn't disappoint anyone--he was thoughtful and kind all the time.

Shit. This is happening. I gulped, the air seeming thicker than the usual crisp fall night. Crickets chirped around us, and the lingering fans still hung outside the stadium chatting loudly. I could only blink, the threat of emotions seconds from spilling.

Too much.

"I—I," I said, unable to form words. I shook my head and focused on the sidewalk. I wasn't ready to talk about this. Us. The hurt, the mistrust. Not…yet. "Freddie."

"Hey, it's okay." He cupped my face and gave me a half smile before taking a step back. The warmth of his touch lingered on my cheek. "We don't have to talk now. I meant what I said. Every day, I'll fight."

I sniffed, the ball of emotions wedging itself in my throat. "I have to uh, head to Daniella's. She's having a small party."

"I'll walk you there."

I shrugged, held my bag tighter, and headed toward her apartment. Freddie stayed next to me, not once touching me or saying a word. Each step rustled his jeans, and the breeze picked up his clean, woodsy scent every few seconds. The ten-minute journey went faster than I would've liked, and he brought me up to the door.

"Thanks for letting me walk with you." He shoved his hands in his pockets and stared at me like he was trying to see into my head. "Have fun and do what you need to do. I love you. I'll see you tomorrow, okay?"

I couldn't respond or move. Do what you need to do? Did he mean... go wild? Have fun? "Aren't you worried about what I'll do?"

"No." He smiled. "Because I know you."

Then, Freddie left the lobby of the apartment building and disappeared onto the street. If he was trying to get me to miss him, it worked. I wanted him here, even if I wasn't ready to talk.

He said he loves me. Twice.

With a shaky breath, I went into Daniella's and told the girls everything. We were having a team-only party with vodka and our favorite dance movies, but Freddie didn't need to know that. However as the night wore on, I couldn't help but wonder what he meant about seeing me tomorrow.

I was looking forward to it.

"I can't believe you talked me into doing this class with you." Daniella groaned as we arrived at the southern part of the quad. In the spirit of team bonding *and* fundraising, I put together a schedule of teaching Zumba classes and charging two bucks per person. They'd be forty minutes long and right on the quad.

I loved running these classes. Plus, they raised money *and* spread awareness of our team. "You'll be great. I bet we get a decent crowd."

"Everyone was talking about it on socials, so hopefully." Daniella yawned big. "Feel any better about Freddie?"

"Mm." That was a non-answer, but I wasn't sure. I'd thought about him all night and what happened. He'd always been clear about his baggage and issues with Maddie, just as he knew how my reputation hurt me. He'd messed up, owned it, and was willing to fight for us. Was I?

I could *picture* being with Freddie next year. Starting my own business and coming home to him. Sharing dinners with him, going on trips. He fit into my life, but how many times would baggage enter our relationship?

"Well, this should be interesting." Daniella arched a brow and jutted her chin toward the back of the small crowd. I followed her gaze and sucked in a breath.

Freddie was there.

So was Michael, Van Helsing, Cal Holt...ten hockey players were here. Freddie waved at me with a silly grin.

He wore athletic shorts and a gray shirt, looking way too good. He walked toward me, almost tripping on his own feet. "Cami, hi."

"Hey?" I eyed him, unable to stop my laugh. "Are you... attending the session?"

"Yes." He nodded so fast, looking quite proud of himself. "I got Michael and some hockey guys too. Here, I have their funds." He shoved money at me as the tips of his ears reddened.

"Freddie, you don't have to do this. I know you aren't coordinated."

"I'm not. Not at all. I'll embarrass myself, but that's the point." He gulped. "I told you I don't dance, but I didn't do a lot of things before you. I want to be this guy, the one to try new things with you. So, I'm doing Zumba."

"Alright." I smiled at him, but his face softened. "What?"

"You look beautiful. It's really hard to not kiss you right now. I should…get back there. Yes." He ducked his head, a blush tinging his cheeks.

It was so goddamn cute and reminded me why I'd fallen in love with him in the first place.

Daniella looped her arm around mine and leaned toward me. "Any guy going through Zumba deserves a second chance."

"I was leaning that way already."

"Good. He seems like a great guy who just made a dumb choice. Tell me, if he does move to Chicago, would you really do long distance?"

"Yes." I stared at Freddie as he chatted with Michael. "I would. I love him."

She let out a little holler as everyone faced us. Daniella set the stereo up and introduced us, but I kept my eyes on Freddie. He stared back at me with a goofy grin and bright red cheeks.

"Okay y'all, we're going to practice some moves for those beginners. Shuffle left, shuffle right, back step, back step. Hop, hop, hop. Hips, hips, arms, arms, pop, snap, thrust. Alright?" I modeled the moves twice. "From the top!"

Watching the crowd of thirty was hilarious. So many missed beats and flailing limbs. Daniella and I each wore huge smiles as we went through the motions again. The third time, we blasted the music.

It was a crisp fall morning, but sweat still beaded my forehead as we danced. I couldn't stop watching Freddie and how he moved so badly. He was three beats behind everyone and ran into Michael five times. For whatever reason, it was the sexiest thing to see him trying something so far outside of his comfort zone for me. His gaze met mine, and he grinned so big, my stomach burst into butterflies.

Suddenly, I couldn't wait for the class to be over. I wanted to talk to him, to tell him I loved him too and that we'd be okay. That I could visit him up in the city on weekends when there wasn't a game. We'd make it work and be happy in our own way. I could dance, and he could explore the city. He understood me so well and I him—we made each other stronger and better.

The rest of the class went by slow, but when we finished, everyone clapped and cheered.

"Yo, that was sick!" Van Helsing, the hockey captain said. He walked up to Daniella and fist bumped her. "Nice work, D."

She rolled her eyes. "Shut up."

"I mean it. This is cool." Van Helsing high-fived me too. "Simpson."

I nodded, curious at how his gaze kept moving toward Daniella. He stepped closer to her. "We still sharing a ride home for the holidays?"

"Seems like my only choice." She met my eyes and shrugged. "His sister and I were best friends in high school. I've known Van a *long* time."

"Don't say it like a bad thing, D."

"It is a bad thing." She elbowed him. "I know too much."

"Nah." He pulled her in for a half-hug, making her yelp.

"You're sweaty and gross. Stop!"

I had a million questions for her, but my attention moved to Freddie. My wonderful, out-of-place, gentle giant who stood with his hands on his hips and sweat dripping down his face. He approached me with hunched shoulders. God, he was so tall, I loved it.

"I can't believe you went through the class." My cheeks hurt from smiling. He was so horrible that the memory would bring me joy for weeks after this. "You were terrible."

"I know. Michael cussed me out twice." He let out an awkward laugh and swallowed so hard his throat bobbed. "You make it look so easy."

"I am trained to do this, ya know."

"Very obvious." He ran a hand over his hair as his gaze

moved from my eyes to my lips, lingering there to the point my skin heated. "Are you doing okay?"

The gentleness to his tone had me moving closer to him. "Better now."

"Good. Good." He nodded and matched my step so our feet were an inch apart. "I really hope you got everything you needed from Audrey. I know what she meant to you and how badly it hurt."

"I did, yeah." My throat got all weird and clogged with emotion as he reached out a hand, but it never connected with me. It fell against his thigh. "I still can't believe you came to this class, Freddie."

"I told you." He breathed heavy and wiped his glasses on the hem of his shirt. He put them back on his nose. "I'm on my sorry-tour for forgiveness. You want me to dance on a table for you? I will. Dye my hair? Get a piercing? Okay, maybe not that. Well, if that's what it takes, then yes. Name it. I love—"

"Freddie?" I stood and wrapped my arms around his sweaty neck. He stilled and moved his hands to grip my waist. His hands almost met around my lower back they were so big, and I pressed my chest against him.

"Yeah?" he whispered, his entire body tense.

"I love you too."

He trembled before dropping his lips to mine and kissing me. His mouth was warm and salty but safe and perfect. My pulse raced as he slid his tongue against mine, tasting like mint. He pulled me tight against his chest, pressing his hand along my spine as he groaned into my mouth. "Thank fucking God," he said between kisses. He kissed me harder, his teeth clashing against mine in a perfectly messy Freddie way. Like he couldn't kiss me enough, like he *loved* me.

I giggled against his mouth, and he cupped my neck, deepening the kiss to the point my thighs clenched. God, he knew how to make me turn into a puddle. I didn't want to stop, but after some of the guys whistled, I rested a hand on his shoulder and pulled back. "Hell of a kiss, big guy."

"Yeah." He blushed, rubbing his thumb over my wet bottom lip. "I missed you, your mouth, your everything. Please tell me we're together again?"

"Yes." I grinned against his thumb, and he picked me up, twirling me around and everything. "Oh my God, put me down."

"I thought I'd ruined it all when we were just figuring out how good it could be." He rested his forehead against mine. "I'm staying here, by the way."

"Wait, what?" I arched my neck to get a better look at him. "You're not going to Chicago?"

"I'm always so worried about what I think others want and not myself. I want to see you every day and do Zumba classes and go to trivia nights. I want to hang with Camden and Michael and explore new things with you. Moving to a city alone sounds horrible. My parents had been pushing it for so long that lines blurred along the way. What might've been my dream turned into theirs, and I let it happen. I needed to figure that out on my own, and I didn't talk to you about it. I should've. I will next time."

"Hey, I know you will." I threaded my fingers through his sweaty hair, so happy I could burst. He held my gaze, his gray eyes swirling with emotion.

"I see my future with you. A real one."

I nodded, my throat tightening. "Me too."

"I kinda smell. Could we head back to my place? I need to shower."

"That an invitation?" I wiggled my brows.

"It absolutely is." He set me down and grabbed my hand, not paying attention to Michael and the guys totally watching us. He intertwined our fingers and led us from the quad, back to our apartment.

Senior year hadn't started off any way I would've thought,

but damn, I wouldn't change a single thing. I found Freddie, Daniella, and a new love for a team I thought I'd lost. Somehow, despite all the problems, it had turned out to be the best senior year ever. I squeezed Freddie's hand, and he looked down at me, so much love radiating from him, and I knew we'd have years of adventures together.

EPILOGUE

MAY—THE NEXT YEAR

Freddie

Cami still wore her graduation cap and gown as I covered her eyes from behind. "Be patient," I said.

"You're blindfolding me and *not* in the fun way, big guy." She covered my hands with hers and squeezed. "What is this surprise?"

We arrived just outside my apartment door. I kissed her neck, and she let out a little hum. I *loved* that sound, like she was so happy with me. "I'm proud of you," I said against her skin.

She shivered. "You have your master's. That's way more impressive."

"I'm in awe of how you've grown, Cami." I trailed kisses down her shoulder, pulling her against me because I could. She was my best friend in the entire world, and despite us being so different, we fit together.

"Well, thanks." Her voice trembled, and she gripped my arms that had settled on her waist. "Your heart is racing. What's going on?"

I willed myself to relax. The surprise graduation party with just our families was a last-minute idea, but it seemed important to do for her. Her sister had a big fancy data job lined up and all the accolades, but Cami worked harder than anyone I knew.

She brushed it all off, saying it was no big deal, but I saw her struggle and push herself all year. She worked her ass off to lead the dance team *and* double major with twenty-one credit hours. She deserved all the applause in the world, and it didn't matter how many times I told her I was proud, she'd shrug.

"You'll see." I twisted the handle and led us into the room before uncovering her eyes. She sucked in a breath at the balloon arch, the large cake in the shape of a dance shoe, and our families.

"Congrats, Cami!" Everyone cheered.

She tensed in my arms, and for a second, worry had me second-guessing everything. Was I the idiot boyfriend who ignored his girlfriend's pleas? Did I do the exact opposite of what she wanted? Oh, shit. I tried to think of an excuse to kick everyone out but then she laughed.

"Oh my God. Freddie, you arranged this?" She spun around in my arms, cupping my face with her slim fingers. "There's ice cream and balloons!"

I pressed my hands into her lower back, holding her tight against me. "If I'd known balloons would make you this happy, I'd stop getting you flowers."

"Don't you dare stop that." She pressed a quick kiss to my mouth before buzzing around the room in an assembly line of hugs. Her dad, her sister, Michael. Then my parents. Camden. Even some of the girls on the team were here with gift bags and large smiles. My chest got all light and fluttery as I watched her beam at the people closest to her. It was a reminder that she needed celebrations in her life. For the girl who spent most of her life cheering for everyone else, I wanted to be that person for her.

Now, a year from now, and decades from now.

I chewed my bottom lip, sweat pooling on my brow at the direction of my thoughts. We'd talked about living together, conserving water by sharing showers because the earth mattered to me. We joked about how much closet space she'd need, but the conversation never actually went to the real question.

Were we going to move in together as we started our lives?

"I'm so proud of you, Cami." Her dad pulled her into a hard hug, his eyes meeting mine over her shoulder. I stood taller, even though I towered over everyone in the room. I lifted my chin in greeting, and once they broke apart, I immediately put my arm around her. Protective didn't begin to cover how I felt of Cami. I wanted to slay every dragon she ever faced and fix every negative feeling she had. Even though her relationship with her dad was better than it was and always changing, I never wanted to see the look of uncertainty in her eyes. I squeezed her shoulders, and she let out a little sigh, one that went right to my soul.

It was her *content* sigh, the one she made when we cuddled or hugged. One thing had become clear while I'd spent the last year with Cami—staying *here* and not moving to the city was the right move. My life was full of people, and I liked it. Plus, nothing had changed with my dad since we had that chat. We were still close, and he always made sure to ask about Cami.

My mom pulled her into a hug as they discussed her new job. Cami would help run a small dance studio for the summer so she could see all aspects of the business. Then she'd start the process of creating her own. It'd be hard as hell, but I couldn't wait to see her succeed.

Small talk wasn't my thing at all, but I survived listening to Camden and Michael banter about sports with my dad. Everyone ate and drank, and Cami smiled the whole time. That was what mattered. It wasn't until two hours later that the last guest left, and it was finally me and my girl.

"Hey, you." She gave me a bewitching grin, one that had my

heart beating a little faster. Her face was an open book once you actually knew her, and her eyes flashed with heat. "Thank you."

"Of course. I love you and want you to know how honored I am to be with you."

She wrapped her arms around my neck and hoisted herself up on my body. I gladly gripped her ass to hold her against me.

"You are the best fucking person I know." She kissed me once, twice. Quick pecks. It wasn't enough.

I moved one hand to cup her head and tilted her a bit. "Right back at you." I nipped at her neck, loving how she squirmed against me. "Are you happy?"

"What?" She tensed and pushed my head away to look at me. "Why would you ask me that?"

"Because. That's all I want. For you to be happy." My voice clogged with emotion, and my grip around her tightened. "I want it all with you, Cami. I'm going to work every day to make sure you're happy, okay?"

"God, I fucking love you." She kissed me hard then, her cherry lips attacking mine without any grace. This was my favorite Cami—the hungry, out of control one that only I got to see.

She sucked my tongue and groaned, rocking her hips against me as she whimpered. "I want it all. With you. Yes. Now, please reach under my gown."

"Is someone ready for me already?" I slid my hands over her strong thighs and about choked when nothing was underneath.

I grazed my fingers over her ass and her already wet pussy. My heart was going to beat out of my chest and live inside hers. The audacity of her. I loved it. "*Cami.* You've been naked under this the entire time?"

She nodded, and something wicked flashed on her face again. "Yes. Does that make you wild?"

"Oh, baby, you have no idea." I growled. Simple as that. I slammed her back against the front door and spread her legs apart, wide. "You are... just..." I got onto my knees, supporting her so she straddled my face. "Everything."

"You are too, Freddie. You're my everything too. We're in this together, yeah?" Her voice shook just a bit, and I pressed my mouth against her center, teasing her the way I knew she liked.

I licked hard, then soft. Pressing the flat of my tongue on her swollen clit until her legs shook around me. She dug her nails into my hair, begging me for more--like I could stop if I wanted.

My face between her thighs was my second favorite place to be.

I wanted to spoil her rotten, so I did. I didn't rush her orgasm at all. I got her right the brink before slowing a couple of times, and by the third tease, she screamed a guttural sound and fell apart around my face.

"That's my girl," I said, kissing her one time. I barely got done before she tackled me to the ground. This petite thing leveled me in one breath. "Whoa."

"You are fucking perfect." She frantically undid my belt and had my cock out in her hands within seconds. I was hard as steel, and she pumped me a few times before unzipping the gown but not taking it off. It billowed around her and gave me the perfect view of her gumdrop nipples.

"I'm not done spoiling you." I sat up and sucked one into my mouth.

"Later." She lined up my cock right at her entrance and slid onto me with another contented sigh. "We fit together so well." She rocked her hips in a mesmerizing rhythm. My dancer. So graceful and beautiful and kind.

I grunted, digging my fingers into her hips. She liked to do this sometimes, where she rode me and wouldn't bend down. It was a show for me, and it was maddening. "Need you," I growled.

"Patience, big guy." She laughed and arched her back, taking me deeper. My thighs tensed, and my balls tightened at how fucking sexy she was. We made the decision to stop using condoms altogether once she got an IUD, and *fuck,* it was magnificent. Feeling her pussy raw and bare. Every single time was like heaven.

She rocked faster, and sweat beaded on her chest. I wanted to lick it off and tried to sit up, but she shoved me down again. "I'm enjoying myself on your dick. Let me spoil you."

"Unfair."

She winked before *finally* kissing me again. I liked coming this way, our chests pressed together and our mouths desperate for each other. I kneaded her ass hard and pistoned into her from this angle. "Touch your clit."

She did and mewled her familiar sounds. She was close. So was I.

Without breaking our kiss, I opened my eyes and found her watching me. It wasn't weird like I would've thought. It made everything *more.* Her eyes dilated as she orgasmed, and her pussy clenching around me sent me into my own orgasm. But it was her eyes that captured me, drew me in.

"Damn, that felt good." She collapsed on top of me, her breaths coming out in pants. "You are my favorite." She kissed my chest before smiling down at me.

"Move in with me," I blurted out, saying to hell with the entire plan I had. It involved ice cream and a PDF of all the reasons why it was better for the environment. "I want to start a life with you, wake up with you every day, and do this… Cami," I paused, swallowing as my heart beat too fast. "We can still go slow if you want. This isn't an ultimatum. Just know… I want to marry you someday. Have kids. Maybe little dancers? I'm in this for the long haul, and—"

"Yes, to all of it. Oh my god." She beamed. No other way to describe it. Her smile had an extra gleam to it as she nodded. "I want you in my life forever, big guy, and I don't know if you realize this, but I'm a pretty determined person."

"Yes, you are. It's one of the things I love about you."

Her eyes crinkled on the sides as she kissed me again. "We're going to need to work on a story."

"What?"

"I can't tell my sister you asked me to move in with you when your dick was still inside me." She giggled as she slid off me, sitting on the ground next to me with the same goofy smile. "We'll make something up."

"I could tell you the original plan." I sighed, pushing myself to sit up. My own face tingled from joy. "Something about you causes me to lose control."

"I love being the one to make you. I'll always push you, Freddie." She stood up, graceful as hell, and held out a hand for me. The gown hung from her shoulders, but she was still the most beautiful, best person I knew. "Come on, let's go clean up. Then I want to hear about your big presentation about the new process at work this morning. I've been dying to ask how it went."

Right there. This was how I knew she was the one. My popular, dancing girlfriend who fucked me on the kitchen floor genuinely cared about me and my nerdy job. She bought a book called Engineering for Dummies so she could understand what I did more, and it wasn't even fair how happy I was.

As I followed her into the shower, her smile still teasing her lips, I made a plan then and there.

Six months, then I was proposing. People like Cami were once in a lifetime.

ALSO BY JAQUELINE SNOWE:

Coming soon!

From the Top, Central State Book 2

CLEAT CHASER SERIES

Challenge Accepted
The Game Changer
Best Player
No Easy Catch

OUT OF THE PARK SERIES

Evening the Score
Sliding Home
Rounding the Bases

SHUT UP AND KISS ME SERIES: INTERNSHIP WITH THE DEVIL

Teaching with the Enemy
Next Door Nightmare

HOCKEY ROMANCE

Holdout

STANDALONES

Take a Chance on Me

Let Life Happen

The Weekend Deal

ABOUT THE AUTHOR

Jaqueline Snowe lives in Arizona where the "dry heat" really isn't that bad. She prefers drinking coffee all hours of the day and snacking on anything that has peanut butter or chocolate. She is the mother to two fur-babies who don't realize they aren't humans and a new mom to the sweetest baby boy. She is an avid reader and writer of romances and tends to write about athletes. Her husband works for an MLB team (not a player, lol) so she knows more about baseball than any human ever should.

You can find her posting photos of her sweet baby on Instagram or rage tweeting. She tries to update her website as often as she can so feel free to poke around. www.jaquelinesnowe.com

Printed in Great Britain
by Amazon

83627926R10162